Beautiful Trauma

I0630426

BESTSELLING AUTHOR
AIMEE NICOLE WALKER

Scarlett Paige,

Once upon a time, I gave birth to this amazing baby girl. She grew up to be a spirited, strong, and beautiful young woman who decided to be a surrogate for her two friends. Plans were made, seeds were sown, and here you are—precious and perfect. Hearing your first cries was one of the most precious moments of my life. You're a very lucky girl, Scarlett. You have two dads who love you so much. I wish you a lifetime of love, laughter, and adventure. You come from a long line of women who don't know the meaning of the word surrender, and so I wish your fathers much luck. I have every confidence that you'll keep them wrapped around your fingers. You are loved, little lady. XOXO

Prologue

Henry Sullivan

ABOMINATION. DISGUSTING. FILTHY. THREE WORDS NO CHILD WANTS to hear when they confess their biggest secret and heartache to their mother. I knew it wouldn't go over well when I told my mother I was gay and HIV positive, but I hadn't been prepared for the rage and contempt I saw in her eyes. I didn't recognize the woman I'd loved with my whole heart.

"I want you out of my house right now, Henry Todd Sullivan. I don't ever want to see you again."

I collapsed at her feet, wrapping my arms around her legs. "Mom, please don't."

"I'm not your mother. You're no one to me. I regret the day you were born." The fight left me then. I shriveled and died like a neglected flower. She placed her foot against my chest and kicked out, shoving me away from her. "You're not taking anything from this house that I bought you either. I'll let you have the clothes on your back, but that's it."

I wanted to beg and plead for her to understand that no amount of praying would change who I was, but I recognized the look in her eyes. She'd made up her mind. I was an abomination. I was disgusting. I was filthy. I was dead to her.

I walked out of the only home I'd ever known. I was numb to the world around me, so lost in my thoughts I didn't know where I was even going. I kept putting one foot in front of the other until I arrived at the place where I was taught to seek redemption and salvation. Grace Baptist Church stood tall and pristine against the summer blue sky.

"Henry?"

I snapped out of my daze when I heard Geoff Daily's voice. He was my best friend, my first love, and the pastor's son.

Geoff crossed the parking lot at a quick pace, looking both worried and scared. He kept glancing over his shoulder like he was making sure no one saw him. He gripped my bicep and pulled me around to the side of the church, which offered both shade from the hot sun and privacy from prying eyes.

"Henry, you can't be here. Your mom called my dad. He knows. I've just spent the last fifteen minutes watching spittle froth around his mouth as he forbade me to see you ever again."

"I'm sorry," I said weakly. "I don't want to cause you any problems. I'll just get going."

"Go where?" he asked gently, reaching up and wiping the tears from my eyes.

"I-I don't know." Hopelessness hit me as hard as a Mack truck. "I have no one." I shook off his touch and stepped away from him. "It's not your problem, Geoff. I can't drag you down with me."

"Cut it out," Geoff said firmly. "You couldn't get rid of me if you tried. Didn't the doctor at the clinic give you the name of a social worker?"

"Yeah, but she's just supposed to help me apply for Medicaid or whatever assistance I qualify for to get help with the meds. I doubt she's going to let me sleep on her couch."

"She might know of a place you can stay until you get this sorted out," Geoff said. "Do you have her card?"

I shook my head. "Her number is saved in my phone though."

The cell phone my mother didn't know I had. I'd bought it with money I earned from my part-time job. "Her name is Gretchen."

Geoff took the phone from my hand, found the contact, and dialed her number. I numbly listened as he laid out my situation and urged her for help. "I don't have anything to write it on, but I have an excellent memory." He listened as she told him a number then repeated it back to her. "Ask for Archie or Esther. Got it. Thank you." Geoff disconnected and immediately dialed the number he kept repeating out loud. I refused to let hope blossom in my heart even if Geoff looked encouraged by the conversation he'd had with Gretchen. "Hello, is this Esther?" Geoff asked when someone answered the phone. "My name is Geoff Daily. My best friend, Henry, was recently diagnosed with HIV and his mother—" Geoff stopped talking abruptly, and I was terrified he was receiving terrible news. Then a huge smile spread across his face. "I like you a lot, Esther." Geoff laughed then listened some more. "Can we come now?" He reached over and squeezed my hand. "We're on our way."

Tears of relief slid down my face. I had no idea where I was going, but I was grateful it wasn't a cardboard box beneath an overpass. "Thank you," I whispered thickly. "Geoff, I..." I couldn't form the words necessary to express my gratitude.

"You'd do the same for me," Geoff said, pulling me into a quick hug. "Listen, I don't want to risk my dad seeing you. Cut around to the back of the property, turn left on the next street, and meet me at the corner. I'll be right there."

I nodded and hugged him again before I started along the side of the church. My knees knocked the entire time I walked toward the meet-up spot, and I'd half convinced myself Geoff was just playing a cruel game by the time I got there. It seemed like I stood there for an eternity waiting for his silver hatchback. Shame swept over me when he pulled up alongside me. How could I doubt this guy's friendship? We'd been through so much together.

Reaching over the console, Geoff linked his fingers with mine.

"You're going to be fine, Henry. You're stronger than you realize, and there are good people in the world."

Fifteen minutes later, Geoff pulled up in front of a two-story house with a wooden sign that declared it as Ryan's Place. "What's this place?"

"It's a transition home for people with HIV," Geoff said softly. "They provide housing and other services to help people in your situation. Gretchen said this is the best place for you. Esther was the lady who answered the phone. She knew what I needed before I could finish my sentence. I think she's just the person you need right now."

I swallowed hard and looked at the pretty flowers and shrubs planted all around the inviting front porch. "What if they don't like me?"

Geoff laughed. "Anyone with common sense will like you, but if these people happen to be complete losers, then you call me. I'll come back and get you. I'll tuck you away in a hotel someplace until we figure out what to do."

"No cardboard box?" I asked, trying to joke but sounding pitiful.

"Not as long as I'm breathing." Geoff started to open his door, but I reached over and placed a hand on his arm to stop him. I didn't know where the conviction came from, but I needed to take these final steps alone.

"I got this," I said, trying to sound convincing. "You made the phone call and broke the ice. I need to learn to stand on my own two feet. There's no better time to start."

"Are you sure? I can stay long enough to see you get settled."

"No," I said more certainly. "I'll text you later and let you know everything is okay. Love you, Geoff."

"Love you, H."

I offered a watery smile then wiped my tears, squared my shoulders, and walked toward the porch. *Abomination. Disgusting. Filthy. I regret the day you were born.* If my own mother couldn't love me, who could?

The front door opened when I stepped onto the porch. A tiny woman with gray hair and the kindest eyes I'd ever seen smiled up at me. "Oh, my lost lamb. Are you Henry?" Unable to speak, I nodded. "It seems like you found us just in time." Delicious aromas wafted out of the open door, and my stomach growled, reminding me how long it had been since my last meal.

Esther was a retired nurse who lived down the street and volunteered at the transition home. She'd been a widow for a while, and instead of wallowing in grief over losing her Morty, she transferred her love and devotion to the boys of Ryan's Place.

A deep hunger for so much more than food prodded me to open my mouth and speak. "In time for dinner?" I asked.

"That too," Esther replied with a sweet smile. "Come in and make yourself at home. There are two empty rooms upstairs—one at the end on the right and the other across the hallway on the left. One overlooks the front yard, and the other overlooks the back. If you choose the back room, be cautious of Mr. Robbins. He has no regard for the neighbors and doesn't bother pulling his shades when he undresses. I guess he thinks since our residents are gay, they don't mind an eyeful of his drooping twig and berries. I've tried telling the old goat that being gay doesn't mean you want to see every man without clothes, but there's no teaching some people."

I chose the room overlooking the front yard. It wasn't very big, but it was immaculately trimmed with pretty bushes and flower beds which gave lovely bursts of colors. I learned the next day the residents were responsible for cutting the grass and weeding the flower beds. I'd had plenty of experience doing those tasks because my parents had insisted that having chores made kids more responsible. I liked staying busy because it kept my mind off the current state of my life. Esther liked my willingness to help, and we spent many hours bonding those first few days.

I knew she wanted me to open up and talk to her about what was troubling me, but I couldn't. The person I'd trusted most in the world had rejected me and turned me out on the street. Part of me knew Esther was different, but I wasn't capable of trust right then. She never pushed; she just gave me infinite, patient love.

The owner of Ryan's Place, Archie White, worked from home as an accountant in addition to his duties running the transition home. One day I passed his office and heard him mumbling swear words as he frantically searched for something on his desk. Whatever he needed was hidden amongst the stacks of files and piles of paper. I thought it was a miracle he ever got anything accomplished.

"Can I help you sort this out, Archie?" I asked timidly.

He'd blinked at me behind stylish glasses for a few seconds before he accepted my offer. I helped him file the miscellaneous receipts on his desk, determine which invoices were still outstanding, alphabetize and organize his files, send out invoices for his accounting services, and set up a daily planner for him to stay organized.

"You're a lifesaver, Henry," Archie exclaimed enthusiastically when we finished. I basked in his praise, loving how good it felt to be useful and appreciated.

A week later, Archie's desk was just as cluttered as it was before my help, and he was just as grumpy. That's when he decided to offer me a position as his personal assistant. Even with my new responsibilities, I still made time to do physical chores because I needed to physically exhaust myself before I could sleep at night.

My transition wasn't quick, and I was still a work in progress, but by mid-December, I was working a full-time job as an assistant for a lawyer friend of Archie's and saving money for my own place. I attended bimonthly therapy sessions to deal with my anger and grief, and it was during one of those sessions that I had an epiphany.

When Esther said I'd arrived at Ryan's Place just in time, she hadn't meant for dinner. I had arrived in time to save my life. If not for Esther, Archie, and everyone else at Ryan's Place, I wouldn't be out on the town celebrating my twenty-first birthday with my best friend. I would've been another sad statistic: a young gay man who didn't think his life was worth living. I knew better now, even if I had occasional setbacks.

"Earth to Henry!" A good-humored shout pulled me from my musings. Geoff smiled and shook his head.

"What?" I asked.

"I said there's a sexy silver fox checking you out."

"Nah," I said, dismissing him. "Doubt it."

"He's been staring at you for fifteen minutes."

"The old guy probably can't see," I quipped.

"Nine o'clock," Geoff said, tipping his head to the left.

I glanced at my watch. "It's eleven."

Geoff threw his head back and laughed like I'd told the funniest joke he'd ever heard. Then his eyes widened, and he sobered up immediately. "He's coming in hot."

"What? Who?"

"The silver fox. He's making his move. I swear, Henry, it's like talking to a seventy-one-year-old man instead of a twenty-one-year-old."

"I'm sorry I don't know what the cool kids say these days. You know I've lived a sheltered life."

"No worse than mine. You just followed all the rules while I broke them."

"That's you. A rebel without a cause."

"Why does that sound familiar? Is it a song title?" Geoff asked. I just rolled my eyes because some people were clueless when it came to excellent movies. "Sit up straight and look sexy," Geoff demanded.

"Look what?"

I thought Geoff was just yanking my chain until the man in question moved into my periphery. I turned my head and stared into bottomless dark eyes. *Silver fox, indeed.* I was thinking of someone older like George Clooney, but the guy smiling at me had the youthful face of someone who'd gone gray early.

"Hello, I'm Ezra." His voice was smooth, cultured, and sexy. "Want to dance?"

"Yes, he does," Geoff said, pushing me until I reached the edge of the booth. I had two choices: stand up or fall on my ass at Ezra's feet.

"Um, hi. I'm Henry."

"It's his birthday," Geoff announced. "Make sure he gets the dance of his lifetime."

A chuckle rumbled from Ezra's chest, making the hair stand up all over my body. He gestured to the dance floor, and I headed in that direction. Once I stepped past him, Ezra placed his hand at the small of my back. His hand felt hot like a brand, and I liked it.

"Dance of a lifetime," I said out loud when we reached the edge of the dance floor. I jerked to a sudden halt when a thought occurred to me, causing Ezra to crash into me. I whipped around and looked up into his eyes. "Dance of a lifetime," I repeated.

"I'm a bit rusty, but I'll give it my best," Ezra said.

"Did Geoff pay you to dance with me?"

A dark, perfectly arched brow shot up. "Excuse me?"

"Did Geoff—"

"I heard what you said. Are you implying I'm a male escort?"

"No! Um, I don't think so."

"I've never talked to your friend before, and I asked you to dance because I saw the way you unknowingly swayed to the music but never made a move to get out on the dance floor. I asked you to dance because I couldn't stop staring at you."

"Oh my God! I messed this up so badly." I sighed and moved to step around him so I could slink back to the table in shame.

"Not so fast, cutie," Ezra said, moving over to block my retreat. "I'm not sure if I should be insulted or really sad you think someone requires payment to ask you to dance."

"Neither sound like a good answer. I'm just going to go. Maybe if I drink enough, I will forget all about this." Suddenly the idea of not remembering Ezra bothered me more than the humiliation caused by loose lips. "On second thought, why don't we start again?"

"I like that. Hello, I'm Ezra. Would you like to dance?" Humor sparkled in his dark eyes, captivating me.

Suddenly, it felt like something more significant was occurring than one guy asking another to dance. It could be something truly amazing or something that could set back all my good progress. Did I dare? Ezra's smile wavered as he waited for me to answer him. I shook off my silliness and returned his smile.

"I'd love to."

It was just one dance, then we'd part ways when he saw how clumsy I was. I'd never have to see him again. What could it hurt?

Chapter One

Henry

Six months later…

BUZZ. BUZZ. BUZZ.

Pulling my phone out of my pocket, I quietly muttered, "Damn it." In my nervous rush to arrive on time for my first summer college class, I'd forgotten to silence the damn thing.

"You're going to want to silence your phone or turn it off," the cute ginger guy sitting beside me said. "My best friend attended this class earlier today and said the professor is a real no-nonsense fellow. He's big on discipline, focusing, and listening. My other friend said he's even grumpier during the evening classes, so we're in for a real treat. Maybe he needs to start taking daily naps."

"Good to know," I absently said while silencing my phone. Since I still had a minute to spare, I tapped the message icon to open the text message from Geoff.

Good luck tonight, buddy. Maybe you can take notes in your human sexuality class and use them to get laid. Dude. Long. Dry. Spell.

I snorted and tapped out a reply. *Fuck you.*

Geoff's reply was instant. *I would, but you shut that down. No more friends with benefits for us.*

I had shut it down because it wasn't good for either of us. We'd resigned to getting off with each other because it was safe. Geoff wasn't afraid of my HIV status, and he knew I'd never out him to his father or anyone else, but the orgasms I had with Geoff felt empty. Once the afterglow faded, I felt guilty for using Geoff and allowing him to use me. We were much better off as friends.

I heard the door at the front of the room open followed by confident footfalls as our professor entered the classroom. Knowing I should put my phone down, I still typed a response to Geoff because I valued him.

True, but I love you.

Love you back, he replied.

Gotta go.

"Good evening. I want to start with everyone silencing their phones and putting them away." The deep, cultured, and controlled voice sent a shiver of awareness down my spine. Dear God, I'd recognize that voice anywhere. Hadn't I heard it in my dreams every night for the past six months?

No way. It couldn't be.

I snapped my head up. *Fuck me.* It was him.

"You won't come until I tell you to, Henry. Say my name. Let me hear that you understand me."

"Yes, Ezra."

My mouth fell open, and my phone clattered noisily to the desk, pulling Ezra's, um Professor Meyer's, dark gaze to mine. He blinked a few times before turning his attention to someone—anyone—besides me, but not before I saw a flash of recognition in his penetrative gaze. *Penetrative.* I bit back a snort. The insatiable man had penetrated me in every possible way during three rounds of mind-blowing, I-didn't-know-that-was-possible sex. My table mate's comment about Ezra needing a daily nap to improve his stamina and mood played in my mind, and I had to bite my lip to keep from giggling nervously.

"My name is Professor Meyer. Welcome to Biology of Human Sexuality."

"Oh God," I whimpered, feeling my dick harden in my pants.

"Pull yourself together, man," ginger guy said.

"If you chose this class because you thought you'd earn an easy grade watching pornography, then I suggest you use either of the two exits at the back of the room. In case none of you reviewed the syllabus before class, let me go over the curriculum for the next ten weeks. We'll kick things off discussing what human sexuality is, and some of you might be surprised to know it's not only about the physical behaviors of sexual intercourse." *Ezra... Fuck!* Professor Meyer paused to allow the smattering of snickers to die down. He glanced around the room, careful not to meet my greedy gaze, then returned his attention to his notes on the lectern.

"We will discuss the anatomy and physiology of both the male and female body, sexual response cycles, gender, attraction and love, sexual techniques and behaviors…"

At the mention of sexual techniques, I was transported back to his high-rise apartment overlooking the glittering Queen City. I couldn't recall what he'd called the technique he used on me—tandem…total…tantric! It started off with a sensual massage and ended up with penetrative sex while staring into each other's eyes, controlled breathing, and the most amazing orgasm I'd ever experienced. It had been more intimate than the typical hookup I'd expected when Ezra invited me back to his apartment after our one dance turned into a dozen.

It's your birthday, Henry. Demand the best.

The best was what he'd given me. I thought it was possible Ezra Meyer had ruined me for other men. I let out a long sigh, earning a gentle nudge from gingersnap. I snapped out of my lusty fog and caught Ezra looking at me. *Did he know where my mind had gone?* No one looking at him would notice the spark of remembrance, but I sure as hell did.

"Then we'll cover sexuality in adulthood and senior years, sexuality and disability, and sexually transmitted infections," Ezra said, wrapping up his overview.

"Gross," a girl at the table behind me vehemently whispered.

"Did you have something to contribute, miss? Is it sex between the elderly, sex for disabled people, or sexually transmitted infections that you find 'gross'?" *He'd heard her whispered response?* Sure, it sounded loud to me because it felt like it was aimed in my direction. What kind of supernatural hearing did he possess to go with his supernatural stamina?

"Um," she said timidly, probably shocked he heard her too. "All of them kind of gross me out, but the last one is the worst. I mean, who wants a sexually transmitted infection?"

I felt my face growing hotter. It took everything I had not to slink down in my chair and make myself smaller. I kept my eyes locked on Ezra and remembered the night we met.

"Let's get out of here," Ezra said in my ear. It might've been a whisper if we were in a quiet setting.

"To get a bite to eat?" I asked.

"I definitely want to nibble on you. Starting with this right here." Ezra traced my bottom lip with his forefinger, his tongue darting out to lick his own lips like he could already taste me on them.

"I'm not sure it's a good idea."

"Why?"

My heart raced, my face heated, and a cold sweat broke out all over my body. This part never got easier, and I didn't think the rejection that followed would either. Even though my viral loads were virtually undetectable after months on medication, I would never dream of hiding the truth from a potential sexual partner. "I'm positive."

"Positive it's not a good idea? Just a second ago you weren't sure. Did I come on too strong? Oh, my nibbling comment was too lame, wasn't it?" Ezra's words expressed insecurity, but it didn't match the confident, knowing expression in his eyes. He wasn't making jokes about it; he was trying to make it easier for me or giving me a way out.

"The nibbling wasn't lame, and I really want to be your late-night snack, but there's something you should know first." I worried my lip between my teeth for a second.

Ezra confidently cupped the back of my neck and slowly lowered his head to mine for a kiss. I had plenty of time to step back from his gentle hold or tell him no, but I wanted his kiss more than I'd wanted anything.

The touch of Ezra's lips against mine was soft and tender, but it still sent an explosion of lust and need spiraling through my body. It had been too long since someone had touched me, and no one had ever made me feel as cherished as he had in the middle of a crowded dance floor with techno music thumping through speakers and bodies thrashing together all around us. Then his tongue slid through my parted lips to tease mine. It was a miracle my body hadn't melted at his feet along with my resistance.

"Miss... I'm sorry, what's your name?" Ezra picked up a piece of paper from the lectern, which I guessed was the class roster. "Maybe I should've taken a roll call first, but I've learned my intro usually scares away the people who signed up for my class for the wrong reasons."

"I'm Emily Thompson, Mr. Meyer."

"It's Dr. Meyer, Miss Thompson," Ezra corrected. "I want you to look around the room and tell me what you see."

She was silent for a minute, and I presumed she was looking around the room, but I remained facing forward and didn't know if she was following orders or engaging in a stare-down with Ezra. "I see people."

"Not disabled people, old people, or infected people?" he countered.

"Um, well no one looks old in here, but it's not always obvious if someone is disabled or has a sexually transmitted infection."

"I'll stand in for the older people in this scenario," Ezra said, earning a few chuckles. "If it's not possible for you to tell upon sight what's going on with someone, maybe you should think before you speak so you're not insulting a person you don't even know. You don't know how a person arrived at this point in their life, and you're in no position to judge them or look down on them."

Most people would've shut up, happy to escape the encounter mostly unscathed, and allowed the professor to get on with his lecture, but there was always at least one idiot in every class. Guess who it was.

"Excuse me, *Dr. Meyer*," Emily Thompson said, disdain dripping from her tongue. "I wasn't judging or looking down on anyone. I was merely saying I wasn't looking forward to those particular study units."

"I don't think you're a good fit for this class, Miss Thompson. It would be wise if we parted ways."

"You're kicking me out of class?" she asked incredulously.

"I'm stating I don't think you're right for this class, and I'm suggesting you reconsider taking it. There will be case studies, field trips, and perhaps personal testimony from people in this room who won't deserve the eye roll and scornful tone you've exhibited."

Field trips? I wasn't sure what to think about that, but my pervy mind conjured up Ezra teaching the class tantric sex using me as his demonstration partner.

"Don't move a muscle, Henry. Just feel me. Feel how hard you make me. Feel the way my dick is pulsing inside your tight ass."

"You're an arrogant asshole, Dr. Meyer. I will officially withdraw from the class, and I'll be sure to pass along my thoughts on your teaching method to the dean."

"Are you aware the dean of this community college is a disabled, older woman you've unknowingly mocked with your derision today?" Ezra fired back.

"Come on, Jen. We're out of here."

"No, Em. I not only need this class, but I also want to take it," her friend said calmly. "I'll call you later, after you've had a chance to cool off."

"Don't bother." Miss Emily Thompson scooted her chair back so fast, it screeched against the linoleum and toppled backward. Then she stomped out of the room and slammed the door loud enough to rattle the windows.

Ezra just smirked and shook his head. "Is there anyone else who feels this class isn't for them? Now is the time to make a peaceful exit." He looked around the room, and I felt the same shiver of awareness I had when he entered the classroom and I heard his voice again for the first time in six months. "Let's get started then. I'll start with a roll call to put faces with names."

My mind started to wander again when he called off the names, but I reeled it back in. Emily's outburst had killed my boner, so I need-ed to focus on something other than memories of the night I spent in Ezra's apartment, or I'd be right back in the same embarrassing place.

"Sullivan, Henry," Ezra said. No inflection in his voice to indicate he knew what my orgasm face looked like. I raised my hand. "Good to meet you, Henry," he said, just as he'd done with every other student.

"Let's get started; shall we?" Ezra pulled a pair of rectangular, black-rimmed glasses from his briefcase and put them on, somehow making him look even sexier. The girl in front of me started to squirm a bit in her chair. *I feel it too, girl.* "What is human sexuality?" he asked, oblivious to the heat he stirred inside me. "Oh, you thought I was asking a rhetorical question," he said, smiling at his silent class. "I'm looking for a volunteer to tell me what human sexuality is?"

"Which part?" Drake, my ginger tablemate, asked. "The develop-mental, the physical, or the emotional?"

"Bingo," Ezra said. "While most of you associate human sexu-ality with the act of sexual intercourse, the term has a much broader scope. Today, we begin discussing the psychological aspects. I'm going to ask you to get in tune with your feelings. I know how much some of you will hate that. Since most of you are probably seeking a so-ciology degree with plans to counsel others, you'll need to excavate your own feelings before you can guide others to do the same thing." He paused when a few students chuckled. "What are the ranges of emotions one associates with human sexuality, and I mean the broad term, not just sexual intercourse?"

Desire, terror, confusion, and elation were some of the terms tossed out there by my classmates. Ezra didn't just let them shout out the emotions without them addressing what part of the human sexuality spectrum they related it to. I was one of only a few who didn't raise their hand and comment—partly because I was nervous and partly because I was just so fascinated by how freely the students around me spoke their thoughts and feelings on the matter.

Before I knew it, Ezra was wrapping up the class and reiterating the assigned reading listed in our syllabus. I knew I should pack my backpack and leave, but Ezra's presence pulled me to the front of the class like a moth to a flame.

Ezra's eyes darted to mine then back away as he watched the students shuffling out. "Is the class not to your liking, Mr. Sullivan?" Ezra asked, sounding stiff and formal.

I glanced over my shoulder and saw the remaining few stragglers slowly meandering toward the exits. "No, sir, that's not the issue."

The door closing behind the last student sounded loud and definite. Ezra turned his dark gaze back on me raising an elegant brow in silent question.

I glanced over my shoulder again to make sure we were truly alone. "Is this too awkward for you? Would you like me to drop the class?"

"Why would I find this awkward or want you to drop the class?"

"Um, because you and I... We—" Shit. Maybe he hadn't remembered me after all. Maybe the recognition I saw in his eyes was just wishful thinking on my part. The guy was sexy as fuck and probably picked up a new guy or two every weekend. Who could keep all the names and faces straight?

"We met at a club, hooked up, and went our separate ways the next morning. I wasn't your professor then, so we didn't break any rules. It doesn't bother me, and I hope it doesn't bother you." Ezra

11

made it sound like it was no big deal he'd made me come five times during three rounds of sex. He wasn't affected by our night together and couldn't see why I would be either. He had no idea he haunted my dreams every single night, nor would he ever find out.

I straightened my spine, squared my shoulders, and said, "Of course not."

"So, you'll stay then?"

"Yeah. The class was fascinating, and I enjoyed it."

"Are you sure? You were pretty quiet," Ezra countered.

"I grew up in a strict, religious home where discussing sexuality was forbidden. I've only been free of the oppressive environment for ten months, so I'm still not up to speed with everyone else."

"You'll get there, Mr. Sullivan. I have every confidence in you."

"Thank you, Dr. Meyer." *Ezra! Yes, Ezra!* I nearly choked when the memory of my last climax came to me without warning. I started walking backward. "I'll see you later."

"In two days," Ezra said, a wry smile tugging the corner of his lip. Had he known what I was thinking?

"Uh-huh. Yep."

"Goodnight, Mr. Sullivan."

"Goodnight, Ez—Dr. Meyer." My eyes widened over my near slip, and my face reddened. "Sorry," I quickly said then turned and got out of there before I said or did something else to make a bigger fool of myself.

I kept walking as fast as I could until I exited the building, not stopping to catch my breath until I reached the car I'd borrowed from my roommate, Jessie. I was glad I'd parked beneath a light post because it helped me see the flat tire before I attempted to drive on the rim.

"Could this night get any worse?"

Chapter Two

Ezra Meyer

I RETREATED TO THE SANCTITY OF MY BORROWED OFFICE AFTER HENRY left. The space wasn't much to look at with its beige walls, equally drab tile floors, a desk that was older than me, and a sketchy chair that squeaked and pitched every time I sat down, but it was service-able. The only somewhat personal touches in the room were an artifi-cial plant with an inch of dust coating the leaves and a mirror hanging on the closet door—both items left behind by a predecessor. Reeling from the shock of seeing Henry unexpectedly, the sparse space sud-denly felt like a sanctuary. I collapsed against the closed door, not trusting my legs to carry me to the rickety-ass chair across the room.

Henry.

His wide-eyed innocence had called to me the night we met. In a room full of preening peacocks, there was a sweet dove unaware of his beauty. He'd laughed with his friend and sipped a cocktail he hadn't really liked. Later I'd learned his friend had bought it for him to celebrate his monumental birthday. It was his first alcoholic beverage *and* his first time at a gay club. I would learn he wasn't a virgin, but he might as well have been. Everything about him was soft, gentle, and kind, even if self-doubt and uncertainty lingered in the depths of his eyes.

Oh, his eyes. If it's true they're the windows to our souls, then Henry's windows were constructed of stained glass in various shades of green and a pop of lemony yellow. The black iron separating the panes of glass would represent his pupils, and the yellow glass would represent the striations around them. Pale green would embody his lovely irises, and the forest green hue would perfectly match the dark band around them.

At the club, I'd thought his hair was an ordinary shade of dark brown, but the winter sunlight the next morning picked up strands of the various shades of red mixed in, reminding me of a burnt Serengeti sunset. Unable to resist, I'd slid my fingers through hair so soft and smooth it rivaled the finest fabrics from the silk market in Beijing.

"Christ. I'm thinking like an English lit professor." A pretentious, well-traveled one. "There aren't always hidden meanings behind words, actions, and appearances. Sometimes the curtains are just fucking blue, sometimes eyes are just fucking green, and hair is just fucking auburn and well-conditioned." But the color of his irises alone wasn't what had enthralled me. His eyes announced every thought crossing his mind, and I hadn't been able to get enough of him. Still reeling from a hideous breakup, I was in no position to offer Henry anything beyond hot, horny sex, so I'd reluctantly let him go the next morning.

Feeling rattled to my bones, I turned and checked my reflection in the mirror and was pleased that none of my turmoil showed in my expression. I glanced down at my hands and saw they were steady too. Inside, though? It was a completely different story. My pulse raced, guts clinched, and my dick had stayed at half-mast during the entire class. I normally walked around while interacting with the students during my lectures, but I'd stayed hidden behind my lectern so no one, especially Henry, could see how he affected me.

Just hearing him slip and say my name had caused me to grip the side of the podium hard enough to break it. My dick had gone from mostly interested to full-blown, let's-fuck mode.

Yes! Oh my God! Ezra! Ezra!

The man had chanted my name like it was his salvation, and I wanted to save him and cast him away at the same time. Pushing him away had been the only option available to me at the time. Yet, when our first round of fucking had ended, I pulled him closer instead of putting him in a cab. I had wanted to challenge Henry and open his mind to the sexual principles I'd learned over the years, and he was the most willing pupil I'd ever taught anywhere—classroom or bedroom. Neither of us could get enough.

I'd hurt Henry's feelings in my classroom, and although it didn't sit well, there was nothing I could do about it. I couldn't jeopardize my career because Henry made me horny. God, I hated how callous and cynical I sounded. I'd once had Henry's wide-eyed wonder as I explored the world, but I'd learned most beautiful things wound barbs around your heart like wicked vines. They would either squeeze the life out of your heart or slash it with the barbs until you bled out. I didn't want that for Henry; I wouldn't be a source of pain to him. So, no matter how much Henry tugged at my heartstrings, I couldn't allow anything further to happen between us.

I turned off the light and exited my office, checking my phone for important emails and texts as I walked toward the staff parking lot in the rear. I deleted the sales ads in my inbox and dialed my best friend, Ryder, after reading his text message that said: *Call me!*

"Thank God!" Ryder said dramatically when he answered. "I thought you'd never call me."

"What's wrong? Did something happen to Lucien or your family?"

"What? Heavens no. The urgency in my text was from hunger, not because someone's life is in peril. I swear to God, Ezra, I can feel my stomach eating itself."

"Jesus. You're so theatrical." My best friend had switched careers from art conservator to romance novelist—a damned good one, I might add. I'd recently finished reading his latest book and suspected he was partly to blame for my overly romanticized thoughts. "Why the hell are you starving yourself, and why aren't you asking your sexy man to feed you in bed?"

"He's out of town again, and I'm on a deadline with this book. If I stop writing long enough to cook something, then I'll lose my train of thought and wreck my mojo. Do you know how many words I've written today?"

"I'm guessing a lot."

"Almost ten thousand. That's a first for me. I. Can't. Stop."

"Okay, I understand you want to stay focused, but do you realize how late it is?"

"It's not that late; I could—Oh! Did I wake you up?"

"It's nine forty-five, not three o'clock in the morning. Haven't you ever heard of Door Dash or GrubHub?"

"Yes, but what I really want isn't available on those apps, and the pizzeria stopped delivering at nine. Besides, the owner would spit on my pizza if I ordered it myself."

"Spit on your pizza?" I asked incredulously. "Save the drama for your books, Ryder."

"I'm serious, Ez. I dated her son in college, and although our breakup was amicable, I acted like a complete dickhead when I returned to Cincinnati last year. I was lonely and wanted Archie to pick up where we left off like six years hadn't passed. When I found out he was seeing someone else, I might've tried to cause a tad bit of trouble."

"A tad bit? Now you sound like my grandma."

"Fuck you, Ezra. Do you want the rest of the story or not?"

By this time, I'd reached my car and climbed behind the steering wheel. "Hang on. Let me start my car so I can transfer the call to Bluetooth."

"Better yet," Ryder said. "I'll order the pizza online and put it under your name, and you can pick it up and bring it over."

"Will I get to eat any of the pizza, or do I just get to sit there and watch you take bites in between weaving your wild story?"

"Of course, I'm sharing it with you."

"Dinner and a story," I said dryly. "How can I pass that up? Text me the address of the pizza joint and what time it will be ready?"

"You won't regret this, Ez."

Famous last words. "See you soon, Ry."

Ryder's text came a minute later. The pizza would be ready just after ten, and according to my GPS, it would only take me ten minutes to get to Mamma Maria's. Rather than stay parked in an isolated lot, I put my car in drive and drove around the side of the building. The faculty and student parking lots were separated by the brick building, but there was only one entrance and exit for everyone to use. When I drove around the building, I expected to see the student lot empty, but there was a single car there. It was hard to tell what color the car was supposed to be because it was a patchwork quilt of faded or chipped paint and rust, which had corroded the metal around the wheel wells and the front and back bumpers. The trunk stood open, and a person was bent over peering inside it. I could only see long, lean legs encased in dark jeans. The Chucks the stranded person wore could belong to anyone since the shoes were gender neutral.

Instead of continuing to the exit, I turned my car toward the stranded student. There was no way in hell I was leaving without making sure this kid had a ride home. As soon as headlights turned toward the stranded car, the kid straightened up and looked in my direction.

The cone of light shining down from the post above looked more like a spotlight, and who was standing in the center? Henry fucking Sullivan.

"Fuck me," I said tersely. Learning the stranded student's identity only tripled my protective instincts. I didn't have to give him a ride, but I needed to make sure he had one. I parked beside him then killed my engine. "What's the problem?" I asked when I got out.

"Oh, hello, Ezra, um Professor Meyer." Henry looked even more nervous than when he'd approached me after class. I didn't wish car trouble on anyone, but I would prefer it was the source of his increased agitation rather than the confrontation with me or seeing me again so soon afterward. "I came out and found a flat tire on Jessie's car."

"Who's Jessie?" I didn't ask which tire since the ones on the passenger side looked fine. I didn't inquire if he'd found a spare while he rummaged around in the trunk. I went straight to the heart of the matter. *Who the fuck was Jessie, and why was Henry driving his car?*

"My r-roommate." Henry had probably mistaken my possessive growl as irritation. The truth rested somewhere in between jealous as fuck and pissed off.

Christ, Ezra. My thundering had made the boy stammer. *He's no boy, and you damn well know it.* I released a breath and started over again. Softening my voice, I said, "Did you find a spare tire in the trunk? On a late model car, the access to it is most likely beneath the carpet."

Henry straightened his shoulders, and his voice lost all traces of unease and trepidation when he said, "Not all of us can afford fancy Audi sedans and luxurious high-rise apartments overlooking the Ohio River."

"I'm not insulting your boyfriend, Hen—Mr. Sullivan. I'm merely stating older vehicles often had removable carpet in the trunk which you pull up to access the spare tire. I can help you change it."

"You're just a jack-of-all-trades, aren't you? There's no carpet and no spare tire." His assertiveness was starting to work on the tenuous hold I had on myself. His innocence had captivated me, but his defiance challenged me. If he wasn't my student, I would bend him over the trunk and remind him who was in charge. The errant thought made my dick twitch.

"Triple A?" I asked, pleased my internal struggle wasn't evident in my tone. "Phone a friend, perhaps?"

"I don't have Triple A, and I doubt Jessie does either." Right. If Jessie couldn't afford a car built in the twenty-first century, then it was unlikely he could afford roadside assistance.

"I am a member, and I will happily call for service. They'll come out and change the tire for you."

"No," Henry said adamantly. "Jess doesn't like owing anyone, especially a stranger."

"Well, what do you propose then? I can't just leave you stranded in a parking lot. Do you have a friend you can call to pick you up?"

"I have friends," Henry said defensively. "They're just not picking up or responding to text messages right now."

"I'll order a Lyft for you then," I said, pulling out my phone.

"I can't let you do that, Professor Meyer." I hated the formality but knew I had to insist he maintain it as a reminder of who I was to him. I'd never even allowed myself to entertain lustful thoughts about a student, let alone have a sexual relationship with one. I saw firsthand the way it could ruin careers, relationships, and reputations. No hot fuck was worth it.

"You're not *letting* me do anything, Mr. Sullivan." I tapped the Lyft app on my phone. "Kindly give me the address of where you're going."

"It's not—" His words died when I glanced up from my phone, and he saw the ferocious expression in my eyes. "Forty-four sixty-eight Grant Street."

"That wasn't so hard." *Wait.* I'd just entered the same address into my GPS. "You want me to drop you off at a pizza joint?"

Henry rolled his eyes. "It's not just a pizza joint; it's *the* pizza joint, which you must know if you have the address memorized."

I shrugged. "I've never eaten at Mamma Maria's. My friend just ordered a pizza online and asked me to pick it up on my way to his house."

Henry's posture grew rigid. "What friend?" He sounded jealous, and against my better judgement, I liked it. A lot.

"It's none of your business, Mr. Sullivan. Shut the trunk, lock up your boyfriend's car, and get in. Don't give me shit about it either since we're going to the same address right now."

"Fine."

Henry's pout was adorable and his borderline stomp when he reluctantly did as I asked made me want to lay him across my knees and spank the disobedience out of him. My amusement swiftly died when Henry slammed the door closed after he flopped down beside me; not because I was worried he'd hurt my car, but because I was trapped in a confined space with his crisp, citrusy scent, reminding me of the lemon orchards in Italy's Amalfi Coast. *Jesus, I was doing it again.*

"Follow the highlighted route," my GPS said when I restarted my car and shifted it into drive.

"You can turn the navigation off since I know where we're going."

I exited the navigation app, and other than Henry giving me directions, we rode in silence for a few minutes.

"You have nicer things than a professor at a community college should be able to afford," Henry said, breaking the silence.

"It's not wise to assume things about people, Mr. Sullivan," I said sternly. "I'm a professor at the University of Cincinnati, which partners with several community colleges in the area. I'm only here for the summer semester to teach this class since I'm trying to prove to the dean that Biology of Human Sexuality would be a valuable course to offer our students."

Henry snorted. "So you're using us like guinea pigs then?"

My hands tightened on the steering wheel. What had happened to the doe-eyed, sweet man who loved to please me? "I'm not using anyone, Mr. Sullivan. I'm well versed with the material, so I don't need to conduct experiments. The dean wanted to see facts and hard numbers before making the final decision on whether it's a good fit."

"Like enrollment, attendance, and grades?" Henry asked.

"Precisely."

"No wonder you were so strict. If you need good enrollment numbers, maybe you shouldn't have tossed that Emily girl out of class."

The memory of the student's scornful remark and the snide look on her face made me angry all over again. "And have her say hateful things that hurt people's feelings. I saw the look on your face and the way your body tensed. You and the others in the classroom don't deserve to have someone degrade you like that—unknowingly or deliberately. A college is a place for higher learning, but some people will never rise above ignorance, no matter how smart they are or how long they go to school."

"Thank you," Henry said softly. "I wasn't aware you noticed my reaction."

I'm always going to notice you. "You're welcome. As for my strictness, I'm a stickler about my time. It's a precious commodity, and I don't like it wasted by people who aren't going to take the class seriously. I'm a very reasonable professor as long as people are giving my class the attention it deserves. Show up on time, keep your phone off, participate in class, and do your assignments. Respect me, respect my classroom, and I'll return the respect to my students."

"Field trips?" Henry randomly asked. "What kind of field trips?"

I knew his mind had conjured up kinky things, and I wanted to keep him guessing. "That's for me to know, and you to find out."

"As long as I don't need a permission slip signed by my mother," Henry quipped.

I heard a hint of sadness and wanted to know more, but we had arrived at Mamma Maria's. Besides, getting to know Henry Sullivan was off the table. The sounds he made during orgasms frequently echoed in my dreams and getting further involved with him was a complication I couldn't afford.

"That won't be necessary," I said, parallel parking in front of a quaint pizza place.

Henry released his seat belt and offered me a shy smile. "Thanks for the ride." His face turned a pretty shade of pink, and I knew his words triggered the same memories in him as me. That night in my apartment, Henry and I had both learned what he was capable of doing, and sitting astride my cock, both cowboy and reverse cowboy, was his favorite position.

I cleared my throat and tried to smile without baring my teeth like a hungry wolf. "No thanks are needed."

Henry got out of the car, and I followed him into the pizzeria at a leisurely pace. Henry headed through swinging doors leading back to the kitchen while I approached the counter. After a few seconds, a woman with curly hair piled on top of her head came out of the kitchen carrying two pizza boxes. *Damn, Ryder really was starving.*

My eyes kept darting back to the kitchen doors swooshing back and forth, trying to catch one last glimpse of Henry. Did he work here?

"Are you Ezra?" she sweetly asked, snapping me out of my musings.

"I am."

"I'm Maria." She looked to be my mother's age, but the gray and white curls I saw woven through the black said she embraced her age rather than fought it. I inherited my early-gray genes from my mom, who started dying her hair to cover a white streak in high school. My mother would go to her grave with whatever black dye her stylist used, but I thought she would look just as beautiful with white hair. "Thank you for bringing my boy home." *Her boy?* Henry looked nothing like Maria, but maybe he took after his father. *Wait.* Did that make Henry the younger brother of Ryder's ex? Like she read my mind, Maria said, "He's not my biological son, but I couldn't love him more if he were." I nodded. "Would you tell Ryder it's not stealthy to order pizza under aliases then pay with his credit card? It's a waste of energy he could spend in better ways. Let him know I don't hate him, and I wouldn't spit in his pizza. I'd love to see him and hear all about his wedding plans."

I tossed my head back and laughed at the ridiculousness of the evening, which was what I needed to dispel the tension holding me in its clutches. "Yes, ma'am. I will do that."

"Good." She reached for the pen she'd tucked behind her ear, and wrote something down on a green, red, and white postcard before she signed it with a flourish. "Here you go. This is a Mamma Maria's gift certificate from me to thank you for your kindness."

"No, please, I can't accept it. I was already coming here to pick up Ryder's pizzas."

"It was so much more than that, and you know it. Henry told me you offered to call Triple A to have the tire fixed even after learning it wasn't his car. That goes above and beyond what most professors would do for their students." Lord, the woman acted like I was a saint, but she'd be horrified if she knew I was mentally stripping Henry naked for more than half the ride to her pizzeria. "I will not hear of you taking no for an answer."

I recognized a losing battle when I saw one. "Okay, I will accept your kind gesture."

"Thank you."

Henry never returned to the dining room, so I either had to find an excuse to linger or accept I'd see him in a few days in class. He was obviously in a safe place, so I thanked Maria once more and left the pizzeria.

I took a photo of the pizza boxes and sent it to Ryder. He immediately replied with a drooling emoji. Even though I felt completely off-kilter, I laughed and pulled away from the curb, hoping two days would be enough to shore up my defenses against a lithe body, sensual lips, and eyes that haunted me in my sleep.

Chapter Three

Henry

"SORRY, I'M LATE," I YELLED, BURSTING THROUGH THE FRONT door of Hastings Law firm. My boss, Desmond Hastings, who was unexpectedly sitting at my desk, clutched his chest and slumped against the back of my chair.

"Lord, child, I only came out here to find some staples, not die of a damn heart attack so that better be a peace offering in the pastry box and drink carrier in your hands." A ninety-pound Rottweiler came from behind my desk to check out the commotion. Luckily, the beast recognized my voice so she wasn't snarling and barking like she would if a stranger had foolishly busted through our door. "Justice wants a treat too."

"Does my sweet girl want a treat?" I asked. Justice walked over and pressed her nose against my canvas grocery tote. "Yes, I am restocking your biscuit stash." I looked back up at my boss. "Sorry, I'm late."

Des looked at his knockoff Rolex watch Jimmy Schlick, aka Slick Jimmy, had given him as payment for his legal services last month. "You're not late; it's only—Wait. It can't be six because I wasn't even out of bed at the ungodly hour. That son of a bitch gave me a faulty watch. I'm going to remember this the next time he gets arrested and needs a lawyer."

It was nine fifteen, and I was supposed to arrive at eight thirty. "I did bring a peace offering, and I'll make up the lost time during my lunch break." I set the coffee carrier and pastry box on my desk.

"The hell you will, Henry," Des said, rising to his feet. Maintaining eye contact with him meant I had to tip my head back since he stood at six and a half feet tall in men's designer dress shoes. When Desmond dressed in full drag, he became Dez-d-Moaner, and her six-inch heels made the queen seven feet of satin, sequin, and sass. The transition from the well-dressed, African American lawyer to an Amazon goddess was surreal. "You work too hard at your two jobs, and now that you've gone back to school, you're going to need the hour each day to catch your breath or study. I'm afraid you're burning your candle at both ends, and I don't want to see your bright flame dwindle to a puny pilot light."

I snorted. "Okay. I promise not to make a habit of this. I just had a rougher first night at college than I anticipated."

"Were your professors raging dickheads? They tend to be strict at first then relax once they've established the rules and tone they want for their class." Des slapped his forehead then rolled his eyes. "What am I saying? This isn't your first rodeo."

I laughed, and Des's perfectly arched eyebrows rose high on his forehead. "The two years I spent at bible college are at the opposite end of the spectrum from the class I attended last night."

"Were you really going to become a pastor?" Des asked, tilting his head to the side.

"That's what my mother wanted for me, and if I wanted financial assistance from her, then it was my only avenue. It wasn't my passion though."

"What was unique about the class last night?" Des asked. He wasn't making polite conversation; Des truly cared about me. Maybe it was exhaustion stirring up my emotions and making my eyes sting, or perhaps it was one of the times where the gratefulness I felt for him overwhelmed me. Des, mistaking my misty eyes, scowled as he rounded my desk and gripped my shoulders. "Who do I need to rip apart?" he asked in a growly voice. "Is your neighbor making trouble for you and Jessie again?"

I laughed and shook my head. "No, the warnings you gave him last time were sufficient."

"Then what is it, lamb chop? What has you so upset that you're late to work? You're never late."

I opened my mouth to answer, but the office door opened.

"Is this a bad time?" the visitor asked in a snide tone.

I couldn't roll my eyes because it would only make the tension between Des's boyfriend and me worse than it already was. The smile I gave Sean was serene and patient, the exact opposite of the seething I felt on the inside. Des could do so much better. "Not at all," I said sweetly. "I was just telling Des about my first night back at college after nearly a year off."

"Oh, how titillating," Sean said sarcastically.

"Sean, what do I owe the pleasure of this visit?" Des asked cooly. *Uh oh.* Trouble in paradise. *Again.* How could anyone as intelligent and compassionate as Des be attracted to a user like Sean Penderson?

"Pleasure is the reason for my visit, darling," he cooed, strolling toward us, forcing Des to remove his hands from my shoulders and step back. Everything about Sean was fake or carefully orchestrated from his hair color, eyelash extensions, and colored contacts to the way he walked.

"Now isn't a good time for me, Sean. My first appointment is due to arrive any minute."

"You have time to talk Henry down from whatever crisis he's landed in this time, but you don't have time for your boyfriend?" Sean's wounded boyfriend performance was Oscar-worthy.

"Ex-boyfriend," Des countered.

Oh! That was new. I had a sudden urge to pop a bag of popcorn in the microwave in our small kitchenette so I could watch the show. They'd had plenty of arguments and almost-breakups during the eight months I worked for Des, but they'd never broken up. I was dying to know what Sean had done to finally push Des over the edge.

"Baby, I didn't mean what I said. Can't we go to your office and talk this out in private?" Sean possessively placed his hand on Des's chest.

"Sean," Des said, gently removing Sean's hand and stepping back from him, "this isn't the time or place to discuss it."

"I see," Sean replied stiffly. "Perhaps, we can have dinner tonight. I can make reservations at Rinella's. Eating at your favorite restaurant always puts you in a good mood."

"I already have reservations for Rinella's tonight, Sean. I told you this last night."

Sean's dry laugh was flat and devoid of humor. "Oh, that's right. Henry's back-to-college dinner. How could I forget such a monumental moment?"

"What?" I asked, looking between the two men. Des looked thunderous while Sean looked smug.

"You just had to ruin his *surprise* dinner, didn't you?" Des asked his boyfriend. *Ex-boyfriend.*

"Oh," Sean exclaimed, covering his mouth and turning murderous eyes on me. "Was it supposed to be a surprise?"

Since Sean and Des were no longer dating, I didn't feel the need to suppress the snark I wanted to unleash on him. "Clearly, which was the point of your visit this morning." It wasn't the first time he'd deliberately ruined a surprise or wrecked plans Des made for me. "You're such a bitch, Sean. Get out of here before I let Justice eat you."

The dog had sat quietly watching the show but stood when she heard her name. Growling low in her throat, Justice slowly walked toward Sean. The dog hated Sean as much as I did or more. He was the reason she occasionally got locked out of Des's bedroom.

Sean squealed and backed up. "Call her off, Des."

Des snapped his fingers. Justice stopped and sat on her

haunches, but she never took her eyes off Sean. One false move and she'd be on him.

"If I were you, I'd slowly back out of the door," I suggested. "No sudden moves, Sean."

"You think you've won, Henry, but Des will get tired of you and toss you aside just like he does with all the pretty boys who came before me. You're no one special. I'm the only one he's chosen to keep. Des is just angry with me right now, but it will pass, and he'll want me back in his bed before the end of the week. I only need to bide my time until then." Sean paused just on the other side of the doorway for dramatic effect.

"Hold your breath while you're at it," I suggested then crossed the room and slammed the door in his face. I turned around and faced Des, whose broad smile would do funny things to my stomach if I weren't already hung up on a different man who was also way out of my league. "Des, if you take that arrogant son of a bitch back, I'll—" The phone on my desk rang, interrupting my threat. "Don't run off. I'm not finished with you." I crossed the room and picked up the phone from its cradle. "Hastings Law; how can we help you?" I asked.

"Good morning, precious. Is my sweet boy with a client, or does he have a minute to talk?"

"Good morning, Mama Hastings," I said, looking over at Desmond. He waved his hands then tapped his busted watch, signaling he wasn't prepared to speak to his mother right then. Des's first client was due to walk through the door any minute, and his mama was a hard one to get off the phone when she called. "He has a client right now, Mama Hastings. I can give him a message when he's through." Des steepled his hands in prayer and mouthed *thank you*. "I have a few minutes though, and you won't believe what happened here this morning."

Des narrowed his eyes and would've flipped me off, but Mrs. Robbins walked through the door, so he silently waved her into his office instead.

"Do tell, precious. By the delightful tone of your voice, I'm hoping my son has seen the light and got rid of that no-good, self-hating homosexual he called a boyfriend." *God, I loved this woman.*

My workload was light, so I grabbed a cup of coffee from the carrier, and a rainbow-sprinkled chocolate donut from the box. "Oh, yeah," I told her.

I was still buzzing from caffeine, sugar, and pettiness when I met Geoff for lunch at a food court halfway between our two offices.

"Check you out," Geoff said, giving me a once-over as I approached the table. He'd arrived first and already ordered our food.

"Tell me; are my feet still on the ground?"

"Oh my God. Did you and Des smoke a joint one of his clients gave him as payment?"

"No one pays Des in weed," I said. At least not that I knew about anyway. "You know I've never smoked pot a day in my life. I've never been drunk either." Except for the one time Ezra got me stoned on his pheromones and fucked me senseless. "Des and Sean *finally* broke up. I don't know any of the dirty details, but Mama Hastings and I are so thrilled."

"Do you have a thing for your boss?" Geoff teased, pushing a tray with my chicken Caesar gyro, kettle chips, and Sprite across the table to me.

I snorted. Des and I were close, so a lot of the people in our lives assumed we were circling one another waiting for the right time to make our move. I loved Desmond Hastings with all my heart, but I wasn't *in love* with him. I was certain Des felt the same way about me too. "No, but I do have a thing for my professor."

"After only one day back at school. What's he like?" Geoff asked.

"You've met him," I said coyly.

Geoff took the bait. "How? When?"

"Think back to a cold day in mid-December. A boy became a man, and—"

"Holy fuck," Geoff loudly said, earning many glares from the people eating around us.

I leaned forward and softly said, "I don't know if it was holy, but it was ethereal for sure."

"The sexy guy who picked you up at Vibe is a professor? *Your professor?*"

"My Biology of Human Sexuality professor," I said.

Geoff just stared at me for a few seconds with his mouth gaping open. "What happened? Did he recognize you?"

"Uh-huh," I said then sank my teeth into my gyro. I made happy noises while I chewed and tried not to laugh at Geoff's irritated expression.

"And?"

"Eat your lunch, Geoff." He rolled his eyes but took a bite anyway.

"I waited until class ended then approached him to see if he wanted me to drop his class."

"Why?" Geoff said around a mouthful of food.

I made him wait while I carefully ate three chips and sipped my Sprite. "Because it's an awkward situation." I leaned closer to Geoff and lowered my voice. "I look at him and picture him naked. He says certain words and I remember just how much I liked feeling him inside me."

"Whoa," Geoff said. "I didn't know you were hung up on him. I just thought you were too busy to date any of the guys who ask you out."

"I'm not hung up on him; it's just that…"

"He ruined you for other guys?" Geoff asked.

I released a sigh. "Maybe," I admitted.

"That's too bad. You have a whole lot of life ahead of you, and I'd hate for you to live it lonely." Sometimes I forgot the depth of emotion and insight Geoff hid behind his easygoing smile. "What happened when you offered to drop the class?"

"He took me to his office and bent me over his desk."

Geoff choked on his sip of Coke. "Really?" he asked after sputtering for a few minutes.

"Oh, wait. That was the fantasy I played out in the shower this morning, which caused me to be late for work."

Geoff lobbed a French fry across the table, smacking me square in the chest. "Jerk."

I caught the fry before it landed on my lap then ate it. "The truth is a bit more humiliating," I admitted then repeated the conversation for Geoff.

Anger flashed in my friend's eyes. "Sexy, silver fox sounds like a pretentious player."

"I thought so too until he gave me a ride after class when I discovered Jessie's car had a flat tire in the parking lot."

"A ride to a destination or a ride on his dick?" Geoff asked through narrowed eyes.

"A ride to Mamma Maria's." I filled him in on our second interaction of the night.

"Don't tell me you worked last night too," Geoff said.

"I only stopped in the kitchen long enough to help them get caught up on dishes and grab a bite to eat before I went upstairs to my apartment." Maria had lived there for a decade or longer, but her apartment became available when Archie moved in with his fiancé and Maria moved into his old room at Ryan's Place. Archie still managed the house during the day, but he'd hesitated to move out because he hadn't wanted to leave the home without management at night. Maria loved fussing over the residents, so it was a win-win for everyone.

"What did Jess say about the car?"

"Well, a miracle occurred overnight while I slept. I found Jess's car parked behind the restaurant next to the delivery cars like usual."

"Ah, the professor had it towed even after you told him not to."

"He had the tire fixed and had the vehicle towed," I corrected. "Jess is still on the road with the band and doesn't have a clue it happened. I'm going to keep it that way. If the professor wants reimbursement, then I'll pay him back."

Geoff snorted. "I just bet you will."

"Asshole."

"Don't even bother denying you wouldn't thank him from your knees."

The thought had crossed my mind, but I pushed it aside almost immediately. "Do you want to hear how I learned about Sean and Des's breakup?" I asked, changing the subject.

"Hell yes," Geoff said. "Don't leave out any detail." My friend didn't bother hiding how eager he was to hear about Des kicking Sean to the curb. He might not be ready to admit it, but Geoff had a major crush on Des. I'd caught Des ogling Geoff plenty of times when he visited me at the office.

An idea started forming in my mind. "What are you doing tonight?"

"Not a damn thing. Dad has his bowling league thing, and Mom is leading the ladies' bible study group at the church, so I have a few free hours. What did you have in mind?"

"Thanks to Sean, I know Des set up a celebration dinner for me tonight at Rinella's. He always pads his reservation number because there's always a last-minute invite. I'm inviting you."

"Oh," Geoff said excitedly before his happiness faded. "I don't want to impose. If Des wanted to include me, he would've asked."

"He didn't invite you because he knows how uncomfortable you get in a setting where you're the only one who's not out yet. He knows how important you are to me, and he'd never intentionally exclude you from my celebration dinner. I'll talk to him as soon as I get back to the office. What do you say?"

"If you're sure…"

"I am."

"What time should I be there?"

"That's a good question. I'll have to find out and text you."

We finished our lunch and parted ways. I was too busy scheming during my walk back to the office and not paying a bit of attention to where I was going, which is how I turned a corner and walked nose first into someone's chest.

"Shit!" I said, rubbing my nose.

Firm hands gripped my shoulders. "Are you all right, Henry?"

Recognizing the voice, I snapped my head up and looked into dark eyes glittering with concern and arousal.

Chapter Four

Ezra

"Oh, hi, Ezra," Henry said breathlessly. It was the same thing he had said to me when he woke up in my bed. He sounded both surprised and elated—then and now.

Then, I'd rolled him over and kissed him fully awake until his dick was as hard as mine. I'd had him once more before I fed him and put him in a Lyft. Facing Henry on the sidewalk, I wanted to kiss him just as bad, but I wouldn't allow it. My hand, acting independently of my brain, cupped Henry's face. I ran my thumb over his full bottom lip, wishing I could nibble it with my teeth before sucking into my mouth. My brain screamed no, but my head was already lowering to take what I wanted.

"Do that shit in private," a man said, slightly jostling me with his shoulder when he passed. Normally, I would've been pissed the homophobe thought he had a right to tell me what to do and fumed he had physically touched me in any way, but I was grateful it stopped me from doing something stupid like make out with my student in broad daylight on a public street.

Dropping my hands from Henry, I took a step back. "Are you okay, Mr. Sullivan?"

Henry's eyes changed from dazed to destroyed in seconds. "Sure, but it would've been my fault if I wasn't. I should've been paying attention to where I was going. At least we didn't knock heads."

I needed someone to knock some sense into me. "What had you so distracted?" I asked, even though I should've wished him a good day and kept walking.

"It's silly and a little embarrassing." Henry shook his head then smiled. "Hey, I was going to thank you tomorrow night, but I'll do it now since we're both standing here."

"For what?" I asked, pretending I didn't know what he was talking about. I would rather he tell me what had put the sappy smile on his face before he'd crashed into me.

"For paying to fix Jess's tire and having it towed back to the pizzeria. You didn't have to do that," Henry said softly, looking at me with doe eyes.

I needed to disavow him of the notion I was a knight in shining armor. "I don't know what you're talking about, Henry. I dropped you off at the pizzeria and went to my friend's to catch up and eat pizza."

"Okay, Professor Meyer, I'll let it go since you clearly don't want credit for doing a nice deed. I'll see you in class tomorrow."

I nodded. "Take care, Mr. Sullivan." I stepped around Henry and walked away from him while I still could.

I needed to find something to keep my brain occupied on my day off, so I called my father to see if I could steal him away for the afternoon to play golf. Knowing he would be at work, I dialed his direct line. He picked up right away.

"Hello, Son. Were your ears burning?" My father's deep, jovial laugh never failed to put a smile on my face.

"No, should they have been?"

I heard a click and knew he'd picked up the receiver, switching off the speakerphone to talk privately. "I was just talking about you to an old friend over lunch. We've both recently moved back to the city, and we made plans to get together for dinner tonight. Your mother and I would love for you to join us."

I smiled and shook my head. "Let me guess; they have a single, gay son around my age who would be perfect for me."

"Did you already talk to your mother? Why didn't she tell me she'd already invited you to dinner?"

"No, Dad, Mom didn't call me and invite me to dinner. I've become very adept at detecting her matchmaking attempts," I said drolly.

"Well, this time it was my idea. Look, Son, I'm not expecting miracles to happen tonight, but it wouldn't hurt for you to join us for dinner and possibly make another friend."

I laughed. It was true my parents' matchmaking attempts had failed to find my "one true love," but it had led to several new friends. Ryder was one of them. "You're in luck because I don't have classes tonight, and I haven't made any plans."

"Perfect," Dad said, and I could picture him rubbing his hands together. "We're eating at Rinella's at seven thirty."

"I'll be there, but can we please not make a habit out of this?" I asked. "If I'd made plans, I wouldn't have canceled them."

"I wouldn't have asked you to change your plans," Dad countered.

"Are you too busy to sneak away for a round of golf?"

"Never," Dad replied. "I'll meet you at the country club in an hour. It will give me plenty of time to humiliate you over eighteen holes and still allow you time to get cleaned up before you meet us for dinner."

"I'm the only one who'll need to clean up first?"

"Please, Son. I won't even break a sweat on the course today."

I admired his confidence, but he wasn't the only one feeling particularly strong. "We'll see who's at the top of their game, old man."

"You'll eat your words."

"Care to make a wager?" I challenged.

Dad chuckled. "What's life without risk? Name your prize."

"Your Aston Martin."

Dad laughed hard and long. "You think I'm going to give you my prized possession if you beat me at golf? I mean, it would take a miracle for it to happen, but still…"

"I didn't mean we'd play for keeps. If I win, I get to borrow the car during a weekend of my choosing."

"Son, I've never let another living soul drive my car."

"Then you'll play especially hard to ensure it never happens," I countered.

"You're on."

"There's my sweet boy," Mom said when I walked into Rinella's. Simone Meyer glowed with an inner radiance you couldn't buy in a bottle. Her aura was angelic, but her smile was delightfully wicked. Mom had dressed in a casual floral dress and high-heeled sandals. She'd recently had her hair cut into an asymmetrical bob that showed off her gorgeous bone structure and made her look even more youthful. "I heard through the grapevine you had an amazing day on the golf course."

"The best I've played," I replied, returning her hug then kissing her cheek. "Isn't that right, Dad?"

My dad's thunderous expression didn't fool me. Paul Meyer looked every bit like you'd expect a CEO of an investment company to look. The slight graying at his temples made him look distinguished, the bespoke suits he wore to work showed off his wealth, and his drive for success was evident in his sharp, blue eyes. Beneath the polished exterior beat the heart of a man who'd come from the wrong side of town, clawed and fought his way through school, and built his company from the ground up. He never forgot where he came from nor did he take anything for granted. My father donated huge sums of his salary to charitable causes near and dear to his heart. He was street savvy and Harvard educated, both fierce and brilliant. He worked hard but loved harder, and there was never a time in my life when I didn't know he loved Mom and me above all else. I wished every day I could find a love like theirs, but so far, my dream had eluded me.

"I'm proud of you," Dad said gruffly, earning a jab from Mom's elbow. He had also dressed casually for the evening in dark jeans and a pale blue polo shirt.

"Are you really going to let me take the Aston Martin for a weekend?" I asked.

"Wasn't that the bet we agreed upon?"

"It was," I replied.

"Have you ever known me to go back on my word?" Dad asked smoothly.

"Never."

He nodded. "You have your answer then."

"Oh boy," I said, rubbing my hands together. "I can't wait. I'll have to plan an epic road trip."

"I think a four-day weekend before fall classes start would be a great idea," Mom said.

"I agreed to a weekend, not a four-day weekend," Dad told her.

"You didn't specify the terms and exclusions in your agreement, so you don't have a leg to stand on, dear," Mom said sweetly.

"Yes, counselor," Dad stated then kissed the cheek she offered.

I was sure Dad had more to say about losing the bet, but the other half of our party arrived before he had the chance. "Son," Dad said, "I'd like you to meet Carter, Maris, and Jared Blake. I'm sure you don't remember Jared, but the two of you were quite inseparable when you were toddling around at dinner parties."

"Maybe seeing me in a diaper will trigger a memory," Jared said. It suddenly got so quiet you could've heard a pin drop before awkward laughter erupted from our parents. I doubted the foursome was aware that diaper wearing was a particular kink, but Jared knew because his face turned as red as a cartoon character's before it burst into flames. "Oh my God," he said, turning to his mother. "I told you not to take me out in public. No good ever comes of it."

His mother's laughter turned from awkward to delighted. "Ezra is a handsome guy, so it's okay you tripped over yourself. If he's anything like his parents, he won't hold it against you."

"I definitely won't," I assured them. I had to admit; I found Jared's dark, curly hair, amber eyes, and shy blushes attractive. He was my age and came from a similar background, which usually prevented awkward topics and lulls in conversation. "I don't know about any of you, but I'm starving tonight. I beat my dad at golf today for the first time in my life. Not only did I beat him; I smacked him down really good."

"Care to double down on our bet?" Dad asked, pulling my attention back to him.

"I've already won," I reminded him. "Why in the world would I give up my prize?"

"I'll make the prize much better," he replied.

"I'm listening."

"Beat me again, and you can borrow the Aston Martin for a month."

I wanted to jump all over the opportunity to drive the luxury car for a month but realized my chances of beating my dad two games in a row were slim to none. His smug smile said he knew it too. He was goading me into losing so I wouldn't get my chance behind the wheel at all.

"That's as shady as some of the legal briefs coming across my desk lately," Mom said. "Think it over, Ezra."

"I don't accept the challenge," I said proudly. "I'll take my four-day weekend and be happy with it."

Dad smiled proudly then slipped his arm around my shoulders. "Smart boy."

The hostess showed us to a table in the back where our parents snatched seats to ensure Jared and I were forced to sit beside each other. I offered him a genuine smile while he just shook his head over their obvious behavior. The hostess handed us menus and said, "Sven will be your waiter, and he'll be with you shortly."

I set my menu down without looking at it and started to reach for my water glass before realizing it was empty. Across from us, our mothers practically had their heads pressed together while looking at the entrees on the menu and discussing what sounded good, which gave me an excellent view of a rather large gathering across the dining room. It was a damn good thing I hadn't taken a sip of water because I would've choked on it. I'd gone six months without running into Henry Sullivan then suddenly saw him three times in less than twenty-four hours. The universe had it out for me.

Feeling my regard, Henry looked in my direction. His eyes widened, and his lips parted, and even though I was too far away to hear him, I knew he'd let out a delightful little gasp like the first time I licked the rim of his pucker. I knew I was right when the person sitting next to Henry suddenly looked at him before looking in my direction. I recognized the guy from the club. It was Henry's best friend who'd taken him out to celebrate his twenty-first birthday. It seemed like the large group was celebrating something at Rinella's too. If I wasn't mistaken, Henry seemed to be the center of attention, which I knew he didn't like. Henry's *friend* seemed to be especially handsy. Was that Jessie?

"You must eat here a lot if you're not even looking at the menu," Jared said, pulling my gaze away from Henry's table.

"He gets the same thing every single time," Dad said.

"Spaghetti and meatballs," Mom added.

"I've tried other things here, but the meatballs are my favorite." I shrugged. "I've already mentioned the appetite I worked up today, and a hearty plate of spaghetti and meatballs will restore my energy." My eyes drifted back to Henry's table when everyone except my dad laughed at my joke.

Henry was too busy talking to the man on his other side to notice I was looking at him again. The handsome African American man looked to be around my age and was dressed in a suit that would rival the ones my father wore to work. The affectionate way Henry looked at the man was returned tenfold, yet I didn't get a romantic vibe from them. A waiter carrying a tray of drinks stopped at their table, momentarily blocking my view. When he walked away, I saw Henry take a sip of a pale-yellow cocktail. He nodded his head and took another sip. Henry licked his lips and looked at the glass in surprise like he hadn't expected it to taste so good. Instead of setting the glass down, he took a longer sip. The two men on either side of him exchanged smiles and possibly a private joke.

I snapped out of my trance when the waiter stepped up to our table. "Hello, I'm Sven, and I'll be taking care of you this evening. Can I start you off with drinks?"

"I'd love a mojito," Maris said.

"Oh, that sounds good. I'll have one also," my mom added.

Dad and Carter both ordered whiskey on the rocks, Jared ordered a glass of red wine, and I ordered a Sprite.

"Not much of a drinker?" Jared asked me.

"Never developed a taste for it," I said casually.

"He prefers to stay in control of his faculties at all times," Dad said, raising his glass of water to toast me.

"That's also true," I confirmed.

Conversation between our families was easy and fun. We talked about the places we'd traveled to recently, and I learned Jared loved the same cities I did. Like me, he loved the Old World feel and beautiful architecture of Italy. If anyone noticed my attention straying to the table across the room, they didn't mention it.

"Have you ever visited the lemon orchards on the Amalfi Coast?" Jared asked. "The fruit is huge and so much more vibrant than the ones we grow here."

"It was one of my favorite places in Italy," I admitted.

Thinking about lemons reminded me of Henry. I glanced back over at his table and saw he'd started on a second drink. His flushed face and goofy grin said he was feeling the effects of the first drink and probably didn't need the second. Henry's supposed friend was too busy looking at the dapper man on his other side to notice when Henry slid back his chair and wobbled as he rose to his feet. He stood there for a second, seeming to regain his equilibrium before he started walking toward the restrooms.

Henry wasn't stumbling or staggering by any stretch, but he didn't look sure-footed to me. No one at his table seemed to notice, which was why I had no choice but to set my napkin on the table and scoot back my chair.

"Excuse me for a moment," I politely said, addressing my dinner companions. "I'll be right back."

I headed straight for the men's bathroom, although I didn't know what I'd do or say when I got there. I pushed open the door and saw Henry bent over the sink, splashing cold water on his face.

"Are you okay, Henry?"

He slowly lifted his head and met my gaze in the mirror. "No, Ezra, I'm not okay."

Chapter Five

Henry

EZRA TOOK THE FEW STEPS SEPARATING US, AND I TURNED TO FACE him, not caring about the cold water dripping down my face. Leaning my ass against the porcelain sink for support, I met Ezra's dark, turbulent gaze. Curiosity and concern for me warred with his need for self-preservation. I didn't know why or how I knew what he was feeling; I just did.

Ask me why I'm not okay, Ezra. Please ask me why.

Ezra said nothing as he searched my eyes for a few moments before letting out a short groan of frustration. He ripped off a paper towel from the dispenser then gently patted my face dry. Even though our flesh didn't touch, it was still the most intimate moment I'd shared with another person since leaving his apartment six months ago.

The gesture suddenly felt too intimate, reminding me of the care Ezra had given me after each round of sex. Gentle bathing, soothing words about how lovely I was, and how much he'd enjoyed the gifts I gave him. *Me?* He thought I was a gift to *him?* The kindness he'd shown me in his apartment had made me feel special, but alone in the restaurant bathroom after everything that happened over the past twenty-four hours, Ezra's actions majorly fucked with my head. I averted my eyes, avoiding his penetrative gaze. Ezra tossed the paper towel in the trash bin, but instead of stepping away from me, he placed his left hand on my hip. Bracketed between his body and the sink, I didn't feel trapped or threatened, I felt...safe and grounded, which only fucked me up more.

The warmth of his skin seeping through my shirt made me gasp. I jerked my head back up and our eyes collided once more. In a matter of a day, I'd seen Ezra look at me with cool indifference, lust, and worry.

"Why aren't you okay?" Ezra asked softly.

Moments before, it was what I wanted him to ask. I'd had just enough alcohol to make me feel brave, but after his tender ministrations and his anchoring touch, I just wanted to get away from him before I made a huge fool of myself. I shook my head and attempted to step away from him, but Ezra tightened his hold on my hip.

"Tell me," Ezra said firmly.

Like someone snapped their finger, my liquid courage came roaring back. "You, Ezra. You're my problem."

He flinched but didn't drop his hand from my hip or step back. "Me?"

"Yes. You and your fucking mixed signals are making me crazy."

"Mixed signals?"

"Are you going to repeat everything I say?" I asked, shocking both of us with the defiance in my tone.

"I believe I need you to elaborate on the mixed signals I'm sending you, Henry."

"Ah, the professor wants examples, does he?" I asked. Later, I would be stunned by my assertiveness, but I was too pissed to care about consequences right then. "Okay. I'll give you specifics." I took a step forward until there was no gap between our bodies. "Last night in your classroom, you looked right through me like you didn't know the taste of my cum. It hurt my feelings, but I understood the position we were in and respected your moral code." I took two more steps forward, forcing Ezra to step back. "Then you showed me kindness when you took me to the pizzeria. I told myself it wasn't personal, and you would've done it for any of your students stranded in the parking lot." Two more steps and I had Ezra at the door of an open stall. "But then you went and replaced Jess's tire and had the car towed home."

"I don't know what you're talking about," Ezra said.

I gripped the collar of his polo shirt and pushed him inside the stall. "Stop it. You denying it only confuses me more. If your actions didn't matter, then why deny them?" Kicking the door shut, I closed us inside the tiny space. I knew Ezra wasn't claustrophobic because of the intense make-out session we'd had on the elevator ride up to his apartment. "One minute your words and actions imply I don't matter to you, but then you do or say something that makes me think you care a lot. You would've kissed me on the sidewalk earlier today if that jerk hadn't interrupted us. Would it have stopped at a kiss?"

"Henry, don't mistake my kindness for something it's not."

"You couldn't keep your eyes off me tonight, Ezra. You say one thing but do another, and it tears me up inside. If you don't want me, then stop looking at me like you can't get enough of me. If you do want me, then you should definitely do something about it."

Pressing me against the closed bathroom stall door, Ezra leaned forward until his lips hovered close to mine. "Alcohol has made you bold tonight, Henry, and you're playing with fire."

"Make me burn."

A growl signaled his surrender, and Ezra captured my mouth with a rough, possessive kiss. His tongue swept inside my mouth like it belonged there: licking, teasing, and mastering mine. I gripped his biceps for support when my knees threatened to buckle. Sensing my struggle, Ezra tightened his grip on my hips and pressed his body harder against mine, making it impossible to miss our erections straining behind our zippers. *This!* Why the hell were we trying to deny this?

Ezra tore his lips from mine then lowered his head, pressing his nose just below my ear. He inhaled deeply. "You smell so fucking good." I tipped my head back against the door, exposing more of my neck to him. "I've never tried a lemon-flavored cocktail before, but I sure do like the way it tastes on your tongue."

"It's a lemon drop," I said between gasps. "It's the first cocktail I've enjoyed."

"I could tell how much you liked them," Ezra said, nibbling and licking a path from my jaw down to the base of my throat. "You're not used to alcohol, and you drank the first one too fast. That's why you were wobbly on your feet when you stood up."

Realization started to cool my feverish brain and body. "Is that why you followed me in here? Were you afraid I was drunk? Were you worried I'd pick the first guy who walked through the door to back into a stall and fuck?"

Ezra lifted his head and stared into my eyes. "We're not fucking, Henry." The disappointment in his voice comforted me, and unfortunately, it also spurred me on.

"No?" I asked, pitching my hips forward and rocking my erection against his.

Ezra dropped his hands from my hips and stood back. He closed his eyes, seeking to regain his composure, or maybe he just didn't want to look at me anymore; either way, it was what I needed to get a grip on myself. I should've lied and told him I was fine instead of challenging him the way I had.

The bathroom door opened, and footsteps echoed on the tile floor. "Henry, are you okay?"

How many men were going to seek me out in the bathroom and ask if I was all right? Ezra's raised brow said he wondered the same thing.

"I'm fine," I told Geoff. "I'll be out in just a minute."

Geoff had been so preoccupied with chatting up Des that he hadn't mentioned Ezra's presence across the dining room or how little I contributed to the conversation around me. I was pretty sure he hadn't been aware I'd left the dining room, and I was positive he didn't know I'd backed my professor into the stall with me. If Geoff came closer, he would've seen two sets of shoes through the gap between the bottom of the stall door and the bathroom floor, or he might've heard both of us breathing heavy. Of course, my humiliation was doing a great job of killing my boner.

"Are you sure? I wasn't aware someone ordered you a second drink."

"I'm not sick. I promise."

"Okay, then. I'll give you some privacy."

"Thank you."

Neither Ezra nor I said anything until the bathroom door closed behind Geoff. I had planned to leave the stall as soon as the coast was clear, but Ezra's scowl kept me rooted to the spot.

"Is that Jessie?" Ezra whispered roughly. "Were you in here making out with me while your boyfriend flirted with the other guy?"

Setting Ezra straight would've been the wisest course of action, so I did. Sort of. "That's none of your damn business, Ezra." I had no intention of telling him who those two men were.

"It's every bit my business, Henry. The last thing I need is to have my reputation shredded because I find myself caught up in your juvenile games. Maybe you guys have an open relationship, and I'm not judging anyone, but I'm grateful he interrupted us before I crossed the line."

"I didn't ask you to follow me to the bathroom to check on me, Ezra. You chose to do that on your own. You decided to dry my face like you cared and ask what had upset me. You're the one who wanted me to elaborate, and you're the one who kissed me."

"And you're perfectly innocent in all this, I assume," Ezra said dryly. "You didn't back me into the stall and tell me to make you burn?"

"Yes, I did those things, but you could've resisted me or refused to accept the challenge. You didn't, and now you're pissed at me."

Ezra released a low, frustrated growl and ran his hand through his hair. "I'm not pissed at you; I'm pissed because I want you."

My anger deflated. "Yesss." The word hissed out of me like air leaking from a balloon.

"I can't allow anything to come of it, Henry."

Hurt and rejection swelled inside me until I thought I would choke on them. "I understand," I whispered softly.

Ezra cupped my face and traced his thumb along my jaw. "I don't think you do."

"Then enlighten me, Ezra. Isn't that what professors are supposed to do? Tell me what's so wrong with me."

"Sweet Henry," he said gently, "the fault lies with me. You're too good for someone as jaded as I am." I didn't believe him and had planned to tell him so, but he placed his finger over my lips. "The answer is no."

I saw the conviction in Ezra's eyes and knew he'd made up his mind. Him pinning me up against the door and kissing me until I was drunk on his taste was a temporary slip of control that would never happen again. It was his sordid goodbye, perhaps.

"Goodbye, Ezra," I said, stepping forward so I could open the door and escape his penetrating gaze. My words sounded formal and final, not the tone and temperament you'd expect from someone you planned to see the following night.

"I'll see you tomorrow night, Henry."

Leaving the cramped space was awkward and impossible to do without bumping into him, but I did so as quickly as I could with the least amount of touching. I plastered a smile on my face when I returned to the table of friends who'd gathered to help me celebrate. I felt Ezra's presence when he reentered the dining room, but I didn't look up or acknowledge him for the rest of the meal. I tuned in to the conversations around me and tried my best not to let anyone see how rattled I felt.

After dinner, Geoff drove me across town to the pizzeria. "You want to tell me what happened between you and the professor in the bathroom stall?"

"No," I said. "I was hoping you were so distracted by your flirting with Des that you hadn't noticed."

"I wasn't flirting with Des and stop trying to deflect the conversation," Geoff said.

"There is nothing to deflect because nothing happened, Geoff."

My best friend sighed. "Henry, I hope you know what you're doing with this guy."

"I'm not doing anything with him, so you have nothing to worry about."

I must've sounded convincing because Geoff let it drop without further comment. We promised to have lunch later in the week when he dropped me off. I was pulsing with nervous energy and had no one to talk to with Jessie still on the road. Rather than go up to my apartment to overthink things for hours, I headed to Mamma Maria's kitchen to put the energy to good use. The internal debate and decision to drop Biology of Human Sexuality could wait until I wasn't feeling so raw.

Chapter Six

Ezra

THE ENCOUNTER WITH HENRY PLAYED IN MY MIND ON AN ENDLESS loop. His assertiveness had struck a chord, awakening some-thing deep and primal inside me. While I liked the blunt way Henry spoke to me and boldly maneuvered me into the private stall, I loved the way he submitted to me when I regained control of the sit-uation. I didn't think Henry was even aware of the needy moans that had escaped him when we kissed. Fuck! He'd practically melted into my arms, and it was addictive. *He* was addictive.

After I'd rejoined my dinner party, I tried my best to avoid look-ing in his direction but couldn't seem to stop myself from glancing over on occasion. Not once did I catch Henry sneaking glances at me, and if I hadn't known better, I would've thought he completely put me out of his mind. I did know better because there was no way this *obsession* was one-sided. I'd felt the way he reacted in my arms—the heat of his arousal radiating off his body and his erection pressing against me. Henry knew I was there, he felt the same pull as I did, but he resisted it.

Henry: 1

Ezra: 0

No amount of listening to music, watching television, or reading books could distract me from the war raging inside my mind, body, and soul. Henry dominated my every thought, and I didn't like it. Only one man had ensnared me so, and it ended in a fucking disaster which had made me the cynical man who pushed lovers away before an attachment could develop. I hadn't regretted strings-free encounters until Henry.

Henry: 2

Ezra: 0

The next morning, I woke up determined to put Henry out of my mind and knew staying busy would be the biggest key to accomplishing the goal. I normally took a solid six to eight weeks off each summer to travel and see the world, but teaching the summer class at the community college put a damper on that. While I had commitments at the college four days a week, they weren't enough to occupy all of my time. Summer enrollment was much lower than the normal school year, so I only taught six classes each week—half of my usual students and classes. I had too much free time on my hands. I could only handle so much golf and tennis at the country club with my parents before I lost my mind. All my friends worked during the day, so I couldn't rely on them to distract me from making a huge mistake. Well, one of them worked at home and set his own schedule and might be willing to take pity on me.

"Why are you calling me in the middle of sex?" Ryder said when he answered his phone.

Smiling at his annoyance, I said, "I'm not having sex. I don't think you are either or you wouldn't have answered the phone."

Ryder snorted. "Of course not. Lucien is still out of town."

"Then who exactly am I interrupting?"

"Jeremy and Rosco," Ryder said with an exaggerated voice that had to have included an eye roll.

"Are you counseling them or something?" I asked, playing dumb. At least annoying my friend kept my mind busy while entertaining me.

"So you did tune me out when I droned on and on about my book characters over pizza the other night," Ryder said wryly. "Don't feel bad; it happens all the time."

"I didn't forget, nor did I tune you out, Ry. I'm just distracting my brain at your expense."

"I could tell you were zoning in and out, but I didn't push you to talk. I'm pushing you now."

"There's this…"

"Guy?" Ryder supplied. "Wait! Don't answer that yet. Come over and have lunch with me."

"I thought you were in the middle of writing a hot sex scene between Jedi and Ricky."

Ryder chuckled. "You think you're funny, don't you?"

"I made you laugh, didn't I?"

"Always," Ryder agreed. "Yes, I was writing a steamy sex scene, but the guys don't mind hanging out naked for an extra hour or two while I fix lunch for a friend. Be here in thirty minutes." He disconnected the call without saying goodbye or giving me a chance to decline.

"It better be a good lunch," I said to myself when I returned the phone to my pocket.

If I hadn't already cheered up at the prospect of spending time with Ryder, seeing his disheveled appearance when he answered the door would've yanked me right out of my funk. "Holy fuck. You look like shit," I said, taking in his blue plaid boxers and coffee-stained white tank top beneath a pale blue silk robe. Ryder wore flip-flops on his feet and a devil-may-care smile on his face. He looked like I felt.

Ryder ran one hand through his hair to tame his bed head and flipped me off with the other. "I guess I'll eat the chicken pecan salad on croissants all by myself."

My empty stomach growled. The only thing I'd managed to swallow after a night of restless sleep was too many cups of coffee, which had only sent nervous jitters through my normally calm system. Aiming my most charming smile at him, I said, "I take it back."

"Okay then," Ryder acquiesced, opening the door wider and stepping aside for me to enter. "Let's eat out on the patio by the pool, and you can tell me all about the guy who has you rattled."

"How do you know this is about a guy?"

One of Ryder's blond brows shot up. "Isn't it always?"

"Yeah, I guess."

I followed Ryder through the lovely home he shared with his fiancé. Ryder veered off to the kitchen to retrieve our lunch, and I continued to the rear of the house. Duke and Duchess, their German Shepherds, were sunning themselves on the patio when I stepped out. The regal dogs rose to their feet and fondly greeted me but soon forgot my existence when Ryder walked out of the house holding two plates of food in his hands.

"Neither of these are for you," he told his dogs. "If you're good, you can have some of the shredded chicken I set aside for fajitas tonight." Like they understood every word, the shepherds returned to their spots in the sun. "I give it five more minutes before they jump in the pool."

"Seriously?"

"I never knew how much German Shepherds loved water until we brought these beasts home. We can't keep them out of the pool, they come running every time one of us turns the water hose on, and Duchess actually jumped into the bathtub with me last night."

"I don't believe it," I said, shaking my head.

"I know," Ry agreed. "Most dogs avoid a bathtub at all costs."

"Oh, I didn't doubt Duchess's love for baths; I found it hard to believe you bathed last night."

Ryder snatched back the plate he'd just set in front of me. "More for me, I guess."

"I'm kidding, but surely you've looked in a mirror today?"

"I did when I brushed my teeth, but I couldn't care because an idea for my next chapter struck me right when I was gargling mouth-wash." Ryder shrugged. "I only meant to go to my office long enough to jot the idea down before I forgot, but the next thing I knew, I was writing the chapter instead of making notes."

"I'm sure that happens often."

Nodding, Ryder said, "Too often when Lucien isn't home to re-mind me to act like a functioning adult." Ryder slid my plate back in front of me. "What's going on with you, Ez?"

I took a deep breath then spilled everything about the fateful night in December. He hadn't known the first thing about Henry. I wasn't in the practice of telling him about my conquests, but I told him how I'd felt propelled across the crowded club to ask him to dance. I confessed to taking Henry back to my place and keeping him there until almost noon the next day. "The guy never completely left my mind, Ry. That hasn't happened in a very long time, and it left me reeling. I avoided going back to Vibe so I wouldn't run into him again. I've managed to avoid him for six months then WHAM! Henry starts turning up everywhere."

A frown creased Ryder's brow. "Is he stalking you?"

"No! Nothing like that. Henry hasn't orchestrated our encounters."

"How can you be sure?" Ryder asked.

"I never gave Henry my full name nor discussed my occupation with him. I'm listed as Dr. E. Meyer in the school's directory and opt-ed not to include a photo, so it's not likely he—"

"Wait! Are you telling me Henry is one of your students?" Ryder asked me. I nodded. Both his blond brows inched toward his hairline. "One of your Biology of Human Sexuality students?" I nodded again, and Ryder snorted. "Dude, I read the material for your class. You're about to have some seriously awkward moments."

"It gets worse," I said, averting my eyes to my plate.

"Worse, how?"

I spilled the rest of the tea.

Ryder placed his elbow on the table and rested his chin in the cup of his palm. "What are you going to do now?"

"I'm going to eat lunch," I said wryly. "Then, I'm going to stay busy so I don't think about how fucked I am."

"Fucked because you're worried about your job, or fucked because you want to drag this Henry guy back to your bed and never let him leave?"

"You think the only two options are covering my own ass to preserve my job and holding Henry hostage in my apartment?" I asked with a smirk. "The truth lies somewhere in between, I think."

"What are you going to do?" Ryder asked.

"That's the million-dollar question, isn't it?" What was I going to do? Knowing I was hours away from seeing Henry again both thrilled and terrified me. I couldn't have him, but I couldn't *not* have him either.

I hid in my office like a coward for as long as I could, not strolling into my classroom until the last minute before class was due to start. Attendance was mandatory and counted for a decent chunk of my students' grade, so I started each class by glancing around the room and documenting who was missing. I dreaded the moment my gaze connected with Henry's, but it seemed I had nothing to worry about because Henry wasn't in his seat, nor did he arrive to class late.

I should've been relieved for a reprieve from the strain of being in the same room with him while ignoring the magnetic pull I felt toward him, but I was worried instead. I had confused, hurt, and angered Henry, so it made perfect sense he needed time to figure out if he wanted to stay in my class, but more than that, I hated the idea of knowing I caused him distress.

The following day, I fully expected to receive a notice from the school that Henry had withdrawn from my class, but it never came. It didn't come the next day nor had it arrived the following Monday when he was due to sit at the center table in the third row. Finding his seat empty again triggered a range of emotions to swirl inside me, forming a cyclone that grew larger and more devastating with every passing minute. Worry, anger, disappointment, and even rejection tossed me around in the maelstrom, battering me from every angle. I made the classroom my life raft and clung to it desperately, but by the time the last student filed out, I was left breathless and feeling unreasonably broken.

Was that how Henry felt? If so, why? We had one night of meaningless—I couldn't finish my thought because it was a bald-faced lie. Nothing about my night with Henry was meaningless, and pretending it was hadn't gotten me anywhere but chasing my tail. Knowing I shouldn't want Henry didn't change the fact that I did. Understanding I wasn't good for him didn't stop me from driving to Mamma Maria's after class ended. I already knew he lived in an apartment above the pizzeria after accessing his student records to find out where to have Jessie's car towed to.

I easily found the door to the apartments at the rear of the building and was pissed to find it unlocked. A person didn't have to ring a bell and get buzzed in; they only had to turn the knob and walk up a dimly lit staircase to the two apartments above the pizzeria. According to Henry's records, he lived in 201B. I stood in front of the door with my hand raised to knock for a solid minute before rapping my knuckles against it.

An overwhelming urge to run washed over me; I was too old to be making foolish mistakes like this. What the hell would I say if he answered? Self-preservation kicked in, and I started to step away from the door just as it suddenly jerked opened, revealing a young woman with platinum hair liberally streaked with pink and purple highlights. She had piercings in her eyebrows, nose, ears, and her ruby red lips were tipped up in a snarl.

"Is Henry home?" I asked politely.

"Who the fuck are you?" she demanded to know.

My reservations fled, replaced by irritation. Who the hell was this girl answering Henry's door, and why did she think she had the right to treat his visitors so rudely?

"I'd like to talk to Henry, please."

"Answer my question first, asshole."

"Listen here, I—"

"It's okay, Jess," Henry said from somewhere behind her.

Jess? As in Jessie? That little shit never corrected me when I'd assumed Jessie was his boyfriend and probably got a laugh every time I brought it up.

Jessie looked over her thin shoulder at Henry to be sure. I couldn't blame her because his voice had sounded lifeless. Whatever she saw in Henry's expression must've satisfied her because she opened the door fully and stepped aside, giving me my first look at Henry. His pale face and the dark, half-moons under his eyes made me gasp in shock.

"I don't look that bad," Henry said, rolling his eyes.

"You look worse than bad," Jess said. "I leave town for a week, and you look like an extra from a zombie movie."

"Jess," Henry said, tipping his head toward the hallway that probably led to their bedrooms.

Seeing he wanted to speak to me privately, Jessie looked between us for a second before staring me in the eyes. "If I find out you're the source of his pain; I'm going to tear you apart. Am I clear?"

"If I'm the cause of his pain, I'd deserve nothing less."

Satisfied I meant it, Jessie exited the living room. I crossed the threshold and shut the door behind me. I was curious about Henry's apartment but couldn't tear my eyes away from him to glance around. I wanted to cross the room and take him into my arms, but I didn't budge. I had no right to push him away one minute then gather him close the next. I was doing just what he'd called me out for the previous week.

"Did I do this?" I asked softly. "Should we call Jessie back in here?"

Henry stared at me for several heartbeats before he shook his head.

"No, I'm not the source of your obvious distress, or no, we shouldn't call Jessie back in here?"

"No to both," Henry said with a soft smile. "You're not fully to blame anyway."

"Can we talk?"

"Is this about missing class, Ezra?"

I pinned him with a disbelieving look. "You think I drive around to my students' apartments when they miss school?"

"I know how important this class is to you, and my poor attendance reflects badly on you," Henry said.

"I'm not here to discuss your absences, Henry."

Henry tilted his head slightly then studied me. "Then why are you here?"

How did I answer him? Did I tell him I didn't know, or did I tell him the truth? Maybe not knowing why I came was the truth. No, I could lie to myself all I wanted, but I couldn't lie to him.

I crossed the room until I stood directly in front of him. Even though I wanted so badly to touch him, I kept my hands to my sides. "I couldn't stay away."

Henry: 3

Ezra: 0

Chapter Seven

Henry

I COULDN'T STAY AWAY. EZRA'S WORDS SHOULD'VE SOOTHED THE TURMOIL inside me, but instead, they only churned it up more. Who the fuck did this guy think he was? Push. Pull. Push. Pull. I'd had enough of it.

"You couldn't stay away?" I asked. "What the hell does that even mean, Ezra? You tell me you want me but nothing can happen between us. You want me to stay away from you, but when I do, you seek me out."

Ezra ran a finger over his eyebrow. I'd seen the gesture before when someone was annoyed, but Ezra wasn't giving off that kind of vibe. "I never said I wanted you to stay away from me, Henry." His voice was calm and patient, reminding me of one of the Sunday school teachers I had as a kid.

"That's right. You're jaded, and I'm too good for you." I didn't bother to suppress my eye roll. Who the hell did this guy think he was anyway? "You implied I should flee for my safety before you corrupt me. I think the ship has already said."

"You don't believe me," Ezra said, his lowered voice hinting of danger. "Is this your way of pushing me? First, you physically push me into the bathroom stall, and now, you're mentally challenging me to prove whether I'm too jaded for you. Nothing good comes out of that, Henry. Neither for you nor I. Leave well enough alone before you get hurt." *Too late.*

"You're the one who showed up at my door, Ezra. What's the matter? Horny? Are you about to reveal your *jaded* side to me? Perhaps we should take this conversation to my bedroom then."

Ezra closed the distance so fast I didn't have time to react. He cupped my jaw firmly and held my head still, forcing me to look into his hot, dark eyes. *Maybe he wasn't as calm as his demeanor had led me to believe.* "Do not presume to think you know me after one night in my bed, Henry," Ezra growled. "I didn't warn you away only to come here and fuck you a week later. I might not be the right man for you, but I'm not a cruel monster either."

I jerked my chin free from his grip and took a step back. "Then why are you here, and don't give me that lame shit about not being able to help yourself. I've never met anyone with as much self-control as you possess." I ignored his derisive snort. "Tell me the truth or leave."

"I was a hundred percent honest. I was worried about you, and my conscience wouldn't allow me to ignore the gut feeling telling me you weren't okay." Somehow that hurt me more because it highlighted how much he cared about me as a person, not just as his student or another hole to plow. "I can see I was right to check on you. You look remarkably thinner than you did last week, and you scarcely had any extra weight you could afford to lose. The dark circles under your eyes broadcast your exhaustion. What's going on, Henry? It's obvious you're not taking good care of yourself. When was the last time you slept or ate?"

"Fuck you. I don't need a Professor Higgins in my life to rescue me."

Ezra's left eyebrow lifted dramatically. "You know *My Fair Lady*?"

"Archie loves classic movies, and it's one of his favorites."

"Archie?" The brow rose higher.

"See," I said gesturing to his tight body with both hands. "You react this way every time I mention another guy. Do you hate the idea of me with another man?"

"I do," he admitted.

"I thought you said you weren't a cruel monster."

Ezra released a long, shaky breath. "I'm not a monster, nor am I a liar. Knowing I can't have you isn't the same as not wanting you. If you don't want me to admit I hate the idea of another man touching you, then don't ask those types of questions."

Growling in frustration, I turned my back and took a few steps away from him. I needed room to breathe and think, which was impossible when I was within touching distance of him. "I think I hate you, Ezra."

I expected him to respond quickly, and when he didn't, I turned around and faced him once more. His dark eyes had lost their spark, and the pallor of his skin shocked me. The idea of me hating him had affected Ezra deeply. Needing to clear the air, I sighed and returned to stand in front of him. Knowing that touching him would be a mistake didn't stop me from doing it anyway. I placed my hand on his crisply pressed shirt and felt his heart pounding in his chest.

"I didn't mean what I said, Ezra. It was a childish thing to say. I'm sorry. I'm just frustrated by the circumstances."

Ezra accepted my apology with a nod. I expected him to remove my hand or step away from my touch, but he didn't. I wanted to press my advantage by caressing the firm flesh beneath my palm, but I didn't. "Is that why you're not eating, sleeping, or attending my classes?" he asked, breaking the silence.

"I'm eating and sleeping," I said. "I'm having a hard time adjusting to my new busy schedule. Working two jobs and—"

"Two jobs?" Ezra asked.

"I missed the deadlines to apply for some grants and scholarships offered through the school, so I work as a personal assistant for a lawyer during the day, and I pick up shifts downstairs a few hours during the week and on weekends to make some extra money."

"You can't sustain this kind of pace for long, Henry. You're burning your candle at both ends. When was the last time you ate?"

"I don't need you to rescue me."

Ezra stepped closer, trapping the hand still resting on his chest between us. He gripped my hips hard and possessively. "We all need rescuing once in a while." My mouth parted, allowing a silly sigh to escape. I'd missed his hands on my body so much. Ezra stared at my mouth so long I expected him to lower his head and kiss me, but instead, Ezra stepped back and dropped his hands from my hips. "You're run-down, and that's not good for you. Are you taking your medication properly? Have you been to the doctor to have your viral loads checked?"

He and Jessie would make one hell of a nag tag team. She'd taken one look at me when she arrived home off her tour and freaked the hell out. "You sound like you're familiar with HIV complications."

"You're not the first person I've met who is positive, Henry. Mistreating your body by not eating and not sleeping is asking for complications you don't need. It will make you more susceptible to colds and—"

"Enough, Ezra. I went to the clinic yesterday and got checked out." As annoyed as I was by him trying to be a father hen, I admired that he didn't back down from the reality of my situation. The only people in my life who weren't afraid to bring it up were Des, Jess, and my friends at Ryan's Place. Everyone else, including Geoff, pretended like I didn't have a virus that I would have to manage for the rest of my life. "I promised my doctor I will do better at managing my time and stress, and I will. I'm great at organizing, so I just need to stop chasing my tail and sort things out."

"I'm glad to hear it, but you didn't answer my question."

Confused, I tipped my head to the side while I replayed our conversation. *Oh!* He meant the question about when I last ate. I didn't want to tell him the truth because it would only make him mad and lecture me even more. "I ate earlier." It wasn't a lie.

"I would ask you to define 'earlier,' but I won't waste time or energy." Ezra pulled out his phone and started tapping on it.

"What are you doing?"

"I'm ordering you dinner to be delivered here. I'll order enough for two, so your hellcat can join you." Ezra glanced up from his phone. "You had a fun time at my expense over Jessie, didn't you?"

"I did," I admitted with a shrug. Ezra's scowl made me grin. "Don't ask if you don't want to hear the truth."

"Touché." Ezra returned to tapping on his phone. "I don't want to hear any protesting from you either. You're going to enjoy this dinner then get a good night's sleep. I want you to email me tomorrow morning so we can work out a time to meet."

"To discuss the classes I missed?" I asked.

"That, among other things regarding your academic future. It's obvious to me how important earning a degree is to you, and I want to find ways to help you. I can't promise you anything, but…"

"Ezra, would you do this for any other student?"

He slipped his phone back inside his pocket and looked me dead in the eyes. "No." I wasn't sure I liked his honesty. I didn't want to be his charity case. "I would offer encouragement, of course, but I'd refer them to a counselor or someone in the financial assistance department. Our situation is different."

"How so?"

"Because I like you, Henry. You are a person who deserves wonderful things, and I want you to have them. I don't know enough about my other students to say the same thing."

"Oh. Do you not want to know about your students?"

"At the risk of sounding like a complete asshole, no. Getting to know my students on a personal level clouds my judgement and blurs lines. I am only interested in their academic success, nothing more." Both his body language and tone of voice were cold, stiff, and unyielding. I didn't recognize this version of Ezra.

"There's more to the story," I said. "You've seen someone get hurt when those lines were blurred, and judging by your vibe, it ended very badly."

"Henry, I can't—" Emotion choked his voice, and Ezra shook his head.

"It's okay, Ezra. You don't have to tell me. I just want you to know I understand." Too bad comprehension didn't make the hurt and disappointment go away. "This is just a bump in the road for me, right?" I tried to sound convincing, but Ezra's frown let me know I missed the mark.

"I want us to get past the mutual attraction we have for one another, but that doesn't mean I don't care about your success. I want to help you."

"Ezra, I don't want to be a charity case or someone you help because you feel guilty."

"Don't mistake my kindness for remorse, because you couldn't be further from the truth. I feel partly responsible for adding stress to your life, and the least I can do is buy you something to eat."

I remembered the breakfast he made for me: fluffy scrambled eggs, bacon, fried potatoes with peppers and onions, and croissants. I'd sat on a bar stool and watched him make coffee in a French press and squeeze fresh oranges to make juice for me. I recalled the way he cared for me after sex. I'd never felt so pampered and spoiled in my life, and it made me feel special. *He* made me feel special just by looking at me. I wanted to think it was because I meant something significant to him, but I realized Ezra was hardwired to take care of people. If I'd learned anything from getting tossed onto the street by a mother who was supposed to love me unconditionally, it was that people were either nurturers or they weren't.

The type of care and concern Ezra put into looking after my well-being wasn't something he learned from watching others. I thought my mother was a nurturer, but I'd been wrong. Ezra was uncomfortable around me, but he put it aside to take care of me. He saw a need and he filled it. If I weren't careful, my sexual desire for Ezra could morph into something much more powerful and deep, making it much harder to get over what happened between us. I couldn't allow that to happen. He was adamant there was no future for us, and I had to accept it and move on.

"Fine," I said after a brief pause. "I will accept your kind offer, and we'll consider the slate clean."

"A truce then."

"Yes," I agreed.

"Thank you, Henry." Ezra sounded relieved, and I admit I felt better than I had since the ordeal had started. It wasn't like my urge to jump him had gone away, but I finally realized his determination was deep-rooted. Student and professor was the only relationship we could have, even if we both wished it could be different. Ezra hadn't said as much out loud, but the soft look in his eyes had spoken louder than words ever could. "I ordered you dinner from my favorite bistro. It will be here in thirty minutes. I included a generous tip for the delivery driver, so you don't have to worry about that either. Make sure you get plenty of rest." He'd checked on me, was satisfied I was more or less okay, ordered me dinner, and was prepared to dust off his hands and congratulate himself on a job well done.

"You don't even know what I like to eat, and you didn't ask me about food allergies," I said, stalling him. While I acknowledged I'd never have him again, it didn't mean I was ready to see him walk out the door.

Ezra nodded to acknowledge I was right. "Perhaps I was a bit too heavy-handed." He pulled his phone out of his pocket and tapped for a few seconds. "It's not too late for me to change your order. Do you have any allergies?" I shook my head. "Would you like to look at the menu and pick out your own dinner?"

I actually liked the idea of Ezra picking out something that was solely for me. "I was teasing you. I just thought it was odd you presumed to know what I liked."

"I have a good track record when it comes to figuring out what you like." Ezra's eyes widened like he couldn't believe he'd spoken the words out loud. That made two of us. There was no way to pretend he wasn't referring to the time I was in his arms and he was inside my body.

"Touché," I said, mimicking his response from earlier.

"I'm just going to get going," Ezra said, gesturing to the door. "Are you going to email me in the morning and set up your appointment to meet with me?"

"Yes, Professor Higgins."

Ezra smiled. "Goodnight, Henry."

"Goodnight, Ezra."

We stared at each other for a few seconds before Ezra turned and walked out of my apartment. I stood there shell-shocked for a few minutes until I heard the creaky hinges of Jess's bedroom door opening. A few seconds later, my friend poked her head out of the hallway.

"Is the coast clear?"

I snorted. "Are we really going to pretend you weren't eavesdropping this entire time?"

Jess shrugged casually, and her off-the-shoulder T-shirt slid lower, exposing more of her pale shoulder and the bold colors in her dragon tattoo. "I can't help it if the walls are thin. What's this I heard about food?"

"Ezra ordered a late dinner for me because he's worried, and he made sure there was enough for you also."

"He's a keeper," Jess said.

I narrowed my eyes at her. "This coming from a person who won't allow anyone to do nice things for her."

"That's my burden, not yours." Jess's sad smile made my heart ache; her words made me want to pick up a sword and slay all the monsters who'd hurt her. "You've found a guy who obviously cares about you."

"It's not like that," I said, shaking my head.

"The hell it isn't," Jess countered.

"I'm serious, Jess. I can't allow myself to think Ezra could ever be mine."

Jess flopped on our ancient sofa and patted the cushion beside her. "Tell me why, Hen."

I sat beside her and said, "I wouldn't know where to start."

"At the beginning," she encouraged.

So I did. By the time our food arrived, Jess was fully caught up on everything that had happened between Ezra and me. I accepted the bags from the delivery guy and confirmed Ezra had covered the tip.

"The food smells fucking delicious," Jess said when I set the food on the table. She immediately unpacked the cartons, unshyly accepting part of a gift I collected from someone else. "This is better than Christmas."

We had homemade chicken and noodle soup, delicious salads made with crisp vegetables, rolls, and raspberry lemon cheesecake. It was the best meal I'd had in a week.

"I don't buy it," Jess said around a bite of cheesecake. "This," she said, pointing to the empty containers, "isn't the act of someone who is trying to make themselves feel better about upsetting you. One or both of you are in denial."

"Eat your dessert and hush," I teased. I couldn't afford to let myself believe there was more to Ezra's actions. Too bad my subconscious wasn't on board because I dreamed of straddling his lap while he fed me bites of what I suspected was his favorite dessert. The next morning, I relived my favorite fantasy of Ezra in the shower and wondered how in the hell I could meet him in his office without staring at his desk and getting a boner.

Chapter Eight

Ezra

I FOUND MYSELF LOOKING FORWARD TO MEETING WITH HENRY REGARDING his future more than I should have, but there was no denying the excitement humming through my body. Since leaving his apartment forty-four hours ago, I'd replayed our conversation in my head at least two dozen times. It took several trips down memory lane before I stopped reaching for my dick and started paying attention to something other than the sexual push and pull between us, and when I did, I realized what puzzled me about Henry.

His determination to take charge of his life felt desperate with a twist of reckless thrown in for good measure. Henry's desire to be in control seemed at odds with his natural submissive inclinations. He had relished the ways I took care of him after sex and melted beneath my pampering touch, but that wasn't the man who stood in front of me the previous night or the week before during our bathroom confrontation. Was Henry having an identity crisis, or did he think he had to suppress his leanings to succeed in life? What he needed to know, and what I was dying to teach him, was that he could be both submissive and assertive. There would be times he needed to stand tall and not back down and others when he could let his guard down and place himself in his lover's hands. I wanted to be the one to guide him, but it wasn't to be.

He'd astutely noticed that my determination to resist getting romantically involved with him came from a more personal place than professional ethics. His curiosity had shone in his eyes, but he never pushed me. Even if the student-teacher conflict didn't exist, I wasn't the guy for him. I had too much baggage dragging me down, and I wouldn't want to subject him to it.

Knock. Knock.

"Come in," I said.

The door eased open, and Henry poked his head around. "Is now still a good time?"

"Of course," I said, waving him in. "I would've emailed you if something came up." *Something other than my erection every time I think of you.*

Henry pushed the door fully open and stepped inside. "Do you want the door open or shut?"

Leaving the door open would've been the wisest decision, which was why I said, "You can close it." With Henry came his intoxicating, fresh scent, and I tried to inhale it without giving myself away. "You look much better." Henry's skin still looked too pale for June, but the dark circles were much improved, and his stained-glass eyes looked sharp and focused.

Henry set his backpack on the floor then sat in the chair across from my desk. "I'm feeling much better. Thank you for the delicious meal you sent over. Jessie and I enjoyed it."

I noticed the slight way Henry's lips trembled when he said his roommate's name. "You think you're funny, don't you?"

Henry shrugged then said, "Sometimes."

"You and Jessie are both welcome."

Henry reached down and pulled a binder out of his backpack and set it on my desk. "She also appreciated the four new tires on her car, even if she was confused how they came to be there. Four new tires, Ezra. Really?"

"I don't—"

"Nope," Henry said firmly. "Whatever happened to us being brutally honest with each other, even if it makes us uncomfortable?"

"Fine. I replaced all four tires on Jessie's car."

"I'm embarrassed I didn't realize the extent of your generosity last week. I thought you'd only replaced the damaged tire."

"All four tires were nearly bald, and I couldn't—" I didn't want to finish the sentence or have him read too much into the truth.

Seeing right through me, Henry said, "You couldn't what? Allow me to drive an unsafe vehicle?"

Staring into Henry's eyes, I only saw bewilderment. He couldn't understand why I would care so much. If I were honest, I would tell him I didn't know why either. Something about him just reached me on an elemental level. Without thinking, I simply reacted to him. I wanted to fulfill all his needs, even the ones he didn't realized he had. "Yes, that's why I decided to replace all four tires. I didn't know how often you drove Jessie's car, and I didn't like the idea of you becoming stranded someplace."

"I'm not a pitiful child, Ez—Professor Meyer."

Leaning forward, I placed my elbows on my desk. "Of course not."

"Despite how I appeared to you this week, I can take care of myself."

I tilted my head to the side and studied the scowl on his face. "But do you like it?"

Henry's brow furrowed. "Excuse me? Do I like taking care of myself? As opposed to what? Having someone else tell me where I need to be every second of the day? Listening to what other people think I should do with my life instead of what I want to do with it?" His voice rose in agitation with every question he asked. "My life might be a bit chaotic right now, but I'm living it my way. I cannot afford to slow down or slack off. I need to find a way to build up my stamina to fuel my mind and body. You said you have some ideas." He opened the binder he was using as a planner. He grabbed the tab marked

"June" and opened his planner to reveal a monthly calendar layout. He turned to the next page that read: Goals and Objectives. Taped to the middle of the page was a blue envelope with my name on it. Henry untaped it from the paper and slid it across the desk to me. "That's Jess's handwriting. I wasn't aware she'd put it in my planner."

I picked it up from my desk and playfully held it to my ear. "Should I be worried?"

Henry shrugged. "She likes you."

I opened the envelope and pulled out the folded note inside it. The unlined, cream paper had flowers and butterflies in the four corners connected by whimsical vines. The colors were bold and beautiful like the person who wrote the note.

Ezra,

I want to thank you for your kindness. I know you bought the new tires because you were worried about Henry's safety, which makes your thoughtfulness even more special to me. He's such a beautiful person, but you already know that.

I don't have a lot of money, but I insist on paying you back. I knew you wouldn't tell me the debt I owed you, so I called a buddy who's a mechanic. He told me the tires you put on my car cost around $500 without labor. I wrote you a check for $100. I will pay the rest as soon as I can.

Jessie

P.S. The threat still stands. I will break your face if you hurt my Henry.

I smiled and put the note back inside the envelope then set it inside my top desk drawer. I was eager to know how the two met, but I wouldn't ask. "She's a spitfire."

"Are you going to tell me what she said?" Henry asked.

"Was the envelope addressed to you?" I countered.

Henry glared at me. "No."

"Then, no, I'm not going to share the details of our private correspondence."

Henry retrieved a pen from his backpack and said, "I'm ready to get down to business then."

I bit my bottom lip when it threatened to curve into a smile. "The first thing I want to address is the one weighing heaviest on your mind, and that's paying for school. I assume you've taken out some federal loans to help you cover the cost of your summer classes." Henry nodded. I slid a piece of paper across my desk.

He picked it up and looked at it. "What's this?"

"I comprised a list of options you can look into for your fall semester. Some of them are work programs that pay toward your tuition, some are renewable scholarships, and others are grants."

Henry frowned. "I already work two jobs and don't have time to work another one. I doubt my grades are good enough for scholarships, and there are others who need the grants more than I do."

Henry's dismissive attitude and negativity irked me. "Working at the university would take the place of one or both of your other jobs. How do you know you're not eligible for scholarships or deserve the grants without looking into the programs?"

Henry studied the paper without meeting my glance. "I don't, I guess." After a few seconds, he lifted his gaze and offered a wry smile. "I guess it doesn't hurt to try."

I nodded. "That's much better."

"What kind of jobs does the university offer?"

"You'd have to check out the website, but I think they range from teaching assistants to working in the cafeteria or maintenance."

"That doesn't sound too bad," Henry said.

I slid another piece of paper to him. "These are your makeup assignments. I find myself in a quandary, Henry."

"What's that, Ezra?"

"Professor Meyer," I corrected.

"Then it's Mr. Sullivan to you," he countered pertly.

I gave him my touché nod. "I don't want to mark you absent because it makes it so much harder for you to get your grade back up, but it feels unethical because I wouldn't make the exception for anyone else. I find myself in the unique position of being the catalyst for your absence, and it seems unfair to penalize you for my lack of control."

"Stop blaming yourself and don't make an exception for me. I wouldn't turn down the opportunity to earn extra credit, but I don't want anything from you for free."

I was a horrible person for imagining Henry's extra credit involved him kneeling in front of me. The skin on my face and neck burned from my dirty thoughts.

"Not *that* kind of extra credit, Professor Meyer. I wasn't propositioning you."

"I do know that, Mr. Sullivan."

"Then why the red face?" Henry asked, smiling devilishly because he knew I was going to tell him the truth.

"Just because you weren't offering your personal services as extra credit didn't mean I didn't imagine it," I said boldly. Henry swallowed hard as his face heated too. "I will give the extra credit idea merit, but it would need to be something I would offer to other students who miss classes for extenuating circumstance."

"I won't be upset if you decide not to give me a chance. I can buckle down and get my grade up other ways."

"Let's talk about you buckling down. You mentioned finding ways to build up your stamina to fuel the energy you need to work and go to school. I have some suggestions."

Henry quirked a brow. "Did you print off a diet and exercise plan for me, Professor Higgins?"

His feistiness turned me inside out. "Now that you mention it…" I said, smiling when Henry's eyes widened. "I didn't design a plan for you, Henry. I want to help you, not control you."

"You do have suggestions though."

"I do," I agreed. "I've had the privilege to travel all around the world and study various disciplines that have made me a stronger person."

"You mean like the iron-clad control you wield like a weapon?" Henry asked.

"Weapons were created to harm people, and I don't use my control in that capacity." Of course, my past boyfriends would disagree with me on that point.

"I didn't mean to insult you, Professor Meyer. What are some things you suggest I do to increase my stamina?"

"A healthy diet, lots of sleep, exercise, and meditation would build a strong body and mind."

Henry scowled. "Exercise? I don't have the extra time to visit a gym or the extra money for a membership if I did."

"You can't afford to skip the gym," I countered. "Most local facilities give a hefty discount to college students, and you only need thirty minutes a day. Go to sleep and wake up earlier. Meditate, exercise, and eat a protein-rich breakfast to fuel your day. It will improve every part of your life. You'll have more energy, sharper focus, and you'll sleep better too."

A sly smile spread across his face. "Plus, there will be a ton of cute guys at the gym."

I bit the inside of my cheek to keep from growling. "Yes, it's fertile hunting ground."

"You sound like an expert," Henry said then shook his head. "Forget my last remark. I don't want to know about your hunting habits. Tell me about meditation."

I pulled a book out of my briefcase and handed it to him. "I've tried all these techniques over the years, and I like some of them a lot more than others. I thought you might like to borrow the book and give some of them a try to see what works best for you."

Henry studied the front and back covers. "You're serious about this?"

I nodded. "It helps you clear the clutter from your mind and find your center. There are many techniques to help combat an anxious or worried mind so you can find peace. Some methods are great ways to start the day, and others work wonders at night, enabling you to fall asleep faster and sleep more soundly. Like with physical exercise, you can dedicate a small amount of time to achieve maximum results."

Henry flipped the book open to the table of contents page. "I'm going to give this a shot." He swallowed hard then lifted his head to meet my gaze. "I spent my entire life under the controlling thumb of my mother and her religion. She threw me out when she found out I was gay and HIV positive. I was luckier than most because I had Ryan's Place. Archie and the team saved my life, and I want to pay it forward and help others like me." Henry held up the book. "I don't care if I feel silly trying these techniques as long as they help me achieve my dreams."

"So, Archie is your Professor Higgins?" I asked, keeping my tone light to hide the rage seething inside me.

Henry tilted his head back and laughed. "Oh my God! He'd love that comparison so much." I wanted to meet this Archie that both Ryder and Henry spoke so highly of. Henry sobered and said, "For too long, I've focused on all the wrong things. I thought about all the things I lost and none of the things I gained. My life resembles a runaway train on most days. There are times when it feels like it's too much for me to handle, then I realize I don't want to focus on the trauma anymore. Bad things happened to me, but they don't have to define me. I'm not where I need to be yet, but I get further and further away from the trauma every day."

"Knowing your worth and understanding what you want and don't want are huge steps. Things are hectic and tough right now, but I believe in you. Look at the sites I gave you and apply for all the grants and scholarships to see if something works out for you. Don't assume you're not eligible or unqualified. Apply for a job at the school to knock off some tuition. Most importantly, take care of yourself."

Henry held my gaze for a few seconds before he broke eye contact to look at his watch. "I better get going. I know it's not unusual for professors to meet with students, but I'd rather play it safe," he said, putting his binder and ink pen back inside his backpack. Henry rose swiftly to his feet and smiled. "Thanks for your help, Professor Meyer."

"You're welcome, Mr. Sullivan. I'll see you in class in a few minutes."

Henry turned when he reached the door then smiled when he caught me ogling his ass in his skinny jeans. "You'll let me know what you decide about the extra credit?"

"You'll be the first to know."

Henry opened the door and sauntered out with an extra sway to his narrow hips.

Henry: 4

Ezra: 0

Chapter Nine

Henry

*B*AM. "YOU GOTTA BE KIDDING ME." I BANGED MY FIST ON THE VENDing machine once more. *Bam. Bam.* "I need some fucking chocolate!"

"Is there a problem, Mr. Sullivan?"

My fist froze inches away from the glass before I could pound it again. I turned slowly and faced Ezra. "Problem? No."

"Then why are you damaging school property?" His firm, authoritative voice sent shivers straight to my balls. I'd gladly accept five minutes naked and alone with Ezra instead of the candy bar I purchased.

I turned and looked at the last Twix bar stuck in the machine. "I need some chocolate."

"So I heard. You think banging on the machine is the best way to achieve it?"

"I don't have another dollar on me right now to buy the bag of chocolate cookies above it to see if it knocks my Twix loose when it falls."

Ezra smiled wryly. "Let me take a crack at it."

"You're going to hit the vending machine?" I asked incredulously.

Ezra was the only person I knew who could make a snort sound haughty or eloquent. He reached inside his pocket and pulled out four quarters. "I'll go with your other option. I could use a sweet treat too." Ezra put the coins in the machine and punched the code for the bag of cookies. We watched as Ezra's mini Oreos bounced off my trapped candy bar and fell into the collection tray at the bottom while my Twix remained dangling above. "Damn. I thought for sure that would work." Ezra bent over and retrieved his cookies then offered them to me.

"No," I said, shaking my head. "I won't take your cookies from you."

His arched brow lifted, and his dark eyes seemed to dare me. "Would you consider sharing them with me instead?"

Picking my backpack up off the floor, I shouldered it and turned to face Ezra. "I wanted to speak to you anyway. That's why I arrived early."

"Is everything okay?" he asked, his voice soft with concern.

"Everything is great."

"Let's go chat in my office. We probably have at least fifteen minutes before anyone else shows up in that part of the building." Ezra held out his hand, gesturing for me to exit the breakroom. "Did you do anything special over the Fourth of July break last week?"

My face heated, and the right side of my mouth lifted in a smirk. "Define 'special,' Professor Meyer."

Ezra's lips parted, and his breath hissed from him. "I wasn't asking about your conquests, Mr. Sullivan," he whispered. "Be mindful of our surroundings."

I nodded and started past him, second-guessing my decision to have a private chat with him in his office.

"Hold up," Ezra said firmly. "Why are you limping?"

"I'm not limping." Maybe I was a little. "It's just a little twinge."

"It's a definite limp," Ezra said, suddenly sounding angry. "Come on." He headed toward the door, assuming I would obey his command.

"I'm not sure I want to go anywhere with you when you're growly like that," I told him.

Ezra halted then turned around to face me. His cheeks were pink, and his eyes shimmered with an expression I knew all too well—arousal. Was that why he was so mad? We'd managed to behave appropriately around one another for the past few weeks after our last meeting in his office. Had I somehow broken our tenuous truce?

Ezra crossed the distance between us with a long, confident stride. "I remember how fond you are of making me growl, so stop wasting our time. My office now." Ezra pivoted and walked out of the breakroom.

I waited a few minutes to allow both of us time to calm down. His words had triggered a primitive reaction in my body that my mesh gym shorts didn't disguise very well. Ezra had left his office door slightly open for me, so I pushed it closed behind me once I entered the room.

Ezra's elbows were on his desk, and his fingers formed a steeple resting against his dimpled chin. It looked like he was praying for something—patience, peace, or that I would disappear and not return. The last thought made my breath hitch in my throat, and I leaned hard against the door.

"Are you okay?" Ezra asked, rising swiftly to his feet.

I held up my hand to prevent him from coming over to me. We both knew what would happen if we were in touching distance of one another. "I'm fine; I promise."

Ezra sat back down, and I limped over and carefully lowered myself in one of the free chairs in front of his desk. His office was so damn small I might as well have straddled his lap in a broom closet. He opened the pack of mini Oreos and tilted it toward me so I could help myself. Once I took a few, Ezra reached in a pulled out a few cookies for himself. "Why don't you tell me how you hurt yourself." He popped the cookies in his mouth.

"It's from Brad. He's helping me become more flexible."

Ezra choked on his cookies for a few seconds then washed them down with a long sip of water. Most guys I knew swigged drinks, but Ezra's throat moved up and down elegantly, hypnotically. "Brad?" he croaked out.

"My yoga instructor. That's why I wanted to talk to you."

"You came to tell me about your yoga instructor?" Ezra asked in disbelief.

"Not Brad and his yoga class specifically, Professor Meyer, but I wanted to thank you for the talk we had two weeks ago. I started exercising, eating better, and meditating as you suggested, and it's made a big difference in my life. I have more energy and focus now."

"More energy for Brad?" Ezra asked.

"More energy *because* of Brad," I corrected. "We aren't screwing." I ate the few cookies I took from the bag then reached for a few more.

"I'm not sure Brad is doing his job right," Ezra said then popped two more cookies in his mouth.

"Because he's not screwing me?" I asked.

Ezra's mouth stopped chewing for a second before it resumed. He swallowed hard then took another drink of water. "I would imagine the gym or yoga studio discourages their instructors from fucking their clients. I meant that Brad isn't doing his job correctly because yoga isn't supposed to hurt. He shouldn't push you past your limits, Henry. You're supposed to start with easy positions and slowly work your way up to the more advanced ones."

"Know something about yoga too?"

"I do. Pilates also. Stop trying to distract me. I want to know why Brad is pushing you too hard." Ezra ran a finger over his brow, which meant he was losing his patience.

"He isn't pushing me; I'm pushing myself. I like learning new positions, and I took things too far during a session at home this morning. My hamstring isn't happy with me right now."

Ezra rose from his chair again. "Stand up and let me look at it."

"No," I said, shaking my head. "I'll go to the clinic if ice and ibuprofen don't help."

"Henry, stand up."

"Stand up, bend over, and put my hands on your desk? Is that the position you want me to get in?" I don't know what made me say it, but I decided to blame the devil. Maybe Ezra was my personal Lucifer; if so, I wanted him to lead me into temptation.

Ezra rounded the desk wearing a stern expression on his face. I stood up to face him. I liked that he wasn't much taller than me, but Ezra didn't need a tall stature to dominate a room or a situation. "Actually, yes," he said silkily. "That's exactly what I want you to do."

"This is ridiculous," I said, but I bent at the waist and placed my palms flat on his desk.

Ezra crossed to the door and locked it, making my dick twitch with the possibilities. He moved my chair back a foot then sat in it, putting his eyes level with my ass. I jolted when I felt his warm hands on my bare thighs. "At least your gym shorts make this easier. Imagine if I needed you to drop your pants."

"You're a cruel man, Ezra."

"I just can't seem to help myself when it comes to you." Ezra carefully probed the back of my thigh, pushing gently with his thumbs. I hissed when he found the sore spot. "Right there?" I grunted and nodded. Ezra returned to the area with gentle pressure then moved his thumbs outward from the center, loosening the tight knot.

"Oh," I whimpered. "It's starting to feel better already."

Ezra scooted the chair back farther then lowered himself to the floor behind me. I knew I should call a halt to him touching me, but I didn't want to. I wanted to see how far he would go. Ezra tugged my shorts down to my knees, and I thought we might go all the way if pushed hard enough. "I wanted to be able to see the afflicted area because it feels hot and swollen."

"It's definitely hot and swollen. Hard as steel too."

Ezra chuckled but didn't slide his hand up between my legs to confirm my statement like I wanted him to. He returned his focus to the knot in my hamstring. "It looks okay, but you're going to want to ice this down for twenty minutes every few hours."

God, his hands felt so good. I didn't care how wrong the situation was. The only thing I wanted was more of his hands on my body. I hadn't exaggerated the condition of my dick either. I glanced down and saw the wet spot on the front of my light blue underwear. I clenched my jaw to keep from begging him to put me out of my misery, but I couldn't prevent the way my body shivered beneath his careful touch.

"I am the cruelest kind of bastard, aren't I?" Ezra asked softly.

"No," I whispered, but my pounding heart said yes.

Ezra leaned forward and kissed the tender spot on the back of my thigh. "What's your opinion now?"

I whimpered. "Yeah, pretty damn cruel." Ezra made me feel bold and daring, which had to be the reason I straightened up and turned to face him. I needed him to see the way my body reacted to him. Ezra's eyes lingered on my crotch before they inched up my torso until they met my eyes. I gripped my erection through my briefs and said, "I can think of a way you can make it up to me."

Ezra's gaze dropped down to watch my hand moving lazily up and down my shaft. "Who's the cock tease now, Henry?"

Acting with a boldness I never knew I possessed, I released my cock and shoved my briefs down to my thighs. "Who's teasing, Ezra?"

Chapter Ten

Ezra

I tore my eyes away from the pearl of pre-cum beading on Henry's cock head to meet his gaze. He'd never acted this boldly before, and I needed to see the same confidence I heard in his words before I took him down the back of my throat. Henry's gorgeous eyes dazzled with challenge, and a smug smirk slanted across his face. How had I thought I could resist him?

"If you're so worried about what I'm doing with this," Henry said, fisting his cock and stroking it, "why don't you show me what I should be doing with it?"

"Do you think you brought me to my knees with this stunt, Henry?"

He arched a dark brow. *"Aren't* you on your knees for me, Ezra?" Henry reached down with his free hand to give his balls a firm tug.

I sucked in a quick breath. Who was this young man, and what had he done with my Henry? I mentally shook my head. He's not *my* Henry. A long-forgotten voice inside me whispered, *but he could be.* Anger. I needed to get pissed and hold on to it, forcing all other emotion aside so I could get off my knees and send him out of my office—hard, aching, and remorseful. Wispy tendrils of anger formed, but they were as elusive as smoke rings in the wind. I could try to grab them, but they'd dissipate in my hands or shift in the opposite direction. That left me with only one alternative: regain the upper hand.

Henry's smirk trembled but didn't fade when I rose to my feet to stand before him. "Somebody can't stop playing with matches, I see."

Henry's hand tightened around his shaft, and he continued to jack himself. "I didn't plan this," he said breathlessly. I recognized the tremor in his voice and knew he was close to spilling his cum in my office. Acceptance and inevitability washed over me. This was always meant to happen again, whether he planned it or not, but we would do things on my terms.

"You didn't plan to imply that some guy named Brad was plowing your tight ass and making you limp?" I asked. Henry's shuttling fist faltered, and his mouth fell open. I raised my brow, letting him know I was waiting for an answer.

Henry shook his head. "I just w-wanted to th-thank you. I get nervous around you and say the wrong things."

"How were you going to thank me?" I asked, stepping closer and brushing his hand off his cock. Henry would come when I said he could. I slid my hand beneath the hem of his tee and felt the flex of his abdominal muscles. He hadn't exaggerated when he said he'd been exercising a lot. I slid my fingers upward, tracing a path up his torso that made him shiver. "By teasing me with what I want most and can't have?" I circled his nipple then softly grazed it with the tip of one finger. I knew how sensitive his nipples were but refused to reward him for behaving badly. "Had you planned to show your appreciation by telling me about the other men who get to enjoy your efforts?" I stilled my hand so that my palm rested over his heart, which raced desperately for me.

"No, I'm not—" Henry's voice choked with emotion. He placed a hand on the side of my neck, his thumb brushing against my runaway pulse. "I'm not that kind of guy," he finally said. "Y-you jumped to conclusions, and I tried to clear things up right away. I wish I wanted Brad, and I wish I could take guys up on their blatant offers, but I can't."

Blatant offers. The thought alone had me fighting back a growl. I retained enough of my good sense to place emphasis on the most important part of his confession. I leaned forward until my lips were a hairsbreadth away from his. "Why can't you?"

Henry's eyes closed, and his head fell back on a soft moan, exposing his strong throat. Unable to resist his sweet offering, I pressed my lips against his pulse point, loving the way it quivered against my flesh. If we were alone in my apartment, I'd mark him. "You already know the answer, Ezra."

Knowing I was going to lose this battle wasn't enough; I needed to make Henry as crazy as I felt before I released the last vestiges of my resistance. "I need you to tell me, Henry. We promised to be honest, no matter what. Use your words."

Henry's head snapped up, and his eyes glittered with determination. "They're not you, Ezra. Is that what you needed to hear? Do you want to know that I choose to go home and fuck my fist rather than give myself up to someone who isn't you? Does that make you happy?"

"Deliriously so," I said before crashing my lips against his for a hot, searing kiss. Henry moaned into my mouth and dug his fingers into my ass cheeks, pulling me closer so his dick was pressed firmly between our abdomens. It still wasn't enough. Need and lust clawed at my guts as our teeth gnashed and our tongues stroked. Henry began rutting desperately against my stomach, too far gone to care how he got off as long as it involved me. I broke the kiss and stepped away from him while I still had a shred of propriety left. "I can no longer deny what's going to happen between us, but it can't happen here." As if to prove my point, voices echoed in the hallway outside my door. I recognized them as students in Henry's class.

"You can't leave me like this," Henry said desperately. He looked down at my polo shirt he'd rucked up; half of the shirt had pulled loose from the waistband of my dress pants. "You definitely can't go in there with that." He gestured toward my waist, and I assumed he meant my raging hard-on, but he was talking about the huge wet spot from his pre-cum on the front of my shirt.

"Definitely not," I agreed. "It's a good thing I keep a spare shirt in the closet in case of an emergency."

Henry looked over my head, and I knew he was looking at the clock. "We have ten minutes before class. You either put me out of my misery in your office, or I'm going to jack off in a bathroom stall. What's it going to be? Do you want to look at my blissed-out face in class knowing you put the look there, or do you want to see it and regret you weren't part of it?"

The image of Henry jacking off while thinking of me was so fucking hot, but not in a bathroom stall where someone might hear him grunt and come. The alternative wasn't feasible either. I couldn't risk one of his classmates overhearing him grunting and coming in my office. The solution came to me, and I pulled my polo shirt the rest of the way free from my pants and tugged it over my head then draped it over the arm of the chair I'd vacated.

I gripped his wrist then pressed my mouth to his ear. "Pull your shirt off, turn around, bend over my desk and present that sweet ass to me. Bite down on your shirt. If I hear one muffled sound escaping from your mouth, I'll deny us both what we need. Am I clear?"

Henry swallowed hard and nodded. I leaned in and gave him a quick peck on the lips before he tugged his shirt off and got into the position I demanded. If we'd had more time, I would've offered him a sweet reward for following instructions and dropped to my knees to rim his pucker until he writhed, his body silently begged for more. Instead, I pulled a condom and packet of lube from my wallet and tossed them on my desk where he could see them and know what was about to happen. Henry rewarded me with a hard but silent shiver.

I unbuckled my belt then unfastened and unzipped my pants. After shoving my pants and briefs to mid-thigh, I opened and rolled the condom down my erection. Henry's need for me vibrated through his body, and I knew a ten-minute fuck wouldn't be enough for either of us. It was the hand we were dealt at the moment, and I wasn't going to waste another minute without feeling Henry's tight heat clamping around my cock.

I tore open the corner on the lube packet and squeezed a generous amount on two fingers. Goose bumps broke out all over Henry's beautiful body when I pressed the slickened fingers against his pucker. I knew it was partly due to the cool lube, but most of it was from anticipation of having me inside him again. Normally, I'd draw out teasing him, but time wasn't my friend. I worked him open with one finger then two. Henry's hole was even tighter than I remembered, and I wished for something to bite down on, too, so my moaning and grunting didn't give us away.

Henry thrust his hips back, fucking himself on my finger and silently telling me he was ready. I smeared the rest of the lube down my latex-covered shaft then pressed my dick against his pucker. Henry bore down and pushed back, sucking the fat head into his tight heat. I gripped his hips tightly, urging him to slow down. I knew he wanted me to ride his ass hard, but we didn't have the luxury, because people would hear our bodies slapping together. I needed stealth and precision.

With one hand on his shoulder and the other on his hip, I pushed fully inside Henry's tight heat. *Divine.* There was no other word to describe how the connection felt. I carefully pulled out, allowing him time to adjust to the burning stretch and fullness. When only the head of my dick remained inside him, I whispered, "Hold on, sweet Henry." I pushed back in, aiming straight for his prostate.

Henry stiffened and jerked but didn't let out a peep, which only made me hotter and hornier. I wanted to push him past all his limits, but it would need to wait until we were alone in my home. The thought should've startled me, but it felt right, and I didn't have time to question my decision. I kept a steady pace of stroking in and out, making sure to peg him perfectly every time. It only took a few passes before Henry began shaking all over. I shifted my hand from his hip to his cock, letting him fuck my fist while I fucked his ass. Lust built inside me; a dark and sensuous beast whispered that fucking Henry was too much and not enough at the same time. He could be my redeemer or my downfall.

Henry's hole squeezed my cock and his dick pulsed in my hand as his release splattered over it and his essence filled the air. Gritting my teeth to keep from shouting, I thrust forward once more, driving Henry up onto his toes, and filled the condom. I leaned forward, covering his back with my chest and wrapping my arms around him, loving the feel of our hot, sweaty flesh pressing together.

"I'm not finished with you, Henry. Not by a long shot." My darkly whispered words elicited a shiver from him. I loosened my arms from around him then gingerly pulled my softening dick from his ass. My brain was already shifting to hiding the evidence of what happened so we could get on with class and the rest of our evening. I pulled tissues from the box and cleaned Henry's spunk from my hand when what I really wanted was to make him lick it off. *Next time.* I removed the condom, tied it in a knot, and wrapped it in more tissues before tossing it in the trash can. "Use my shirt to clean up," I instructed. "Toss it in the closet when you're done."

Henry rose to his full height and turned to face me while using my favorite light blue polo to wipe his cum off his cock and pubic hair before wiping off the spurts that had landed on my desk. "Are you mad at me?" he asked, looking and sounding worried. I wanted to see him with his face flushed with pleasure, not doubt.

"No, but this can't happen here again," I replied, tugging my pants and briefs back into place. I reached for my wallet again, but this time I pulled out a card with a barcode on it. "Do you remember where I live?" Henry nodded. "Are you driving Jessie's car?"

"Yes, she left for a short tour a few nights ago."

I offered the card to him, and he accepted it. "This is a pass to get into the parking garage." I pointed to the bold back numbers on the top. "This number is the assigned spot for my guest. I want you to go directly home after class, pack a bag, and come to my apartment. You don't need to stop for anything to eat; I'll take care of that."

Henry traced his fingers over the parking slot number. "Ezra, are you sure?"

"I'm positive. Oh, and make sure you leave the card on your dashboard so it's easily visible when the building security passes through the garage and spots a car they haven't seen before. They would call up to my apartment and interrupt us, and we wouldn't want that, would we?" I glanced at the clock and saw I was out of time. "I want you to stay in here a few minutes to gather yourself before you come to class. Your face is giving away your every emotion."

"Yeah? What am I feeling?" Henry challenged.

"Hope. Fear. Hunger, and not just for the Twix bar you had to abandon. Am I right?" Henry nodded. "Then I need you to stay in here until you have yourself under control. Think of your meditation techniques and maybe put your dick away."

"Shit," Henry whispered like he'd forgotten his shorts were down around his knees. "I see what you mean."

"I'm going to grab my clean shirt and get out of here. You follow when you're ready, and I will dock you for being late because of this stunt." Henry's mouth fell open in a silent protest, but I diverted him with a soft kiss on his mouth. "You'll come over tonight so we can talk."

"Talk? I need an overnight bag for talking?"

I crossed to the closet door and pulled it open. I took the navy blue polo off the hanger and pulled it over my head. "First, we're going to use our words to come up with an understanding of what's going to happen between us. Then we're going to use our bodies to communicate until we've worked a month's worth of frustrations out of our system." I tucked the shirt in my waistband and fastened my belt. Facing the mirror, I ran a hand through my hair and made sure there were no outward signs I'd just emptied my balls inside one of my students. Crude? Yes, but that's how the school administration would view what happened with Henry. They wouldn't understand and would reduce what we shared to basic human biology. It was so much more than that though. The last thought rocked me hard, but I just couldn't seem to find a fuck to give at the moment.

Satisfied I looked okay, I turned to face Henry once more. "Don't be too late, or I'll have too much time to think of punishments."

Henry pointed to his dick that hadn't fully returned to its slumbering state. "You're not helping, Ezra. I seem to have no control when it comes to you."

I smiled devilishly. *Let's keep it that way.* "See you in class."

I needed it to be the quickest ninety minutes of my life.

Chapter Eleven

Henry

STUNNED. IT WAS THE ONLY WAY TO DESCRIBE THE WAY I FELT LOOKING at the parking pass card in my hand. *What had just happened?* I replayed the last twenty minutes in my mind while simultaneously willing my dick to forget all about it. I had arrived early to thank Ezra for his recommendations because I felt truly strong, healthy, and independent for the first time. The only thing that would've made me happier was what happened between us once we were alone in his office. I hadn't planned a big seduction; I'd simply wanted to eat a damn Twix bar and thank Ezra before class. Sure, I selfishly wanted to share a space with him for a few minutes, but I never dreamed it would involve my shorts around my knees and Ezra's dick in my ass. My hole twitched at the reminder.

The sex wasn't as surprising as what happened next. Chemistry had always raged between us like an inferno, so it almost felt inevitable it would happen again, no matter what either of us said. But the invite to Ezra's home after class for dinner, talking, and more sex… *Stunned.*

I glanced down my body. Satisfied my dick was going to behave, I pulled my shirt back on then lifted my backpack off the floor and carefully tucked the parking garage pass in a slot inside it. The square of paper felt like the most precious gift anyone had ever given me, so roughly shoving it in my wallet or tossing it in the bottom of my bag to get crumpled felt wrong. Besides, Ezra would undoubtedly want it back and wouldn't like for me to return it in poor condition. The idea of him handing the card to a man other than me had the same effect as dumping a bucket of ice-cold water over my head. The sensation was unwanted and uncomfortable but, in this case, probably for the best. I couldn't afford to lose my head over Ezra, or I'd face a huge set-back. I couldn't assume he would want more than this night.

I inhaled deeply and released the breath slowly. *I can do this.*

I crossed to the mirror Ezra had used to check his appearance before leaving. My reflection showed a man who looked happy and a little dazed. My cheeks still held a hint of a flush, and my lips looked swollen and well-kissed. I would be lying if I said I wasn't nervous, but hiding in Ezra's office all night wasn't an option. Satisfied my re-flection could pass for someone who was agitated from running late instead of recently fucked, I opened the door a crack and peeked out-side. Luckily, no other stragglers were in the hallway about to bust me coming out of my professor's office.

I walked quickly to the classroom and pulled open the door be-fore I could talk myself out of it. Every head in the room turned in my direction because no one was ever late to Professor Meyer's class. The subject was intriguing on its own, but throw in a sexy, charismatic instructor and you have yourself a full classroom. I was probably the only one who'd missed classes or arrived late.

Ezra cocked an eyebrow in mock irritation, and I started to squirm a bit at the back of the room. Everyone but my tormentor would've mistaken my fidgeting as nerves, but Ezra knew what he did to me. He was just a master at hiding it. "So nice of you to join us, Mr. Sullivan. Please find your seat."

I smiled nervously and said, "So sorry, Professor Meyer. I had a bit of car trouble." I averted my gaze and made my way to the table I shared with Drake, who looked at me like I'd lost my mind.

"As I was saying," Ezra said, ignoring my apology and dismissing me altogether, "we're going to begin our next unit and discuss our first field trip." Soft murmurs erupted around the room, and Ezra coolly paused to let them pass before continuing. "Our next unit is Sexual Techniques and Behaviors. I would again like to stress that we are all adults in this classroom, and I expect you to act accordingly. I will not tolerate crude or disrespectful comments, nor will I permit shaming of any kind. You will discover many things in this world that don't appeal to you, but that doesn't mean they shouldn't fascinate anyone else. Are we all in agreement?"

"Yes, sir," we all said.

Ezra nodded and began his lecture. I was mesmerized by the confidence with which he spoke about sexuality, the ways he engaged with his students, and how comfortable they were speaking out. Growing up in a strict, religious home, we never discussed sex. If we pretended it didn't exist, then we wouldn't be tempted, right? So wrong. The subject was only ever mentioned in our church in the context of procreation or sin. That was it: you had sex to make babies, or it was a sin. Sex corrupted the soul and weakened the mind, according to Preacher Daily.

Once again, I remained quiet while most of the other students talked openly about the things they'd felt and experienced, but never in a crude, insensitive, or disrespectful way. Ezra's eyes would land on me occasionally, but I never saw censure or disapproval that I hadn't spoken out loud about my experiences or aired questions I had. I was more comfortable putting my personal feelings in my assignments rather than sharing them with people I didn't know. I wasn't sure I'd ever overcome my hesitation to speak so openly about personal subjects, but time would tell. I wasn't the only one who chose to observe more than participate, and it helped me not to feel isolated.

"This has been a wonderful discussion, but our time is almost up, and I know you're dying to know more about your first field trip." Ezra smiled when we all sat up straighter in our chairs. "Have any of you heard about the Museum of Sex in New York City?" He paused to see if anyone had, and when no one spoke up, he continued. "It's a wonderful museum, and I highly suggest it to anyone traveling to the city. Luckily, the museum now has a traveling exhibit at select cities throughout the country. I'm friends with the director, and I'm excited to announce the museum is opening an exhibit in Cincinnati next weekend."

Friends, huh? What kind of friends?

"It's stirred up a big controversy locally, so I'm surprised you haven't heard about it on the news. Deandra and her crew have been quietly setting up the exhibit, but word has leaked out, and church congregations are ready to protest with signs or pitchforks on opening night. My lucky students get a private tour of the museum before it opens to the public and get to avoid the fray." Excitement rippled through the room, and Ezra soaked it all in. He looked mighty proud of himself, reminding me of our cat Jasper who wanted us to fuss and fawn every time she killed a mouse and dragged it home.

"Do we get extra credit if we counter protest?" Drake asked beside me.

Ezra tipped his head to the side while he pondered it. "Let me get back to you on that, Mr. Duggins. I would need to set rules and get signed agreements from anyone participating so neither I nor the university are held accountable if any of you knuckleheads get arrested." Laughter spread around the room.

"Fair enough, Professor M," Drake said. *Professor M? Back off, gingersnap.*

Ezra glanced at his watch. "That's it for tonight, guys and gals. I'll see you on Wednesday night."

I stood up, shouldered my bag, and made my way out of class. I hadn't bonded with any of my classmates, so there was no need to put my head down to avoid eye contact and conversation. I was just proud that I had by some miracle made it through class without getting a boner. Discussing sexual techniques and behaviors while still wearing Ezra's scent was a dangerous game, but I had set my personal feelings aside and focused on the lecture.

"Sullivan," Drake yelled from behind me.

Damn it. Why tonight of all nights? I slowly turned around and forced a friendly smile. "Yeah?"

Smiling ruefully, Drake held up my textbook. "Forgot something, buddy."

I shook my head and walked over to him. "I can be such an airhead sometimes."

"Nah," Drake said, shaking his head. "You look like there's always someplace you need to be."

"Well, it's true. Gym, work, school, work, sleep. Repeat."

"Oh," he said, sounding disappointed. "You heading to work now?"

"Not tonight."

His amber eyes lit with hopefulness, and I regretted being honest. "You wanna hang?"

"Oh," I said, hoping I sounded disappointed. "I can't tonight; I have plans with a friend." Ezra was *friendly*... Mostly. "Maybe some other night?"

"Sure, man," Drake said casually. "See you Wednesday." He handed my book over and stepped around me to leave the room.

"See you," I called after him. Feeling Ezra's eyes on me, I risked looking in his direction. While his facial expression gave nothing away, the rigid tension in his body spoke loud and clear. He was annoyed. How could Ezra think for a second I'd choose Drake over him?

I turned and left the room and headed straight for my car. I turned on my phone when I got behind the wheel and saw I had a text from a number I didn't recognize.

Dinner is arriving at 10:15. You won't want to be late.

I didn't need Ezra to sign his texts because his haughtiness came through loud and clear. I hit the icon to save the number as a contact in my phone and giggled when I entered E. Higgins to identify Ezra. My laughter died when I saw I only had forty-five minutes to shower, pack my bag, and get to Ezra's house. My phone buzzed with another incoming text.

Don't shower either. I want to smell myself on your skin.

I couldn't form thoughts, let alone type them out, so I sent Ezra a thumbs-up. Then I drove across town to my apartment with shaking legs and a racing heart. Was I making a huge mistake? Hadn't I finally accepted the thing I wanted with Ezra would never happen? *No*, a voice whispered inside my head. It was right. Deep inside, a tiny part of me had always known we weren't through. I remembered what Ezra had said to me about playing with fire. Allowing myself to get closer to him might singe me, but it was a risk I was willing to take. Some scars were worth the battle.

With that conviction pushing aside my fear, I quickly packed and headed to Ezra's fancy apartment with its dedicated parking garage only for residents and their guests. A vacant guard shack and a set of gates just inside the parking garage blocked unwanted visitors from entering. I fished out the parking pass Ezra gave me and held it in front of the scanner like the instructions said. The light switched from red to green, and the gates lifted to grant me access. I followed the signs for the designated parking numbers and pulled into the spot beside Ezra's car.

Is this for real? Am I really doing this? Hell yes, I am.

I set the parking pass on the dashboard like Ezra had instructed, and got out of the car with my overnight bag. I had homework I needed to do, but it could wait until my lunch break the next day. The ride up to Ezra's floor wasn't nearly as thrilling the second time since he wasn't there backing me into the corner, kissing my neck, and whispering about all the filthy things he wanted to do to me. Anticipation climbed higher and higher with every floor the elevator passed until I was breathless when it came to a soft stop. The quiet whoosh of the opening doors sounded really loud in my ears.

Any lingering doubt disappeared when I stepped off the elevator and found Ezra leaning casually against the wall outside his apartment door. He'd changed into a pair of silky-looking black sleep pants and a black tank top. Ezra Meyer was the sexiest man I'd ever met, and he wanted *me*. Why? I didn't know, but I was done questioning it.

Ezra straightened to his full height when I approached. In a dark and delicious voice, he said, "Hello, Henry."

Chapter Twelve

Ezra

I'D WATCHED AS HENRY STEPPED OFF THE ELEVATOR, AND WHILE I wouldn't say he looked doubtful, he at least looked cautious. Then his eyes met mine, and he must've seen what he needed because he stood taller as he approached me, eyes raking over my body. Henry's mouth parted, and a soft sigh slipped out when I greeted him, making me want to sink my teeth into his full bottom lip.

"Hello, Ezra," he said breathlessly when he reached me.

My apartment door and privacy were only a foot away, but I couldn't stop myself from reaching for Henry and pulling him into my arms. "I bet the elevator ride up this time wasn't as exciting."

"I was just thinking the same thing." The easy smile Henry gifted me with was beautiful, and I couldn't resist tasting it. Cupping his neck, I sipped and teased his lips until they parted for me. I didn't give a damn about where we were or who might see us; I only cared about having more of Henry. I deepened the kiss until he melted against me. A ping rang in the hallway, followed by the soft swoosh of the elevator doors opening. I didn't jerk away from the kiss; I ended it slowly with tiny kisses that expressed how much I wanted him with me. Supplicating, stained-glass eyes peered at me through half-closed lids, and I found it nearly impossible to tear my attention away from Henry to greet the delivery man lingering a few feet down the hallway.

Releasing Henry, I kissed his forehead then guided him to my apartment. I didn't want any man to see the arousal in his eyes, even if the guy was only dropping off food and leaving. After opening the door, I ushered Henry through it. "I'll only be a minute. Make yourself comfortable." I turned and greeted the delivery man with a polite nod.

Once he stepped closer, I could see the guy was actually an overgrown kid. "Here's your order, Dr. Meyer. Dad said to tell you he added a new dessert he'd like you to test out for him. On the house, of course."

"Phillipe is your father?" I asked, accepting the large, canvas carryout tote from him. I'd already paid for my food online and added a generous tip, so there wasn't anything for me to sign.

"Yeah, he was surprised to discover he was a father too," the young man said with a laugh. "I am a product of his fake-it-until-you-make-it phase. He faked being straight, but he never quite made it. In the process, he made me, but my mom didn't tell him because they'd already agreed to get a divorce and Dad had accepted an apprenticeship in Paris." If I hadn't known Phillipe so well, I would've found the conversation awkward.

As intriguing as the discovery was, Henry was waiting for me, and the clock was ticking on our time together. Still, being a rude asshole just to satisfy my dick wasn't cool. "It must have come as a great shock to both of you," I said politely. "I'm glad you found one another."

"It did, but I'm glad we found each other too." The young man glanced toward my door. "Have a good night."

"You also," I said, hoping my smile was warm. The kid was excited about meeting his dad, and now I could only think about how I was almost old enough to be Henry's father. It didn't curtail my plans to do very naughty things to Henry once we cleared up a few things. I waited for guilt or self-disgust to kick in, but neither was forthcoming. "Take care," I added before opening my door.

My home was quiet when I entered, and I saw no sign of Henry in the open living room, kitchen, or dining room. I didn't see his shadow amid those on the balcony overlooking the river either. He couldn't have left since there was only one exit, which meant he was either in my home office or my master suite. I was nearly certain Henry wasn't rummaging around in my desk, which meant he was in my bedroom. I wanted to look for him but decided to give him however much time and space he needed to come to terms with what was going to happen between us. I carried our dinner to the smaller, intimate table off the kitchen with the fantastic river view. He wasn't here for a quick fuck, which I'd made apparent when I told him to pack a bag. Maybe he was battling a case of sudden nerves. If he didn't return by the time I unpacked the carryout tote, I—My thought died when I heard the sound of bare feet approaching me. I turned to face him and nearly swallowed my tongue. How the hell did he manage to throw me off guard every single time?

"Is this okay?" he asked, holding his hands up and spinning slowly. "I felt overdressed, and I got in too big of a hurry at my apartment and forgot to pack pajamas." Henry wore my navy silk sleep pants and navy tank top. He must've remembered where I kept my pajamas from his last visit because he'd borrowed a pair then too. He'd sat in my kitchen looking rumpled and smelling like sex while wearing my clothes. It had kept me aroused the entire time I made breakfast. I liked seeing my things on him. I liked it even more when I got to remove them from his body then mark him with my scent. Henry brought out my baser instincts and needs—a primal urge to mate and mark.

"It's perfect," I said, noting my voice sounded raspy with desire. There were things we needed to discuss before I could allow myself to touch Henry intimately again. I might've lost control in my office, but I couldn't let it happen again, and I also couldn't let Henry go. "Are you hungry?"

"For you." The bold words matched the expression in Henry's eyes. He was so different from the man I met nearly seven months ago who could barely make eye contact with me.

"And you shall have me, but we need to eat and talk first." I gestured for him to take a seat.

Henry sat down and looked up at me with a sly grin. "Is this where we lay down the rules of when we can be together?"

Unable to resist, I dropped a kiss on his upturned forehead. "This is where *I* lay down the rules since *I'm* the only one with something to lose here." I opened the container of savory pork tenderloin and forked a generous amount on Henry's plate then reached for the new potatoes. Noticing his stiffness, I returned my gaze to his.

Henry's lips were pursed in thought, and a deep V furrowed in his brow. "Wait. Are you implying I don't get a say in what happens between us?"

Sighing heavily, I scooped potatoes onto his plate. I was fucking this all up. "Of course not, Henry. You're not my prisoner, and I'm not trying to control you. I would never try to suppress your free will. I didn't mean to imply you couldn't be hurt if things go wrong, but it's my *career* on the line."

Henry's shy smile returned. "You were born to boss people around, Ezra."

"It's a habit I picked up early in life," I quipped, winking at him.

"I think bossing people around is a very close second place to your desire to take care of those you care about."

Henry's words hit very close to home, and I nearly dropped the serving spoon. I set the container of potatoes on the table and picked up the green beans. Those were traits I was able to hide or disguise with most people, but Henry saw to the very core of me. I felt a shimmer of hope. *Just maybe…*

"How do you even know I like green beans?" Henry asked, pulling me out of my fantasies. Our gazes met and held. My hand holding the scoop of beans hovered uncertainly over his plate. "I actually love them, and I smell a hint of bacon, so these will probably be the best green beans I've ever had, but it wouldn't hurt you to ask me first instead of assuming I want them. I can also serve my own dinner."

I handed the container of beans to him with the serving spoon. "Fair enough. I will try to do better when ordering dinner."

Henry's mouth fell open again, but he quickly regained his composure and dished beans onto his plate. "This is something you want to do again?"

"Very much, but we have to be careful."

"Because I'm your student or for other reasons?" he pressed. There he went again with his keen instincts.

"Yes, because you're my student." There were a few other reasons, but I wasn't ready to share my tumultuous past with him. I might not ever be prepared to slice myself open for him, and it was something he'd have to accept if we were going to have any kind of relationship.

"Fair enough," Henry said, using my phrase against me. "That's only going to be the case for another month."

"So far," I countered. "We might find ourselves in this situation again if I'm teaching a class you need for your degree."

"We can cross that road if we come to it," Henry said, sniffing the air appreciatively. "Do I smell bread?"

"Yes, how silly of me. Phillipe would never exclude his famous French sourdough bread. I also learned from his son that he included dessert for us to try."

"The delivery boy is the chef's son?" Henry asked. I detected something else in his voice. Was he questioning how close I was to Phillipe? I somehow felt comforted by the notion I wasn't the only jealous one, but it also meant the potential for misunderstandings that could lead to explosive arguments if we weren't open and honest.

"That's what he said when he handed me the bag." I repeated

the story for Henry while I retrieved the mini loaves of bread and butter I'd left in the tote. "I don't know how new the development is, but I'm guessing pretty recent. I've never seen the kid before, and his emotions looked shiny and new."

"Wow," Henry softly said when I set a mini loaf on his plate.

"The bread is delicious," I said.

"Not that, although I'm sure it is. I was just wondering what it's like for Phillipe to find out he has a grown son." Henry sniffed the air and moaned. "Okay, the smell of this bread is making my stomach growl. I need you to sit down and serve yourself dinner so we can eat."

Chuckling, I bent down and kissed the top of his head before taking my seat across from him. "You don't have to wait for me, Henry. Dig in."

"No way," he said stubbornly.

"Was the Twix bar going to be your dinner tonight?" I asked with a raised brow.

"No, Ezra. I've truly learned from my mistakes. I had a hearty salad with seared steak and boiled eggs for added protein for lunch, but I must've burned it off. I just wanted the little kick of sugar to get me through your class."

"But then I went and depleted your caloric reserves even more," I said proudly.

"You don't have to sound so smug."

Satisfied I had everything I needed, I picked up my fork and pointed at Henry's plate. "Eat."

Henry didn't argue; he picked up his fork and took a bite of his tenderloin. He moaned as flavor burst on his tongue. He moved to the potatoes then the beans before he sliced a piece of bread from his loaf and spread a thin layer of butter on top. "Stop staring at me and eat. I'm not the only one who needs protein for the after-talk activities. I assume you didn't invite me over to clean your apartment or play Monopoly."

"Definitely not."

Henry smirked. "Give me your rules and lay everything out on the table for me, Ezra."

I'd rather lay him out on the table, but he was right. I told him we needed to talk, and it's what we would do. "No one at the school can know about us."

Henry nodded. "That goes without saying."

"Nothing goes without saying, Henry. Assumptions kill dreams and ruin lives." I sounded more forceful and grimmer than I'd planned. I cleared my throat. "I haven't done this in a while."

"What exactly is *this*?" Henry asked, gesturing between us.

"I don't know exactly what *this* is, but I know I want you, and I don't want anyone else to have you as long as we're seeing one another. I can try to deny that I don't want to know everything about you, but it would be a lie. You fascinate me, Henry."

Henry snorted. "I'm not a player, Ezra. I know you think there's a line of guys wanting a crack at my ass, but it's not true. I only want you." He tilted his head to the side. "I want the same commitment from you. As long as *this* is going on, there can't be any other guys for you either."

"Agreed," I said quickly. "Honesty is a must. I will try to open up more and share more of myself too. I don't want this to be a one-sided thing where you take all the risks." The more I talked the more I realized our thing was starting to sound more like dating. "If ever I—*this*—becomes too much for you, I want you to tell me. You don't owe me anything. I want you here because it's where you want to be."

Henry nodded. "Same. I want you to tell me if I no longer do it for you. I don't want pity fucks because you're afraid of breaking poor Henry's heart."

The idea of hurting Henry in any way turned the food to lead in my stomach. It felt like my last bite was stuck in my throat, and I had to swallow hard and take a sip of water before I could speak again. How could I tell him he should trust me with his body but not his heart? "I promise, Henry."

Henry studied my face for a few seconds before he said, "I guess that settles it then. Now, let's eat dinner so we can get to the best part of the night."

"Phillipe's dessert?"

"As wonderful as I bet it is, I picked out the spot where I want you to fuck me next."

Grateful I hadn't taken a bite, I asked, "Is that so?" *Imp.*

Henry waggled his brows. "The balcony. I wondered what it would be like the last time I was here, but it was too cold for outdoor sex in December."

"Where's your sense of adventure?" I teased.

"Tucked inside my warm body where my dick would try to hide." Henry's mock shiver made me laugh hard.

Everything about him was more delicious than the gourmet dinner we were suddenly ignoring. The only thing keeping me from dragging him out onto the balcony right then was knowing he needed to eat.

"Food then fuck," I said, pointing at his plate with my fork.

"Yes, Professor Higgins," Henry said demurely, forking a bite of tenderloin while batting his eyelashes playfully.

A familiar thought bounced around in my brain. How had I ever thought I could resist him?

Chapter Thirteen

Henry

I'D TALKED A BIG GAME, BUT I BECAME MORE NERVOUS AS DINNER WOUND down. It wasn't because I'd changed my mind about Ezra fucking me on the balcony; I wanted that more than anything. I just knew this time together would be different. I wasn't in his home on the pretense of having a one-night stand, and this wasn't a quick, unplanned fumble in his office. When Ezra slid deep inside me, he would do so knowing I belonged only to him for as long as he wanted me. I would take him inside my body knowing the same. Those thoughts made my heart race with excitement. Then doubt crept in. How long could he possibly want me? Looking around his luxurious apartment, I had to wonder how long it would take for him to realize I didn't belong in his world, not even as his secret lover.

Ezra had mentioned the possibility of me wanting to leave the relationship first, and I had nearly laughed out loud. I might not have as much world experience as him, but I already knew I'd never find anyone who stirred me deeper—physically and emotionally—than Ezra did. He would be the best I ever had, and I was already worried about losing it—*him*—before we truly began.

"Stop it, Henry." Ezra's deep voice pulled my attention to him. A smile played at his lips, and the mix of humor and lust in his gaze made an intoxicating combination.

"Stop what?" I asked, trying to play it cool.

"I'm not exactly sure what's worrying you, but I can tell something has interrupted your joy of anticipation."

"How could you possibly know that?"

Ezra tilted his head slightly. "Which part? The one where I can tell you're anxious or that you were anticipating me fucking you out on the balcony. Your knee is bouncing, and you keep nibbling on your bottom lip, which are classic signs of anxiousness. As for the other, your desire for me is rolling off you like heatwaves from hot asphalt." He straightened and leaned forward. "Tell me, Henry, will you want something to bite down on, or do you wish for my neighbors above, below, or beside us to hear your cries of pleasure carrying on the wind?"

"Not fair," I said breathlessly, forgetting about anything except the glittering promise I saw in his dark gaze.

"Why? Because I distracted you from your worrisome thoughts? I'm not sorry for that, but I will apologize if something I said earlier has upset you."

I shook my head. "No, Ezra. It's just my inner demons waging war. I want to be here with you, and nothing you said upset me." I hadn't arrived expecting a grand declaration of love. In fact, nothing Ezra said had shocked me. He wanted me but needed to protect his career at the same time. What was so hard to understand about that?

"I know a thing or two about inner demons, Henry. I think we all do. If there are certain assurances you need from me, I'd like to discuss them. I won't make promises I can't keep, and I'd prefer we learn now about lines neither of us is willing to cross before..." Ezra's words trailed off, but I knew he was going to express concerns about me getting hurt. "Let's just avoid any unpleasant surprises."

"Ezra, I don't need assurances, and I'd never want you to make false promises. I think I'm just having a hard time believing something I wanted so badly is coming true. I don't want more than you can give, and I won't try to give you more than I can handle either. Please don't let my quietness ruin our night."

Ezra set his fork down and rose to his feet, extending his hand toward me. I scooted my chair back, giving him room to pull me into his arms. Ezra's body was rigid with sexual tension, and his erection pressed against mine. "Does it feel like you've ruined anything?"

"No," I whispered.

"Are you finished eating?"

"You wanted to tell me I was done eating and command me to lean over the balcony, didn't you?"

"Deny you food after the lecture I gave you two weeks ago?" Ezra asked with a smirk.

"It would reheat," I countered. "I remember seeing a microwave in your fancy kitchen during my last visit." I had a sudden vision of Ezra and me making out in the kitchen while popcorn popped in the microwave. It was such a random, silly thing, but the idea of sharing popcorn while cuddling on the couch seemed both ordinary and extraordinary at the same time. The familiar scene would be more special with Ezra because it was something I'd never allowed myself to dream.

Ezra leaned in and gave me a quick kiss. "I'm losing you again."

"No," I said, shaking my head. "A silly thought just popped into my mind."

"Henry, I don't think you're capable of silly thoughts."

I snorted. If Ezra wanted to know what I was thinking, then I would tell him. "I want to make microwavable popcorn and eat it while cuddling with you on the couch and watching a movie."

A smile tugged at Ezra's lips. "What kind of movie?" he asked seriously.

"Um, a comedy or action movie, maybe." I sounded uncertain because his reaction had surprised me. I guess I expected him to dismiss me outright or say watching movies wasn't part of *this*.

"I like those types of movies too. I think we've arrived at the most important question of the night, Henry. Are you ready to answer it?" I grinned at the over-the-top seriousness in Ezra's voice. "Do you prefer your popcorn plain, with some butter, or the movie-the-ater-butter style?" God, I could see myself licking Ezra's salty, buttery fingers.

"I like the movie-theater-butter kind. I prefer Orville Redenbacher, but you won't ruin *this* if you use a knockoff brand."

Ezra gasped then nipped my bottom lip. "There is no other brand of popcorn, Henry." He smiled fully then, laughter vibrating through him. "Did we survive our first serious obstacle?"

"It would seem so."

"Do you feel better now?" Ezra asked, rubbing his warm hand in circles on my lower back. I knew he wasn't talking about popcorn and a movie. He wanted to relieve my concerns and would patiently do so until I was comfortable. I had firsthand knowledge of how in-dulgent Ezra's patience felt.

"I do," I confirmed.

"Good." Ezra kissed the tip of my nose then lowered his arms and took a step back. Holding out his hand for me, he said, "The bal-cony awaits."

Even though I'd already had Ezra inside me a few hours before, I needed to feel him again. He didn't lead me through the door off the dining room, he guided me through his master bedroom exit where he had a second seating area set up. The space was completely dark except for the light spilling out through the sliding glass door. The balcony had privacy walls at both ends which made it feel like Ezra and I were alone with the river, stars, and moon.

"I keep a lighter for those candles in the tin box. Why don't you light the candles while I retrieve condoms and lube from the bedside table?"

"You don't want me to shower first?" I asked.

Ezra pulled me in tight and ran his nose along my neck, breath-ing me in. "Hell no. I love smelling our sex on your body. We'll take a relaxing bath after I make you utterly filthy."

"Oh God," I whimpered.

Ezra sucked my Adam's apple between his lips then asked, "Are you praying for rescue?"

"Praying my heart doesn't explode before either of those things happen."

Ezra raised his hand and tenderly ran it through my hair. "I have faith in your heart." *I have faith in yours too, even if you don't.* He gave me one more quick kiss then released me to return inside for the supplies.

My hands shook when I struck the match and held it to the wick. The moment felt huge, and I was so worried my bumbling would ruin it. Behind me, I heard Ezra opening drawers and taking out what we needed. He flipped off the bedroom light when he finished, casting the balcony in complete darkness except for flickering candlelight.

"What do those candles smell like to you?" Ezra huskily asked when he returned with lube in one hand and a condom in the other.

I sniffed the air, and at first, I only smelled the lingering trace of sulfur from the match, but then I picked out other scents. "Lemon and vanilla," I replied. It felt familiar, but I didn't immediately place where I remembered it from. "Oh, it reminds me of the candles my mom used to keep mosquitos away."

Ezra chuckled warmly. "You're thinking of citronella, but that's not what I think of when I light them when I lounge out here naked at night."

I swallowed hard. "What do they remind you of?"

"*Who*, not what." Dropping the condom and lube on the table, Ezra pulled me to him. "The subtle lemon fragrance reminds me of you, Henry. I lie out here stroking my dick wishing you were with me."

"Ezra," I whispered.

"So, I no longer wish to see doubt or hesitation in your eyes when you look around my world and wonder if you belong here. I want you here, and that's all that matters. That's the only assurance I can give you right this minute. Understood?" I nodded as tears threatened. Of course, he saw through my fears and recognized them for what they were. "Now we can both live out our balcony fantasies."

The kiss Ezra gave me was gentle, but I felt the power of his desire thrumming through his body, and mine answered in return. I reached for the hem of his tank top, even though I knew he preferred to be in control. I wasn't pushing or testing him; I needed to be able to act on my impulses without second-guessing myself every time I turned around. I wanted to touch and feel his bare chest, so I went for it. Ezra squeezed my hip to encourage me then dropped his hands so I could lift the tank top over his head. I reached for my shirt next, needing to be skin-on-skin with him, but he stilled my hands.

"You don't get to have all the fun." Ezra brushed his lips against mine then removed my tank top, dropping it on the balcony floor next to his.

I moved into him with a confidence I'd never felt before, pressing my bare chest against his, whimpering when our heated flesh met. "Too long," I told him, discounting the quick fuck we'd shared in his office. I'd gotten off with his cock in my ass and my dick in his fist, but I hadn't been able to kiss and touch him freely.

"Much too long." Ezra's agreement ghosted over my lips before he devoured them.

Hands roamed everywhere, relearning contours and textures while his tongue boldly swept inside my mouth to explore me. I'd kissed other guys before, but it had never involved my entire body as it did with Ezra. I figured it was the difference between kissing a boy and a man. My whole being trembled and shook, and I greedily pressed my body tighter against his.

Ezra ripped his mouth off mine and stared down at me. Maybe it was a trick of the candlelight, but I swore I could see the stars reflecting in his dark eyes. "I wanted to go slow and not just shove you down and fuck you, but—" It wasn't like him to sound and look uncertain, and I loved having a bit of power over him.

I brushed the back of my hand over his silk-covered erection then reached between our bodies and slowly untied the drawstring of his sleep pants. Ezra's breath hissed, and his hands tightened on my hips. Feeling bold, I said, "I'm going to strip you down, then I'm going to straddle you on the chaise and ride your cock."

"Henry, you completely unravel me."

"It's only fair since you do the same to me," I said, leaning forward and nipping the flesh above his nipple.

I shoved his pants to the floor then quickly released my drawstring and pushed mine down my hips. Ezra's mouth found mine again as he took the two steps backward needed to reach the chaise.

"Too bad you weren't here on Independence Day. I would've loved watching the reflection of the fireworks on your skin as you moved over me." I opened my mouth to tell him next year but stopped myself before I killed the mood.

"I guess I'll just have to make you see fireworks behind your eyelids then," I told him.

Shaking his head, Ezra lowered himself to the chaise then gripped his dick. I loved the candlelight flickering against his golden skin and nearly became transfixed when he started stroking up and down. This was how he looked when he jerked off thinking about me. It was heady, overwhelming, and mouthwatering. "I'm not going to close my eyes, Henry, because I don't want to miss a single expression crossing your face."

I straddled his thighs and lowered my head for another devastating kiss that seemed to stretch on forever. I kept inching my body closer and closer until no air was between us, and his dick was flush against mine. I gripped the back of the chaise over his head and began thrusting against him, aided by the pre-cum dripping from our cocks.

I caught Ezra's sexy growls, and he collected my needy whimpers. It didn't take me long to reach the verge of orgasm, so I stopped rutting against him and reached for the condom. I didn't ask for permission or wait for his instructions; I tore the packet open with my teeth then removed the circle of latex.

"Roll it on me," Ezra growled. "I need to be inside you."

I might've teased him, but I was too desperate to have him again. I kissed him while clumsily rolling it down his hard length until it fit snuggly at the base of his cock. I pulled free of the kiss and reached for the lube.

"Stretch me open," I said, matching his demand with one of my own.

Ezra was as gentle and considerate as he always was, even if his tight jaw and blown pupils demonstrated how far gone he was. I was his drug, and he needed a fix.

Knowing I was ready, I pulled free from Ezra's fingers and moved to align his dick against my prepared hole.

"Easy," Ezra said softly. "There's no rush this time."

No boundaries either, which made me even more desperate to have him inside me. Ignoring his wishes, I pushed down hard, burying his dick deep inside my ass. I cried out from the pleasure and rightness of having Ezra where he belonged and knowing I put him there.

"Baby," Ezra whispered, broken, gripping my hips. "I...you..."

I'd rendered him speechless, and it was the biggest turn-on I'd ever experienced. Our first time together, Ezra had shown me the ways he liked to be pleased. I decided it was time for him to learn new things about me. I didn't want a slow ride; I wanted to obliterate every damn memory he had of anyone else who came before me and ruin him for anyone who might try to come later.

The desperate, needy look in Ezra's eyes made me feel powerful, and I used it to fuel my hips, trying different angles and tempos until I found the ones that made him grit his teeth or cry out. My hips would falter and lose rhythm at times, but Ezra encouraged me by squeezing my hips instead of trying to take over. I hovered over his face, staring into his eyes; Ezra's gasps puffed against my lips, spurring me on.

I wanted him to come first, but his experience won out over my exuberance. One minute I was canting my hips forward to make him grunt and groan, and the next, I was emptying my balls over his chest and stomach.

I stared at him through stunned eyes, giving him the opening he needed to resume control. Quicker and easier than I thought possible, Ezra reversed our positions so I was on my back, and he was between my spread thighs.

"Do you want a hard fuck then?" he asked, pushing my knees up toward my chest. "Want me to unleash my desire?"

"Yes," I whimpered.

Ezra snapped his hips forward, fast and furiously then fucked me with a relentless rhythm that managed to make me hard all over again. The legs of the chaise rocked loudly against the balcony floor, threatening to break or tip us over.

"Is this what you needed, baby?"

I dug my fingers in the back of my thighs, holding my limp-noodle legs out of the way. "Yes!" I was on the verge of coming a second time when Ezra snapped his hips forward once more, roaring my name as he shook and came. I released my thighs and lowered them so Ezra could collapse against me, pinning my still-hard dick between our stomachs.

"Every person on this side of the building knows some guy named Henry caused the world's largest orgasm," I said proudly.

Unwilling to be outdone, Ezra scooted down my body then blew my dick and mind until I yelled his name too. We lay together in tangled limbs afterward, the night air cooling our fevered bodies which were bound together by sweat and drying cum.

"Ezra?"

"Yes, baby."

I loved the way he called me baby. "Am I filthy enough to earn that bath now?"

Ezra sniffed my neck with another sigh. "I hate that you won't smell like me."

"So wash me with your soap," I suggested.

Ezra lifted his head and smiled down at me. "I like the way you think." He started to lower his head to kiss me but jerked back. "Fuck!"

"What is it? A muscle spasm?"

"Hey now," Ezra said, sounding offended. "I'm not that old."

"There's no age requirement for a muscle spasm. Remember my limp earlier tonight?"

Ezra nodded to acknowledge my point. "It wasn't a spasm; a mosquito bit me on the ass."

He looked so outraged that a mosquito would dare take a bite of his ass. I couldn't stop the laughter building inside me. "I-I'm sorry," I managed to say before the dam broke and it burst from my chest. "I'd bite your ass too if I were her."

Ezra tried not to laugh, but he joined me until he got bit a second time. "That's it," he said firmly, leaping to his feet. "It's time for a bath, then you need to get some sleep." He blew out the candles and crooked his fingers for me to follow.

On our way to the bathroom, I watched in puzzlement as Ezra stopped by his bedside table and picked up his phone.

"Checking your messages?" I asked.

"Adding citronella candles to my shopping list before I forget," he quipped. He looked at me with a raised brow. "Not a single smartass joke out of you about faulty memories at my age."

I held up my hands in surrender. "I wouldn't dream of it." My lips quivered and threatened to give way to laughter yet again.

"Get in the bathroom," Ezra said, pointing to the doorway.

"Yes, sir," I said cheekily then gasped when Ezra's hand landed soundly against my bare ass. I spun around to face him. "Spanking wasn't in the lesson tonight."

"Keep it up, and you're going to get a firsthand lesson in spankings, Henry."

The idea thrilled me to the core, and I suddenly wanted to be naughty—very, very naughty.

Chapter Fourteen

Ezra

"God, this feels amazing," Henry murmured, his head tilted back and eyes closed. Water from the rainfall showerhead I'd had installed over the large circular bathtub gently trickled over us while water from the faucet simultaneously filled the tub. "I've never seen anything like it."

Unable to resist the smooth column of flesh Henry had exposed, I kissed a path from the base of his neck up to his ear. After nipping his lobe hard enough to make him gasp, I claimed his sweet mouth and kissed him until he melted against me like cotton candy.

"The plumbers thought I was crazy when I showed them the picture I found in an interior design magazine. They came up with so many reasons why it wouldn't work, but they couldn't overcome the one that said it would."

Henry chuckled. "Your will to see it happen?"

"Exactly," I said, capturing his lips in a quick, soft kiss.

"I can't believe I missed this the last time I was here. I just thought the double doors led to a walk-in closet."

"That was the original plan, but I paid extra to customize this space." It wasn't cheap either. I'd had the space tiled from floor to ceiling, and the homeowner's association insisted I install extra drains in case the built-in overflow on the bathtub failed. Then there was the cost of creating a walk-in closet space where none had existed before, which cut into the guest bedroom I used as a home office. For the first time since I moved in, I felt my extravagant decisions paid off.

Henry lifted his head. "Why would you spend your own money to upgrade an apartment?"

"I don't rent the space; I own it. This is a condo, not an apartment."

"Oh," Henry said sheepishly. "I guess I'm not familiar with condos. I see a high-rise building and assume they're apartments."

"I can explain how condominiums vary from apartments, or I can tell you how much I'm enjoying using the tub for the first time."

Henry's eyes widened then narrowed. "Seriously?"

I grinned at the suspicious tone in his voice. "Seriously. Why do you have a hard time believing it?"

Henry's body stiffened against mine. "Ezra, your condo is a total fuck pad. This bathtub isn't about getting clean; it's for pretending you're kissing and fucking in the rain or a waterfall on a tropical island. Why would I believe this is the maiden voyage?" His body and tone of voice were tense, and I hoped the truth would ease his worry.

"How many men do you think I've brought to my home?" I asked. Henry scowled and shifted to put distance between us, but I tightened my arms around his lower back, keeping him tight against me. *Where he belonged.* "Would it make you feel better or worse to know the truth? Those inner demons you mentioned earlier are whispering ugly things in your head, right?" Henry released a shaky breath and nodded. "One man, Henry. You are the only man I've brought into my home, shared a bed with, and introduced to my bathtub. If my home is a fuck pad, then it was created just for you."

Henry's mouth fell open in a cartoonish way, and I would've laughed if the conversation wasn't so serious. "How could that be?" he whispered.

"I'm not saying you're the only person I've had sex with since I moved here last year, Henry. What I'm trying to say is you're the only one I wanted to bring home with me. You're the only one I wanted to see lying between my sheets or sitting at my barstool while I cooked breakfast. You're the only one I wanted to hold in my arms in this over-the-top bathtub. You're the only one who occupies my thoughts and dreams."

"Why me?" Henry wasn't fishing for compliments; he honestly couldn't understand his appeal to me. "Never mind," he said suddenly. "Let's not ruin a beautiful—"

I silenced him with a kiss while gathering my thoughts so I could convey them in a way that didn't paint me as some pervert or describe him as some weakling that needed me to take care of him. Henry wasn't weak, and there wasn't anything perverted about our relationship. When I finally pulled back, he was once again relaxed in my arms.

"Besides your physical beauty, there's something about you that calls to me. You have this…innocent quality about you, but then I look into your eyes and see a man much wiser than his years. You find joy in the simplest things and take nothing for granted because you know how fragile and tenuous life is. I know that people have let you down." Henry nodded. "I want to know more about that when you're ready." I smoothed my thumbs over his cheeks and loved the way he leaned into my touch. "You call to the parts of me that want to nurture and protect, and those feelings go much deeper for me than sexual desire alone. You've picked up on that already."

"So, I'm kind of a sexy stray kitten to you?" Henry asked bemused.

I leaned forward and nipped his swollen bottom lip. "You have the sharp claws and feistiness of a kitten for sure. I don't want to take care of you because you're pitiful, broken, or weak; I want to cherish you because no one else has." Tears welled in Henry's eyes and spilled down his cheeks, and I kissed them away. "I want to hold you close and keep chasing away the sadness in your eyes until all I can see is confidence and pride."

"Then what will you do with me once you've created the perfect gentleman, Professor Higgins?" Henry asked shyly.

"I can't foretell the future, Henry, and I won't give you promises I can't keep. Besides, who's to say you'll still want me? There's bound to be a young hunk who—"

Henry silenced me with a hard, quick kiss. "No one has ever made me feel like you do, Ezra. No one looks at me like you do either."

"How's that?" I asked. I wasn't looking to stroke my ego; I needed to know the emotions I stirred inside him. I saw them rising to the surface, but Henry never voiced them because he probably worried he'd push me away. Most of all, I needed to know I wasn't drifting alone in whatever it was developing between us. There was no denying it was stronger and more tangible than infatuation, but it was way too soon to call it love.

Henry's lips trembled when he tried to speak, then a soft, frustrated sigh escaped him. "It's hard to find the right words."

"Then use honest ones."

"You make me feel wanted, cherished, and"—his voice cracked—"*clean*. When I got my diagnosis, my mom made me feel dirty and trashy, which made it easy for her to throw me to the curb. I found a new family at Ryan's Place who accepted and loved me, but there was still something missing. Plenty of guys hit on me, but they bailed the second they learned about my HIV status, but you…" Henry's words trailed off, and he smiled at the memory.

"You'd braced yourself for rejection, but I shocked you with a kiss." I reenacted the hot, sweet kiss I'd given him nearly seven months ago. "Then I told you it was okay and assured you I was on PrEP."

"You made it seem so normal, Ezra."

"It's your normal, Henry. You're not dirty, and you're sure as hell not trash." I was both eager and dreading the day Henry trusted me enough to tell me about his past. I wanted to know all the pieces of him, but I knew with absolute certainty that the truth would enrage me.

"I'm hot trauma is what I am," Henry countered, averting his gaze.

Cupping his chin, I raised it until his eyes met mine once more. "You're beautiful trauma, baby. One day, this trauma will be in your rearview mirror, and all you'll see ahead of you is a bright future." *One that probably didn't include me.* With that sobering thought, I turned off the rainfall showerhead and faucet so I didn't overflow the bathtub and test out my backup systems. "I believe you said something about using my soap to mark you."

Henry sighed then squirmed in my embrace. "That sounds wonderful, but I confess I like the kind of filthy you make me feel, Higgins." His dick started to harden from the friction.

I pinched his ass cheek, making him yelp. "Cut that out before you make me hard again. It's getting late, and you need to get some sleep."

"Sleep?" Henry asked, rutting his dick against my lengthening one. "That's the last thing on either of our minds. I know damn well you're not worried about keeping up with me." His eyes shimmered with a challenge.

"Okay, but don't blame me when you're exhausted, dragging around in the morning, and pissed off because I get to sleep in while you have to go to work."

Henry narrowed his eyes. "I guess you better make it all worth it then."

I answered his dare by washing his body from head to toe. I loved smelling my shampoo in his hair and knowing his skin held the scent of my soap. I tormented him by making him sit out of arm's reach while I took my time gliding the soapy loofah sponge all over my body.

"Please, Ezra," Henry said, pleading with both his eyes and words.

I drained the tub and dried us both off before leading him into my bedroom. Henry slid between the turned-down sheets like he belonged there, and I liked when his need for me surpassed his nervousness. I followed him onto the bed then rolled him onto his back, kissing him until his fingernails dug into my back. My feisty kitten needed to come again.

"Condom and lube," Henry desperately said when I finally lifted my head.

I shook my head. "Your sexy ass has already seen enough action." Henry let out a needy whimper that made me smile. "I'll take care of you, baby." I rolled onto my back and said, "Come up here and straddle my face. I want to suck your cock." Henry's eyes widened, but he climbed up and placed his knees on both sides of my head. "Grip the headboard and put your dick inside my mouth."

"Ezra," he whispered, sounding shocked by the suggestion.

"The idea of fucking my face thrills you, doesn't it, baby?"

Henry nodded. "What about you? I can't leave you hard."

"Before you come, you're going to turn around and suck my dick while I eat your ass and jerk you off."

Clumsy and tentative at first, Henry fed his cock into my mouth. I loved watching his body flush with desire as he gained confidence and learned the beautiful things his body could do. I gripped his ass, encouraging him to let go, and Henry rewarded me with a pace that made his balls slap against my chin. I greedily lapped and sucked his cock until he suddenly pulled back.

"I'm going to come," he panted. Henry's flushed cock looked angry, and I knew he'd come all over my face if I ran my tongue over the sensitive spot just under his crown. I lifted my head to seek him out, but he shook his head and scooted back further. "That wasn't the agreement," Henry said haughtily. He repositioned his body so his head hovered over my cock.

I smacked his ass then gripped his hips, pulling his pert cheeks closer to my mouth. "You're right. I did promise you a rim and a jack."

Henry released a startled cry followed by a throaty moan when I circled my tongue over his crinkled pucker.

I firmly gripped the base of his cock then said, "Get to sucking, Henry, and I might even feed you dessert in bed."

By the time both of us came again, Phillipe's dessert was long forgotten. Instead, I fed Henry the dulce de leche trifle in bed the next morning between sips of coffee. I firmly believed meditation was the best way to start the morning, but Henry's throaty purrs when he indecently licked the spoon could quickly become my favorite new rise-and-shine routine.

Chapter Fifteen

Henry

Tucked in the corner of Dante's Bistro, I reread the text exchange I'd had with Ezra while waiting for Geoff to arrive. *I'm stopping to get popcorn on the way home from dinner with my folks. Need anything else? Want something sweet to go with the salty?*

I'd felt a tiny pang in the region of my heart when he'd told me over the phone about plans he'd made with his parents for dinner. Friday nights had belonged to us ever since we began dating, or whatever you called it, six weeks ago. We squeezed in a few stolen hours throughout the week and chatted every day, but Fridays were special. Maybe we never went out on an official date in public, but we either ordered in a nice dinner or cooked one together at Ezra's place. There would be sex followed by popcorn and a movie then sometimes more sex. We often ended up soaking in his fancy tub before we climbed into bed where we would cuddle and talk for hours about anything on our minds.

Ezra did most of the talking, telling me about his childhood in Connecticut and all the places he'd seen around the world. The furthest I'd traveled from Ohio was Kentucky where I spent two weeks every summer at church camp, so I didn't have much to contribute to those conversations. Ezra never made me feel inferior and was happy to hear about whatever experiences I'd had. Well, all except for learning I'd lost my virginity to Geoff during one of those church camps. He loved listening to my stories about working for Des. I couldn't share specifics about cases, but I could tell him some of the more interesting ways clients paid him. He realized early on that I have a deep abiding love for Des that didn't extend to romantic love.

I always slept over and lingered at his home until it was time for my shift at Mamma Maria's on Saturday. Saying goodbye to Ezra and knowing I might not see him again for another six days got harder every week.

Picking up on my disappointment, Ezra had quickly explained that he couldn't keep putting his parents off when they invited him out. They were starting to get suspicious, and it would be better to have dinner with them so they could see he was doing just fine. Ezra had called it proof of life or something like that. This was news to me because Ezra hadn't told me he'd turned down invitations from anyone to be with me. I was excited that our nights meant as much to him as they did me, but I didn't want him jeopardizing his relationships with people who were important to him, especially his parents. As much as I wanted to believe I wasn't a temporary phase in Ezra's life, I couldn't allow myself to believe I was anything more to him. It would hurt too much when we ended *this*.

Who else had Ezra turned down? How long would he be willing to continue living separate lives like this? There was the Ezra he showed to the world and the one he reserved only for me. The idea of losing our special bond made my chest tighten and my stomach ache, so I reminded myself to cherish the memories we made and be grateful for whatever time we had left together.

I'd injected false cheer into my voice and told Ezra that one Friday apart wouldn't kill us. I suggested getting together for a few hours the following morning because I didn't have to be at work until two in the afternoon. Ezra quickly clarified he wasn't canceling our plans; he was only delaying them a few hours. Then he suggested I meet Geoff for dinner because he didn't like the idea of me feeling lonely.

You're all the sweet and salty I need, I'd replied to Ezra's text.

Have fun with Geoff. I'll see you in a few hours. Ezra had added a few kissy lips which I had sent back to him.

Ezra's parents weren't the only suspicious ones. I'd turned Geoff down enough times that he had threatened to find me and kidnap me if I told him no again. He was stunned when I invited him to dinner, but there was no mistaking the happiness in his voice. Taking the time to soothe ruffled feathers was good for both Ezra and me.

"Dayum," Geoff exclaimed, pulling my attention to him. I was so lost in thought I hadn't heard him arrive. "I honestly didn't recognize you at first, H." He flopped down in the chair and stared at me with wide eyes and a slack mouth.

I looked down at my T-shirt and jeans—things I'd worn to meet him more times than I could count. "What are you talking about?"

Regaining his composure, Geoff smirked and said, "I'm not talking about your clothes, Henry. It's everything else."

I rolled my eyes and shook my head. "Same haircut; same me."

"It's not your physical appearance, although your shoulders do look broader. Maybe that's because you're sitting up taller. You look…" Geoff's voiced trailed off while he searched for the right words to say, or so it seemed to me anyway. "You look more put together, confident, and in control. I haven't seen you since early July and Labor Day weekend is around the corner. What've you been up to the past six or seven weeks? You're never available to hang." Geoff's eyes widened. "Maybe I should ask *who* you're doing instead of what."

"Don't be crude, G," I said, feeling my cheeks turn pink.

"Hey, guys, welcome to Dante's Bistro," a perky waitress said when she arrived at our table. "My name is Shelley, and I'll be taking care of you tonight. Is this your first time here?"

"Yes," Geoff said at the same time as I said, "No." I felt Geoff's stare but ignored him to focus on the daily food and drink specials Shelley rattled off.

"I'll have the bean with bacon soup with a grilled ham and swiss panini and water to drink," I told her.

"With lemon or naked?" she asked me.

"Without lemon, please." I couldn't think of a response with the word naked in it that didn't sound suggestive or conjure boner-inducing images of Ezra.

"I'll have the same thing as my friend, Shelley, but I'll take sweet tea with lemon instead of water."

"All right, guys," she said, picking up the menus. "I'll enter your orders then bring your drinks out."

"Thanks," I said, dreading when she left because I knew Geoff was going to bombard me with questions.

"Who is he?" Geoff asked.

"Who?" I asked, looking around the room.

"Ha ha ha. Very funny. Henry, I love you, but I doubt you discovered this upscale bistro on your own." A playful smile tugged at Geoff's lips, but his words struck my heart like a sharp barb. He must've realized he'd hurt my feelings because all humor leached from Geoff's face, and he reached across the table, resting his hand over mine. "Henry, I didn't mean it to sound like you were some loser with bad taste in restaurants. I was focused more on the affordability than your taste in fine cuisine."

"It's okay, Geoff. It's true I wouldn't have discovered this place without a recommendation from a friend," I said, remembering the first time I tasted Dante's chicken noodle soup when Ezra had sent it to my apartment after confronting me. Eating at the restaurant reminded me of the shift in our relationship, and it was a special treat I permitted myself once a week. Even though I experienced it alone, the memory of Ezra's thoughtfulness was always there to keep my company.

"*Friend*? Why are you hiding the fact that you're dating someone? Are you ashamed? Oh. *Oh*. It's *him*."

"Him?" I asked, wishing Geoff had spotted a friend in the crowd.

"The professor. You're dating your professor," he said too loud for my liking.

Jessie knew the truth about my relationship with Ezra, but only because we lived together, and any food-related gifts he'd surprised me with during the week included enough for her too. If she happened to be on tour, I saved the leftovers for lunch the next day. Jessie never pressed me for information because she could see I was happy. As much as Geoff meant to me, I hadn't planned to tell him about Ezra. I didn't want other people's judgement to taint what Ezra and I had together.

"Could you be any louder? I don't think the table in the back heard you," I hissed.

"Christ, Henry, do you know what you're doing? Isn't that guy a little old for you?"

"Aren't you the one who literally pushed me into dancing with Ezra at the club?"

Geoff released a long sigh. "I just wanted to see you smile and have a good time. I also hoped you'd get laid. Setting you up to have your heart trampled later wasn't part of my scheme. Is the sex great enough to risk your academic career?"

I stood up so fast my chair nearly toppled over. Reaching for my wallet, I said, "I'll cover dinner."

"No!" Geoff said, wrapping his hand around my fist clutching two twenties in it. "Stop, Henry. Please sit down. I fucked this all up, and I'm sorry. Please don't go. I haven't seen you in so long, and I've missed you."

I released a shaky breath then put my money back inside my wallet and returned it to my back pocket. Returning to my seat, I softly said, "No one can know, Geoff. Ezra could lose his job, and before you say he deserves it, keep in mind he truly cares about me. Besides, I took my final exams this week, so he's technically no longer my professor."

"Now what?" he asked.

"I honestly don't know. We're taking things one step at a time."

Geoff tilted his head to the side. "And you're sure no one in your class knows? I can't imagine it's been easy hiding your feelings."

I replayed the past several weeks in my head, checking for instances where one of us gave anything away. No one could accuse me of getting preferential treatment from Ezra. I smiled when I remembered Drake mentioning Ezra's blatant grudge against me for missing classes. I preferred everyone thinking the professor hated me rather than knowing we spent every spare minute naked together. The biggest hurdle had been touring the Museum of Sex exhibit. I couldn't keep my mind from imagining Ezra and myself testing out some of the toys, and I'd nearly lost my mind when I came across the padded spanking bench. Ezra had threatened more than once to redden my ass during our relationship but hadn't done it until we got back to his apartment after the tour. Heat still radiated off my flesh the next morning, and I'd had a hard time sitting, but it was so fucking worth it. I sometimes found myself extremely jealous of the sexual exploring Ezra had done during his travels abroad, but I got over it quickly since I reaped the benefits of his knowledge.

"Earth to Henry," Geoff said, snapping his fingers. "I don't want to sound like a whiny crybaby, but it's my turn for your attention now."

"Sorry," I said, offering a smile. "You're right."

"Love looks good on you, my friend."

My breath snagged in my throat. "Love?" I croaked out.

"Whatever," Geoff said, rolling his eyes. "We'll let you live in denial a little longer. What have you been up to besides bumping uglies with the professor? Are you working out?"

"Yeah," I said. "I work out a few times a week. It helps me maintain my energy levels throughout the week. I've been sleeping a lot better and watching what I eat. It's improved my stamina a bunch."

"I bet it has," Geoff quipped.

Shelley showed up with our drinks, delaying my response. Rather than zing him with a snappy comeback, I wadded up my empty straw wrapper and flicked it at him. Geoff placed both hands over the spot on his chest where it had landed. The silliness chased away any lingering awkwardness from Geoff discovering I was secretly dating Ezra. For the remainder of our dinner, we kept the conversation light, discussing the other things going on in our lives. I noticed Geoff wanted to avoid any conversation involving Des as much as I tried to steer clear of Ezra, so we silently reached a cease-fire.

The food was delicious, and the company was even better. I realized I needed to make time to spend with Geoff because his friendship was important to me, and I was the only person in his life who really knew him. Since Jess was in town and needed her car, I had planned on getting a Lyft over to Ezra's apartment, but Geoff wouldn't hear of it.

"Let me drive you over," Geoff said. "It's not like I'm going to show up at his place and harass him when you're not around."

"If you're sure you don't mind," I said.

"Get in," Geoff said, hitting the remote to unlock the doors. Traffic was as heavy as I'd expected on a Friday night, and it took us twice as long to get to Ezra's apartment as it usually would. "Some big event must be going on," Henry said.

"Something sports related, I'm sure."

"Are you all set for the fall semester? You'd mentioned scholarships, grants, and getting a job at the school. Will that help with tuition?"

"Yes, and I also have federal loans. I'm in a much better financial position than I was for the summer semester. I'm slightly concerned my class load is too heavy, but I'm determined to make it work."

"How are you going to fit in a third job?" Geoff asked.

"Des is letting me cut back to twenty-five hours a week, and then I'll make the rest up as a teaching assistant. I'll pick up extra shifts at Maria's if I need them, but I think I can let that job slide for now."

"It's still a lot, Henry," Geoff said. "Better make sure you get your daily *workouts* to help with your stamina."

"Knock it off," I replied. "You can pull over here, and I'll walk the rest of the way. That way you don't have to go down an extra block before you can loop around and go back toward your house."

Geoff pulled over and put his car in park. "Henry," he said solemnly, drawing my attention toward him. "Please be careful with this guy. I'm not saying Ezra's bad; I just don't want you to get your heart broken."

"Everything will be okay, Geoff." I offered him my brightest smile, hoping it would ease the worry I saw on his face. "Let's meet for lunch next week. How's Tuesday?"

"Perfect," he said, sounding mollified. "Gyro Palace?"

"I'll be there."

Geoff released his seat belt then reached for me. "Love you, H."

I returned his hug, squeezing him tight. "I love you too."

I pulled back, ruffled his hair, then got out of the car. I waved at him then strolled down the sidewalk toward Ezra's condo building. My phone vibrated with an incoming text, and I pulled it out of my pocket.

Just waiting for the check, then I'll be on my way. Shouldn't be much longer.

I must not have been paying attention to where I was going, because I stepped into the path of a pedestrian walking toward me. The impact was hard enough to make me stagger back a few steps.

"I'm so sorry," a man with a deep, British voice said. He'd grabbed my shoulders to prevent me from tumbling. "Are you okay?"

"I'm the sorry one," I said, lifting my head up, up, and up until I looked into the tall man's startling blue eyes. He had to have been at least six and a half feet tall, and his shoulders were broad enough to block the sun. "I should've been paying attention to where I was going."

"Even so, you're the one who took the brunt of the collision. Are you okay?"

"Yeah," I said, waving off his concern. "Thanks, though."

"Have a good night then," the stranger said before he walked away.

I shook my head in disbelief. "You too," I called over my shoulder. The guy raised his hand to acknowledge me but kept walking. I continued on my way to Ezra's, stopping only to exchange pleasantries with one of the concierges who knew me by name.

It was my turn to pick a movie, and I'd chosen *My Cousin Vinny*. Knowing it could be a while before Ezra got home, I hurried into the bathroom and took a shower. Ezra stocked the bathroom with the products I used, including the lemon-scented soap I preferred. I also had a few drawers where more and more of my things had started to wind up. I refused to think of the significance of Ezra supplying my soap and making space for my stuff because it could give me a false sense of security about our relationship. We'd made no plans for a future together; we'd chosen to focus on the present and all the joy we discovered in each other. I ignored the frizzle of doubt that sometimes crept in when I least expected it. I blamed Geoff's unwarranted concern for it resurfacing while I was alone in Ezra's condo.

After a quick shower, I towel-dried my hair and body then wrapped the super-soft towel around my waist and headed into Ezra's bedroom. I stopped midway to the dresser when I realized I wasn't alone. Ezra lay in the center of his bed with his hands tucked under his head.

"Hello, Henry."

Chapter Sixteen

Ezra

HENRY'S BEAUTIFUL SMILE DOMINATED MY ATTENTION UNTIL A DROPlet of water fell from his damp hair and landed on his shoulder. I couldn't tear my eyes away from the drop's journey as it slowly slid down Henry's pec then his obliques, which grew tighter each week from his dedication in the gym and yoga with *Brad*. It was silly to envy a bead of water for touching a man I'd come to think of as mine. The droplet's time with him would be short-lived as demonstrated when it was absorbed by the plush towel wrapped around Henry's waist. Me? I got to have him for as long as he wanted me. Somehow, this guileless young man had found a way to scale the walls I'd built up in recent years. What started as ball-gripping lust had become something so much more meaningful than I'd predicted or thought myself capable of.

"You shouldn't use that voice, Ezra." Arousal had turned his fresh-from-the-shower pink flush to a deeper hue. God, he was so responsive and delicious. I couldn't wait to taste him.

"What voice?" I asked innocently.

Henry narrowed his eyes and took a few steps toward the bed but never came close enough for me to reach him. *Wise man.* "The same one you use when you're ready to fuck. You say 'Hello, Henry' but I hear 'Drop the towel and straddle my face.'"

"Is that so?"

"You know what you do to me, Ezra. You play dirty, and it's not going to work tonight," Henry replied stubbornly. "I've been looking forward to watching this movie with you all week."

The truth was our simple movie dates meant more to me than any extravagant trip or date I'd ever gone on. What started as a need for secrecy turned out to be the most precious time I'd ever spent with a man. Friday nights were about so much more than movies, popcorn, and a night of uninterrupted sex. We talked and teased, and although it was obvious both of us still harbored painful secrets, we learned so much about each other. Henry was enthralled by my traveling stories, which made me want to show him the world. I was fascinated to hear about the people who'd become his chosen family. I learned that Henry and Jess first met at a support group for abandoned kids, and I better understood why Jess was so protective of Henry and insistent on paying her own way instead of relying on others. Henry shared fragments of his strict upbringing and events that led him to the doors of Ryan's Place, but I could tell he held back the most painful parts, and that was okay with me. He'd get there when he was ready. I tucked away every kernel of information I gleaned from him more vigorously than we consumed the kernels of perfectly popped and generously buttered popcorn.

What followed our movies was something I could only describe as spectacular. Henry, with his wide-eyed, almost-innocence, reached something deep inside me I didn't even know existed. It extended beyond my need to nurture and take care of him; it allowed me to accept his thoughtful gestures in return. I didn't shy away when he took my foot in his hands and began massaging it while we relaxed in my bathtub and talked about the week we'd had. I didn't discourage his attempts to make blueberry crepes for me one Saturday morning because his eagerness to pamper me warmed my heart. Henry's crestfallen face when they turned out less than picture-perfect kicked in my protective instincts, and I would've eaten every single one even if they'd been horrible. Luckily, they were delicious even if they didn't look that great.

"I'm not trying to distract you from the movie, Henry."

"You're not?"

"I'm not naked, am I?" I asked.

Henry raked his eyes over my bare chest and sweatpants hanging low on my hips. "You might as well be. Seeing the definition in your pelvis makes me crazy, Ezra; you know this."

"I do," I agreed, lowering my hand and tracing the indentation between hip and groin. "Would you like me to put on a shirt? Are you worried I will distract you from Vinny?"

The expression in Henry's eyes turned from lustful to daring in a blink. "Not a chance." Henry loosened the towel from around his hips and let it fall to the floor. It was doing a poor job of disguising his growing erection anyway. "How about you, Ezra? It's been nearly a week since you've touched me. What would happen if I were to decide that watching movies with clothes on was overrated? Could you make it to the credits without pinning me to the couch and taking me?"

I sat up quickly then flung my legs over the side of the bed to stand up. "I guess I need to level the playing field then." I hooked my thumbs in the waistband of my sweats and pushed them down my hips. I watched Henry's eyes track their movements down my legs until the sweatpants pooled at my feet. "Now we're even."

Henry's gaze snapped up to lock with mine. "Let the games—I mean, movie—begin."

I'd never stood in my kitchen buck-ass naked before, and any awkwardness I might have customarily felt was negated by the sight of Henry's pert ass on display when he rose up on his tiptoes to reach the popcorn bowl in the cabinet.

"Need a hand?" I offered. "I'm only a few inches taller than you, but sometimes a few inches are all you need to get the job done."

Henry smiled at me over his shoulder. "Bringing out the big

guns, I see," he said when his gaze landed on the erection jutting out from my pelvis. Henry winked playfully then added, "You just keep your inches over there."

Fuck, I loved the banter we shared. Our playfulness extended to every form of communication between us—talking, texting, and even sex. Henry just made my heart happy.

I wrapped my hand around my dick and stroked twice. "If you don't need me, then…"

"Oh, I need you all right, but it's going to wait until Vinny saves the day."

"Henry, this movie better be amazing."

He turned fully, the popcorn bowl temporarily forgotten, and placed his hands on his hips. A slow smile—confident and curious—spread across his face. "Or you'll do what?"

"I guess you'll just have to see, won't you?" I quipped.

Henry's head fell back, and joyous laughter echoed around my kitchen. "What you meant to say was you don't know, but you'll have nearly two hours to come up with a plan if I should resist your tempting body."

"Okay, you have me there, but I'll come up with something you won't ever forget."

"You do realize you're only adding fuel to my determination to resist you until the credits play," Henry asked. "I mean, I'll get to watch a movie I love, and I'll get whatever *punishment* you dole out if you don't like the movie. I can't believe I'm saying this, but I kind of hope you hate it."

The microwave pinged, signaling the popcorn was ready.

"Grab the bowl, Henry."

Henry's mouth fell open and a soft gasp escaped him. "You use that same voice when you tell me to grab my ankles."

A low growl rumbled in my chest. "Henry."

"Oh, God. That's the one you use when I'm about to come, and you want me to hold it."

"Christ," I gritted out.

"Okay, that's better," Henry said, smiling impishly. "Annoyed professor voice to the rescue." He pivoted around and got just enough of his fingertips on the bowl to tip it toward him.

Whether to ward off the chill from the air-conditioning or because I wanted to up the stakes and make resistance more difficult, I wrapped the chenille throw blanket around us, forming an intimate cocoon. With Henry's body pressed firmly against my left side, I balanced the large bowl of popcorn on our thighs. Resisting his nakedness was going to be the biggest challenge I'd faced, but I was determined to do it. Until Henry *accidentally* dropped a few pieces of popcorn that just happened to land between my legs.

"Oops," he said, not even bothering to hide his evil glee. "Let me just get that. We don't want to waste any popcorn."

"It would be a travesty," I said as the opening credits began rolling. An evil smile curved on my lips as I recalled the terms of our agreement.

Henry's fingers danced between my thighs, teasing a path toward my balls where the popcorn conveniently rested. "Aha! Found them," he announced, making sure to fondle my sac. I tightened my thighs, trapping his hand. "Surrendering already, Ezra?" he asked breathlessly.

I picked up the bowl of popcorn and set it on the coffee table. "Not at all. I'm just taking advantage of a loophole. You said credits but didn't specify opening or closing." I pushed him to his back, and Henry eagerly parted his legs to make room for me. "Rule number one: be precise when issuing a challenge. You lost; I won."

Henry's vibrant eyes were a kaleidoscope of emotion and color as he studied my face. He raised his hand and traced my jawline with his index finger, stopping to tap the dimple in my chin. "I'm not sure there's a true loser here, Ezra. I think we can admit we've both won."

Shaking my head, I said, "Nope. The current score is Henry: twenty-five; Ezra: one."

Henry snorted. "How the hell do you figure that?"

I ran my hand through his hair. "I break all my rules for you, Henry. Maybe you can give me just this one victory."

"You've been keeping score?" Henry asked disbelievingly. "I think I should be insulted. Shouldn't I?"

His confusion made me laugh. "Nope."

"I might be insulted," Henry said, nodding. "Yeah, I think you need to do some smooth talking here."

I laughed harder. "Just let me have this victory, and I promise to share it with you."

"When did you start keeping tally?" Henry asked, attempting to wiggle out from under me until I gripped his ass and thrust my erection against his. "Oh." His breathless gasp puffed against my smiling lips.

"The confrontation in the bathroom was the first time I realized you had the upper hand in our relationship, and I was seemingly powerless to stop you."

"Me? Upper hand?"

"Henry, you must know by now how completely you unravel me. I want things with you I haven't wanted with another person in a very long time."

He studied my face for several seconds, and a dark cloud briefly passed over his expression, eclipsing his joy. What was it? Disbelief or had I read our growing relationship all wrong? "How would I know that? I mean, it's evident how much you physically desire me, and I can tell you care about me as a person too. But…" Henry's words trailed off, and he swallowed hard.

"Go on."

Henry shook his head. "I don't want to ruin our night."

"You won't," I assured him, knowing this conversation was long overdue because Henry deserved more than I was giving him. "Something is bothering you, and I want you to tell me."

Henry closed his eyes, and I wasn't sure if he was looking for courage or maybe searching for the right words to say. I'd noticed that Henry's boldness typically resulted from a situation that angered or aroused him. This conversation appeared to do neither. He took a deep breath and met my gaze once more. "I'm not asking you for promises or assurances, Ezra, but I would like to know if you see a time where you and I will date openly? Is that something you even want?"

I had to weigh what I wanted with what I could give him. How cruel would it be for me to tell Henry that I wanted to show him off to the world in one breath then tell him it wasn't possible in the very next? Yes, I wanted to date him openly, but to do so could result in consequences I wasn't ready to face. Even if I hadn't broken code of conduct rules, I'd be a laughingstock among the faculty. *There goes another horny professor who can't keep his dick in his pants.* I'd never wanted to be that guy, but I was on the verge of risking the reputation just so I could have my Henry.

"Forget I said anything," Henry said, mistaking my quiet for impending rejection.

"Henry," I said softly. "I'm not ashamed of you if that's what you're asking."

"That isn't what I asked, but maybe it follows the same vein. If I weren't a student at your college, would you want to date me for real?"

The answer was unequivocally yes, and I was ashamed he didn't know it. "Henry, I—" Whatever I was about to say was cut off when my door opened and my parents' voices echoed in the foyer. "What the fuck?" I whispered, scrambling to wrap the blanket tighter around us.

"Ezra!" Mom called out.

Henry's beautiful eyes nearly bugged out of his head with panic, and his mouth fell open in alarm.

"You left your cell phone on the table at the restaurant," Dad said, his voice growing louder as they came farther into the condo. "It's a good thing the manager knows us so well and called to let us know.

You took off out of there like a scalded cat. What was so pressing that you left so fast and didn't realize you left it behind?"

I popped up and looked at them from over the back of the couch. "Um, hi. You might not want to come any closer."

Startled, my parents jerked to a stop. Mom gasped and brought her hand up to her chest while Dad grinned like a loon. Both of them took in my blanket-draped shoulders and flushed face and knew exactly why I'd left the restaurant so quickly and what they'd interrupted.

"Now, I get it," Dad said, wearing an attaboy grin.

"Um, we'll just set your phone down on the table in the foyer and head on out," Mom said, backing up.

"Why don't you leave the spare key I gave you too," I suggested. "I can't have you popping in here and killing the mood whenever I have my boyfriend over." *Boyfriend.* The word came out of nowhere, but I liked the way it sounded. I guess Henry had my answer after all. My *boyfriend* stiffened, and I turned my head to look down at him. Tears gathered in his eyes, and I wanted to lean down and reassure him, but it needed to wait until we were alone again so I could do it properly. I winked to reassure him, and the smile he gave me in response nearly blinded me with its brilliance. I turned my attention back to my parents, who stood there wearing identical dopey grins on their faces. "Do you mind?"

"Not at all," my mother said. She looked at the television and noticed the movie playing. "Oh my goodness. I haven't seen *My Cousin Vinny* in years. I tried to get you to watch this with me, but you never would. It seems like your boyfriend has great taste in movies."

Dad nodded. "Classic movie about 'two yutes,'" he said in an exaggerated New York accent. *What the fuck?*

"The two what? 'Did you say yutes?'" Mom asked in an equally embellished Southern drawl.

Henry started giggling, and I realized they were quoting the movie he loved so much.

As charming as this scene was, I really wanted them to leave.

"Mom. Dad," I said with exaggerated patience. "Can we please talk about the movie later?"

"Sure, we can," Mom said breezily. "How does Sunday night at five o'clock sound to you?"

"Sure," I said, willing to agree to anything at that point just so they'd leave.

"Good. Bring your boyfriend with the cute giggle with you," Mom said, smiling because I'd fallen into her trap.

I could see Henry shaking his head out of my peripheral vision, but I ignored him. "Absolutely."

"It's settled then," Dad said. "We're looking forward to meeting him. Goodnight, Ezra and Ezra's boyfriend," Dad said, placing his hand on Mom's waist and guiding her back toward the door.

"Goodnight," Mom echoed.

"Night," I said.

"Um, goodnight," Henry said timidly.

I heard my parents whispering back and forth but couldn't make out what they were saying. I waited for them to drop my phone and spare key on the table and let themselves out before returning my focus to Henry.

"Does that answer satisfy your question? Yes, I want more with you."

"Don't you think going from secret romps to calling me your boyfriend and taking me home to meet the parents is a big jump?" Henry asked, looking and sounding shell-shocked.

"You were never just a romp, Henry, and no, I don't think it's a big jump. I think it feels right."

"But they might not like me and—"

I cut his protests off with a long kiss, not stopping until we were both breathless. "They're going to adore you, Henry."

"How can you be sure?"

His vulnerability flayed me. "Because who wouldn't adore you, baby?"

Henry swallowed and I saw how badly he wanted to believe me. "Do you honestly want me to meet your parents, Ezra?"

"I do," I replied with conviction. "I didn't just say it because my mom put me on the spot. No one forced me to call you my boyfriend. It slipped out naturally because it felt right. I don't know how this is going to work yet, but I know that I want it to."

Henry nodded. "I want it to too."

After kissing his forehead, I asked, "Do you know what this means?"

"I have two days to freak the hell out over meeting them?"

I shook my head. "My score just went up."

Henry rolled his eyes. "Fine. Henry: twenty-five; Ezra: two."

"You agreed to be my boyfriend *and* meet my parents. Henry: twenty-five; Ezra: three."

Chapter Seventeen

Henry

WHEN EZRA ARRIVED AT MY APARTMENT TO PICK ME UP, JESSIE escorted him to my room, threw open the door, and said, "Fix him! He's been like this since Maria dropped him off after church. I would've called nine-one-one, but I recognize a nonemergency freak-out when I see one." Jessie shut the door solidly, leaving us alone in my room.

"I don't feel too good, Ezra." It was a massive understatement. I felt like I needed to throw up except my nerves had prevented me from eating all day. My pulse pounded at my temples, throbbing in tempo with my racing heart. "Maybe you should go to dinner at your parents' house without me."

"Henry," Ezra said, crossing the room to stand beside my bed. "What's wrong?"

"What's not wrong?" I asked. "I can't find anything decent to wear, I can't get my hair to look right, and I look like I'm about fifteen years old. Your parents are going to think you're having a midlife crisis when they meet me."

"Baby," Ezra said, dropping onto my bed and pulling me into his arms. I rested my head against his shoulder, feeling better than I had since leaving his apartment Saturday afternoon. "It doesn't matter what you wear, your hair is fine the way it is, and you look like a twenty-one-year-old man. My parents are not going to think I'm having a midlife crisis." Ezra's chest shook, and I jerked my head up to look at him.

"Are you laughing at me?" I asked.

"No," Ezra said calmly. "I think the situation is adorable, but I'd never laugh at you. How can I make you feel more comfortable about meeting my parents?" A sobering expression crossed his handsome features. "Would you prefer to meet them another day? Maybe you're not certain about us and—"

I cut him off with a quick kiss. "I want to meet my boyfriend's parents, Ezra; I just don't want them to see a gold-digging hussy when they look at me."

"Gold-digging hussy?" Ezra fell back on my mattress, laughing harder than I'd ever heard him. "G-g-gold. D-d-digging. H-h-hussy. Have you been watching reruns of *Dallas* or *Dynasty*? Or was it *Knots Landing*? Oh my God, Henry. I don't even know where to begin with that statement." I started to get up off the bed, but Ezra pulled me down to lie beside him. "You're not going anywhere. I just need a minute to recover."

"I bet he's heard that one plenty of times before," Jess said as she passed by my bedroom door.

"Is she calling me old?" Ezra asked me. When all I did was stare at him, he yelled, "Are you calling me old, Jess?"

"If the shoe fits, Grandpa."

"Jess!" I yelled, mortified by her bluntness.

Ezra only laughed harder. "Oh. Oh my God," he said, winding down from his trip to delirious town. "Okay, we need to get on the road if we're going to make it on time for dinner. Do you want to go?"

I nodded.

"Great. As much as I love seeing you parade around in tight-fitting boxers, I'm afraid I must insist on covering them up." Ezra kissed the tip of my nose then left me lying on my bed while he crossed the tiny space and rummaged around in my closet. "This is just a laid-back dinner at my parents' house. My dad will be wearing a polo shirt and a pair of jeans or khakis, and my mom will be wearing a casual dress and flip-flops or sandals. Don't let my parents' Indian Hill zip code fool you."

I relaxed enough to let my eyes roam over Ezra's outfit. He'd chosen dark denim jeans in a tighter fit than I was used to seeing him wear and a pale blue, short-sleeved, button-up shirt that looked lovely against his tan.

Ezra slid a few more hangers over then said, "What do we have here?" He removed my Spiderman Halloween costume from last year and held it up so he could look it over. "I'm going to need you to try this on for me someday." The heat in his voice made me shiver. Our eyes met, and I could tell we were seconds away from either forgetting about our dinner obligations altogether or arriving very late. Ezra blinked then turned quickly back to my closet where he tucked the costume away for another day. "Later, Ezra," he said to himself, making me smile for the first time that day. I loved how much he wanted me. "How about this?" Ezra held up a charcoal gray polo shirt I forgot I owned. I had found it during one of my trips to Goodwill with Esther. She knew the best locations and days of the month to find the good stuff.

"Not bad. I have a pair of nice shorts to go with it."

Ezra shuffled a few more hangers over and pulled out the white and gray plaid shorts. "These will work perfectly." Bending forward, Ezra picked up a pair of shoes from the floor. "These burgundy Chucks match the accent stripe in the plaid. We're all set."

I slid off the bed and started getting dressed, which became harder when I had to tuck my stiffening dick into my shorts. "I need you to stop looking at me like that," I told him, gesturing to my problem.

"That's never going to happen, but I'll happily lend a hand." Ezra crossed the room, batted my hand away, and tucked my dick away before he zipped and buttoned my pants. Then he placed both his warm hands against my abdomen, smiling when my muscles quivered beneath my flesh. "Need more help?"

"I think you better wait for me in the living room," I said.

"Probably," he agreed. "You're not going to freak out and escape out the window, are you?"

I snorted. "I wouldn't trust the fire escape." Ezra scowled and headed toward my bedroom window to inspect it. "I'm sure it's perfectly fine, Ezra. I simply meant I wouldn't be testing it out for anything less than an emergency. I might be nervous about meeting your folks, but I'm not going to climb down the fire escape to avoid it."

"Once you're ready, we're going to have a nice chat about why you're so nervous."

"Can't wait," I said with mock cheer.

Ezra narrowed his eyes but didn't say anything else before he left my room. I didn't waste any more time second-guessing my new status as Ezra's boyfriend because I knew he'd come looking for me.

I found him sitting on the couch looking through a copy of Jess's *Rolling Stone Magazine*. He looked up when I entered and smiled at me. "Ready?"

"Yes," I said with conviction I didn't feel.

Ezra reached for my hand and led me from my apartment, not breaking our connection until I was seated in the passenger side of his car. Not one to waste time, he got right to the point as soon as he pulled away from the curb. "Why don't you tell me why you were so panicked? Don't tell me it had something to do with your appearance, and please don't use the gold-digging hussy phrase again. I can't be serious when you say it, and the situation calls for my full attention."

Honesty had been a huge part of our relationship once we stopped lying to ourselves about wanting one another. I could gloss over my concerns and let them rot, or I could act like the adult Ezra believed me to be and talk about them. "I'm worried about their reaction to our age difference and what they'll think when they find out how we met."

Ezra reached over the console and squeezed my hand. "I already told them, Henry."

I snapped my head in his direction. "What? When?"

"I called them last night because I didn't want to catch them off guard and risk their surprise coming across as disappointment to you."

"You told them I'm only twenty-one?"

"Yes."

"They weren't upset?" I asked.

"I think they were a little surprised, but they weren't upset. We're consenting adults, after all," Ezra added wryly. "My parents were more concerned about our relationship harming both our reputations at the school."

"*My* reputation? What do I have to lose?" I asked.

"You could lose the respect of faculty members and gain a lot of scorn from other students. If this blows up, you will be impacted too. Until my mother pointed it out to me, I'd selfishly only worried about *my* standing with my peers and *my* career."

I rotated my wrist and slid my fingers between Ezra's. "You're the least selfish person I know, Ezra. Hypothetically speaking, it would be a lot easier for me to transfer to a new school where they didn't know my reputation, but carrying on a torrid affair with a student would follow you wherever you went."

"*Torrid affair?*" he asked. "What's up with you tonight?"

Grateful for the change in topic, I confessed, "I started reading one of Jessie's romance novels. There was a 'torrid affair' between an heir to a large ranch and a poor girl from a rival farm. Their dads used to be partners until something went wrong. I haven't gotten to that point yet. Kip's mom just lit into Clarissa and called her a gold-digging hussy."

"Somehow, you imagined my mom in the role of Kip's mother?" Ezra asked, trying like hell not to laugh his ass off. "Does that make me Kip then? Is that short for Kipper?" Ezra lost it then, laughing until he was out of breath and tears ran down his face. "I'm so sorry, baby.

I'm used to these little surprises from you, but this one caught me off guard."

"I'm not usually this dramatic. I blame my nerves." I swallowed hard because those nerves were rising up to choke me. "Did you tell them about the other thing?"

"That you have an insatiable sexual appetite?" Ezra's fingers tightened around mine. I appreciated his attempt to keep the conversation light.

I chuckled as he meant for me to. "The other part."

"I didn't tell them you're HIV positive, Henry. That's your story to tell, not mine."

"You don't think they have a right to know you're sleeping with someone who's positive?"

"I don't. It's our business. We practice safe sex, I'm taking PrEP, and you're taking your meds and doing everything in your power to keep yourself healthy and strong."

"Ezra, you know there are risks besides sexual encounters," I countered. "What if I cut myself with a steak knife at their house?"

Ezra glanced over with a raised brow. "Is that something you often do?"

"No," I said, shaking my head. "I was just using it as an example."

"I'm not dismissing your concerns, but maybe we worry about potential injuries resulting in bloodshed if they occur. For now, why don't we start focusing on positive examples."

"Such as?" I asked.

Ezra snickered at my stubborn tone. "What if my parents look past the age difference and school situation and see we have something extraordinary? What if they stop worrying I'm going to die alone and quit playing matchmaker?"

"Does that happen often?"

"Yes, and they're terrible at it. The guys they introduce me to are all nice, but we don't connect. I have made some good friends from their lousy attempts, so they weren't complete failures."

"Oh man," I said, suddenly worried that Ma and Pa Meyer would step up their game to save Ezra from my evil clutches. *Ma and Pa Meyer? Get your shit together, Henry.*

"Oh no," Ezra said firmly. "We're not traveling down that road again." Ezra stopped at a red light then turned and leaned toward me. "Stop anticipating disaster and prepare yourself for a warm welcome from two people who will be excited to see that you make their only child happy."

"I do?" I hated the insecurity I heard in my voice.

Ezra pressed a quick kiss against my lips. "Extremely." The light turned green, and he returned his focus to driving.

I stopped staring at Ezra and looked out the passenger side window. "So, you're saying to knock it off and stop worrying I'll stick out like a sore thumb like Mona Lisa Vito did in Alabama."

"'Yeah, you blend,'" Ezra said, mimicking Marisa Tomei's New York accent.

"I knew you were going to love the movie."

Ezra chuckled. "Yeah, I did. I can't believe I waited so long to watch it."

"If it helps, I didn't see *My Cousin Vinny* until I moved into Ryan's Place. I would never have been permitted to watch it at home."

"It wasn't a violent or sexually risqué movie," Ezra countered.

"No, but it's filled with foul language. My mom thought any exposure to violence, sex, or even swear words would set me on a path to eternal damnation, but all she did was make those things more enticing to me. Well, some of them anyway."

"Ahh," Ezra said. "The ignore-it-and-it-will-go-away parenting technique. It doesn't have a very high success rate."

"Tell me about it."

Sensing that talking about my upbringing was the absolute last thing I wanted to be doing, Ezra changed the subject. "Now that I know you enjoy romance novels so much, I have a few gay romance novels I could loan you."

I looked over at him again, studying his gorgeous face in profile. I loved his chiseled bone structure; it matched the descriptions I'd read in Jessie's romance novels about dukes and other peers of the realm. As with the heroes in the books, I knew secrets and past hurts hid beneath his beautiful veneer. If there was one thing I learned from reading, the highest or thickest walls hid the purest hearts.

"I don't know. I might start getting ideas."

Ezra sat straighter in his seat. "Oh yeah?"

I chuckled. "Not *those* ideas. Well, maybe those too. I was thinking more along the lines of scaling the wall surrounding your heart or possibly tearing it down one brick at a time."

Ezra's lips turned up into a big smile. "Are you going to rescue me like a valiant knight?"

"If that's what it takes. I'll have to borrow someone else's steed since I don't own one."

Hearty laughter burst from Ezra. I thought what I said was more cute than funny, but it had tickled something inside him. "Oh my God. You just reminded me of a story about my parents' first date." He tried to tell me but was laughing too hard to speak in complete sentences. All I made out was "dad" and "motor scooter." His amusement was contagious, and I found myself chuckling too.

My enjoyment dried up the minute Ezra turned into a driveway with an iron gate. He released my hand long enough to push a button on a remote clipped to his visor which opened the gates to reveal a long driveway disappearing into a thickly wooded area.

"We're here," he said excitedly.

"Oh my God," I whispered. *What was I doing?*

Chapter Eighteen

Ezra

"J UST BREATHE, HENRY. MY PARENTS AREN'T ROYALTY, THEY DON'T LIVE in a castle, and you will not have to battle fire-breathing dragons at any point during our visit."

"Uh-huh," Henry said in disbelief. Then his breath hitched in his throat when I crested the hill and stopped so he could see the house, barns, and horse paddocks in the rolling valley below.

"This old farmhouse was built in 1890 when Indian Hill was still a farming community. Over the years, the farmland was sold for real estate development, but this old beauty still stands as a reminder of what used to be. Mom said she fell in love with the property at this exact spot."

"I can see why," Henry said. "Someone put a lot of care and effort into maintaining this property."

"The best part is they did it while maintaining the original architecture of the home. I'm jealous this isn't the home I grew up in." The front door opened, and my mom stepped onto the front porch. "It's too late to turn around now," I told Henry, adding a wicked laugh to try to shake him from the terror setting in as I eased down the driveway. Henry sounded like he was hyperventilating, and I wished I could think of something magical to say to make his panic go away. "At least she's not carrying a shotgun."

"*What?*" he squeaked. *Okay, so that wasn't it.*

"Bad joke, baby. Terrible joke."

"I might never forgive you," Henry said.

"I promise to make it up to you." I shifted the car in park and released my seat belt so I could give Henry an apology kiss, but my mom rounded the corner of the house with three Greyhound dogs close on her heels. "You're not allergic to animals, are you?"

"Only the kind that will eat me," Henry quipped.

"You're safe then. Dad made her give the tigers back to the zoo."

Henry narrowed his eyes. "You have a cruel streak about you, Ezra. I didn't know that until today."

"I'm nervous that you're nervous. I open my mouth to say something encouraging, and the exact opposite comes out."

A shy smile curved Henry's lips as he studied my face. "I like it."

"Which part? The gun-toting mother or man-eating tigers? I think your sense of humor needs work."

He laughed then. "You're always so cool and in control, so it's nice to see you a little rattled."

"Always?" I asked huskily. "I can think of plenty of times when you made me lose—"

Henry leaned forward, cutting off my words with a quick kiss. "Giving me a boner just before I meet your parents would be the cruelest stunt yet."

"You're right," I said softly. "Forgive me?"

"We'll see," Henry said noncommittally before releasing his seat belt and opening the door. "Maybe you want to shut off the car and join us."

Oops. By the time I killed the engine and climbed out of the car, Mom and her three dogs had already converged on Henry.

"Hello, Henry," Mom said, ignoring Henry's extended hand to hug him. "It's so nice to meet you."

"Likewise, Mrs. Meyer."

"Please call me Simone," she said, squeezing Henry's shoulders affectionately before turning to hug me. "Hi, brat."

"Hi, Mom."

Instead of the summer dress I predicted she would wear, Mom wore a white, sleeveless blouse, faded denim jeans, and her riding boots. She smelled like sunshine, grass, and leather which meant she'd just come in from riding one of her beloved horses on the trails through the woods.

"Come on in and get something to drink. Dad is out back fussing over his smoker. He put the racks of ribs on a few hours ago."

"That's what smells so good," Henry said, sniffing the air appreciatively.

"I hope you brought your appetite with you," Mom told him, looping her arm through his and leading him toward the front door. Henry glanced at me over his shoulder, and I gave him a reassuring smile as I followed them.

Dad was casually lounging poolside rather than hovering over his smoker as Mom had implied. He rose to his feet as soon as we stepped onto the patio and offered his hand to Henry. "It's nice to meet you, Henry. I'm Paul."

"It's nice to meet you too."

"I hear you're attending my alma mater," Dad said proudly. He looked at Mom with a smug expression on his face. "I was so excited when Ezra accepted a position at the University of Cincinnati instead of that *other* school across town."

Mom snorted. "Really, Paul? Henry has been here for less than five minutes, and we're going to subject him to our college rivalry." She turned to Henry and smiled. "I attended Xavier University."

"Ah," Henry said. "That crosstown battle is almost as intense as the argument over who makes the best Cincinnati chili: Gold Star or Skyline."

"Skyline," we all said at once.

Dad laughed. "I like you, Henry. Great taste in schools and chili."

"And men," I added.

"Yeah, I guess you're okay too," Dad said, hooking his arm around my shoulders and pulling me to him for a hug.

"Ezra," Mom cheerfully said, "why don't you give Henry a tour of the house and property while I get cleaned up and put the finishing touches on dinner?"

"Want a tour?" I asked, appreciating the excuse to get Henry alone to make sure he was doing okay.

"I'd love one," Henry said.

I threaded my fingers through his and pulled him into step with me. "How long before dinner?" I asked.

"Thirty or forty minutes," Dad replied.

"Plenty of time," I said.

I gave Henry a quick tour of the house, and he got to see a few of Mom's cats lounging in windows, chairs, or stripes of sunlight across the floors. Henry loved the old charm of the house as much as I did, but he especially loved the four-legged beasts he discovered in the barn.

"I've never been around horses," Henry said. "They're gorgeous."

"These are retired racehorses my mom rescued," I told him. "She grew up around horses on her grandparents' farm. Riding is something she gave up for many years to focus on her family and career. She's rediscovered her passion for the magnificent beasts."

"Rescued?" Henry asked.

"These horses had outlived their usefulness, so their owners were going to have them destroyed."

"No!" Henry said, sounding as horrified as I did when I first found out. "Who does something like that?"

"Someone who sees these horses as investments that are no longer paying dividends." My favorite horse, Bourbon Baby, nickered and came over to see me. I leaned into her and ran my hand along her velvety soft nose. "These lucky horses don't have to worry about that anymore though. They get to live out their lives getting pampered and spoiled."

"Are your mom's Greyhounds rescued too?"

I nodded. "Mom detests animal racing of any kind."

"I like your mom a lot, even if she has the same name as Kip's mom."

"What? Are you joking?"

Henry laughed and shook his head. "Nope. I had to bite my cheek to keep from laughing."

I straightened away from the horse then pulled Henry into my arms. "My mom might share a name with the meddlesome, fictional mama in the book, but I assure you, I'm not Kip, and you're definitely not Clarissa." I turned, pinning Henry between the stall door and my body. "Gold-digging hussy or otherwise," I added.

"This is almost like the scene I read last night," Henry whispered against my hovering lips. "Clarissa snuck away from her homestead and met Kip in the barn on his ranch one night, and he laid one on her."

"Laid one on her?" I asked. "One what? Hand? Mouth? Dick?"

Henry rolled his eyes. "I'm just repeating the phrasing in the book."

"Maybe we should rewrite the scene," I suggested. "I like the gal's boldness. It reminds me of a certain someone I know. Tell me what good ole Kip and sweet Clarissa got up to in the barn."

"There was a lot of kissing," Henry said.

Getting into character, I looked up and down the length of the barn. "We need to be quiet, or my folks will hear us."

Henry rolled, repositioning us so that my back was pinned against the stall. "I guess you better keep your moaning down then."

"Oh? What did sweet Clarissa do to Kip?"

"She pulled him into an empty stall, pushed his cowboy jeans down his legs, then dropped to her knees and blew him."

"Really?" I asked, looking for an empty stall.

"Yep, but she didn't let him come. She pushed him down onto a bale of hay, hiked up her skirt, and rode him like a prized thoroughbred."

"How much time do you think we have left before dinner?" I whispered against Henry's lips.

"Not enough to do what you're thinking?"

"You have no idea what I'm thinking," I challenged. Henry's brow shot up. "Okay, I was thinking a quick fuck in an empty stall, but I dismissed it because you know how I like to take my time drawing out your pleasure."

"What do you have in mind then?"

"Want to check out some trails?" I asked.

"On horseback?" he sounded excited by the idea.

"I thought we'd save that for our next visit when the clock isn't counting down toward dinner. How does an ATV sound? Four wheels instead of four legs?"

Henry laughed. "Sure."

I led him to the equipment barn where Dad stored his beloved Wolverine.

"This looks pretty badass," Henry said, gaping at the silver and black utility vehicle. "I've never seen one like it before. It looks much fancier than the one Kip took Clarissa for a ride on."

I laughed. "It's called a side-by-side. It's safer than a regular ATV because it has a roll cage, seats with seat belts, and a windshield to keep the bugs out of our teeth."

"It looks fast."

I chuckled. "Very. Want to drive it?"

"Um, not yet, but maybe someday."

I grabbed some helmets off the pegs hanging above a workbench. "Roll cage or not, helmets are a must, or Mom will have our asses." After checking to make sure Henry's helmet was snug, we climbed into the Wolverine and took off toward the woods surrounding the property. "My parents own a lot of acreage," I yelled over the engine. "Most of it's wooded, but there are some tillable acres. My parents don't know anything about farming, so they hired someone to plant and harvest the hay she needs for her horses. I'll take you up to the ridge so you can see the fields below."

Henry gave me a thumbs-up.

I drove fast on the straight parts of the trails, making Henry whoop in excitement, but took it slower on the curvy or hilly trails to avoid tipping us over. Henry laughed and pointed out the various wildlife he spotted along the way, and I decided to bring him back soon for a horseback ride and picnic.

I stopped the side-by-side just beneath the ridge. We took off our helmets and walked the rest of the way. None of the nervousness Henry exhibited earlier was present. His hand was relaxed in mine, and his stride was loose and happy instead of rigid. Henry had hidden his tension from my parents for the most part, but maybe Mom still sensed it, and that's why she suggested I give Henry the tour, to help ease his anxiousness.

Henry gasped in delight when we crested the hill and could see the hay fields stretching below us. "This is heaven on earth," he said.

I pulled him into my arms. Pressing a kiss to Henry's forehead, I said, "I agree because you're here with me."

"Ezra," he whispered. "You make me feel so cherished."

"Good. The next time I bring you up here, I'm going to bring a picnic basket and a blanket so I can lay you down and cherish you properly."

Henry tightened his arms around my waist and looked at me with adoration. "I want to believe I deserve this—*you*."

"Then believe it," I said firmly.

I knew it wasn't that simple for Henry to cast off the rejection he'd experienced the previous year, but deciding he wanted something was the first step to believing he could have it. I'd take it and use it as a base to work from.

Standing together on top of the ridge, our problems seemed far away. It felt like we were the only two people in the world, and I wasn't eager to leave the solitude or Henry's arms. The realization that I was in love with Henry washed over me, heating my skin like the sun bathing the fields below us in vibrant light. I couldn't think of a more picturesque setting to tell Henry how I felt, but he wasn't ready to believe me.

"Kiss me, Professor Higgins," Henry said in the worst cockney accent I'd ever heard.

Cupping the back of his head, I said, "'You impudent hussy!'" It was one of the few lines I remembered from *My Fair Lady*.

Henry's laughter bounced off the trees and echoed in the valley at our feet. "I guess that's slightly better than a gold-digging hussy."

I began nibbling a path up his neck. "I like you in all your hussy forms," I said, stopping to suck his earlobe into my mouth. I kissed along his jaw until I reached his lips. "Maybe you can sleep over tonight, and you can tell me more about Clarissa and Kip's antics."

Henry frowned. "It's Sunday."

"What better way to start your week than by waking up next to me?" I asked him.

"The only thing better would be to start the week with you inside me," Henry countered.

I gasped, pretending to be shocked. "Shameless."

Henry linked our fingers and led me back down to the Wolverine. "Let's not keep your parents waiting. After dinner we'll go back to your place, and I'll introduce you to the shameless hussy."

"Oh, baby. He might be my favorite one yet."

"Good," Henry said. "I think I'm ready to drive now, Ezra."

I stopped then reached into my pockets and pulled out the Wolverine keys. "Here you go."

Henry smirked. "Oh, that wasn't what I meant, but I can give this a try too."

I nearly swallowed my tongue when I realized what Henry was referring to. He laughed wickedly and continued walking toward the Wolverine.

"Who's the cruel one now, Henry?" I called after him.

Chapter Nineteen

Henry

AFTER OUR DRIVE UP TO THE RIDGE, I WAS TOO EXCITED ABOUT MY plans for Ezra later that evening and forgot to be intimidated by his parents. I should've just trusted Ezra in the first place because both his parents greeted me warmly when they'd introduced themselves. Simone hadn't even waited for us to walk up to the door before she welcomed me to their home. I forgot I was wearing clothes someone else had worn before I owned them. Worries over our seventeen-year age difference and the reality that Ezra was my professor faded because of the way Ezra looked at me up on the hill. For the first time since meeting Ezra, I had real hope that a relationship was possible between us.

Cherished. Adored. That's how Ezra made me feel every second we were together. I thought I had known those feelings before I met him; I thought I knew what it was like to be the center of someone's universe. I was wrong.

"What did you think?" Paul asked when we returned from washing our hands in the powder room.

"I think you own a piece of heaven," I replied.

"I think the piece of heaven owns us," Paul quipped.

"Your home is stunning," I told them. I knew nothing about

architecture or maintaining the integrity of an old farmhouse, but I recognized beautiful when I saw it.

"Thank you," Simone said. "All the woodwork is original. It took the previous owners three years to completely restore the home to its original grandeur after decades of neglect. Unfortunately, the wife was diagnosed with terminal cancer not long after they moved in, and the place was just too much upkeep for the husband to take care of by himself, so they put it on the market."

"That's so sad," I said.

"It really is," Simone said. "Life is precious and fleeting."

Beside me, Ezra whispered, "Carpe diem," in his best Robin Williams voice. I had to bite my lip to keep from giggling. Nothing about the movie was funny, but Ezra finding ways to quote the movie's lines at every opportunity was hilarious.

"*Dead Poets Society*," Paul said, nodding his approval. "Excellent movie."

"Thanks, Dad," Ezra said. "It was my choice last week. Henry had never seen it."

"It is a beautiful but tragic movie," Simone said.

"Very," I agreed. Neil Perry's struggle with a strict, unaccepting father reminded me so much of the last fight I'd had with my mother. Ezra had regretted his movie choice when I burst into tears toward the end, but he kissed away the hurt. Seeing the parallels between Neil's life and mine were heartbreaking, but it also reminded me of the beauty in my life. After Ezra had fallen asleep, I lay awake in the dark more determined than ever to pay my blessings forward to help others.

"Speaking of seizing the day," Paul said, gesturing with a dramatic flourish to the food spread out over the kitchen island. "Let's eat."

The ridge had made me forget my fears, and the first bite of delicious smoked meat made me forget my manners. I didn't lick the barbecue sauce off my fingers, but I was tempted to lick it from Ezra's—parents present or not. I didn't belch or toss the cleaned bones over my shoulders, but I forgot all the pleasantries I'd learned from the time I could sit up at the table. I didn't participate in the small talk exchanged at the table, and I didn't compliment the hosts on their delicious meal. I wasn't even aware of my rudeness until I was halfway through my second plate.

I set my fork down and wiped my mouth with the napkin I'd at least remembered to lay across my lap. "Oh my goodness. This food is so amazing I forgot myself. These are the best barbecue ribs I've ever had, Paul. The potato salad is the best I've had since my grandmother passed away, Simone."

She reached over and patted my hand. "Seeing you enjoy the food so much is the only compliment we need. Paul takes great pride in his ribs. He's thinking about entering them in a Pitmaster contest held at the county fairgrounds later this year."

"Really?" Ezra asked, his voice and eyebrows lifting in surprise. "You've adjusted to country living extremely well."

"Your mother is thinking about entering her jams at the county fair next year," Paul said so fast it almost sounded accusatory.

Ezra smirked. "Dad, you might as well have just pointed at Mom and said she started it."

"I kind of did start it," Simone said sheepishly. "I started dragging him to farmers' markets and pick-your-own-fruit farms. He started playing around with seasonings and spices to make his own dry rub and barbecue sauce, and I started baking and trying my luck at making jam."

"It turns out we're both good at it," Paul said with an amused smirk.

"You made the rub and sauce for the ribs?" Ezra asked, sounding as impressed as I felt.

"They're amazing, Paul. I think you should enter them in the contest. What kind of jams do you make, Simone?"

Simone smiled and seemed happy to discuss her latest hobby. "I make several, but my favorite is the razzleberry, which is strawberry, blueberry, and raspberry."

"It's delicious on everything," Paul told us. "I heat it and pour it over ice cream to make a sundae."

"It sounds divine," Ezra said.

"I'm glad you think so because I'm sending home several jars with you," Simone told Ezra.

"Hey," Paul protested. "You're giving my razzleberry jam away?"

"Honey, you don't need a dozen jars."

"No, but I want them." Paul's petulant pout didn't last long beneath Simone's determined stare. Her expression was so familiar I couldn't help but laugh. Paul grinned at me. "Henry, do you find yourself on the receiving end of a similar glare often?" he asked me.

"All the time," I said, nodding.

"Two stubborn mules," Paul said, gesturing to his wife and son. "Luckily, they always mean well."

"So I've learned," I agreed.

"Tell Henry about the first time you saw that look on Mom's face," Ezra said.

"The first time she aimed it *at me* or used it on my behalf?" Paul asked.

"Both."

"The first time she used it on me was when I asked her out on a date," Paul said. "She took one look at my UC shirt and dismissed me outright."

Simone snorted. "I dismissed you outright because of your horrible timing and your rudeness." She turned at look at me. "Paul was working as a soda jerk at Clancy's diner where my date had taken me for dinner."

"He was a real putz too," Paul said drolly. "Babe, they'd stopped calling them soda jerks once soda fountains started disappearing from drugstores." Turning to me, Paul said, "Back in the day, you'd stop by the drugstore to get your stuff and order a cherry Coke, a root beer float, or a malted milkshake to drink while you waited." Drinking a root beer float while waiting for my meds sounded nice. "Once the drive-in restaurants and diners came along, the soda fountains at drug-stores were forgotten. Kids wanted to hang out with their friends and listen to music on a jukebox or show off their cars at the drive-ins."

Ezra chuckled. "Or motor scooters."

Simone threw her head back and laughed while Paul glared at his son. His look was impressive but nowhere near as intimidating as Simone and Ezra's.

"Laugh it up," Paul told them. "That bad boy got me to work and school eight months out of the year. It got excellent gas mileage, and the ladies liked Steed." *Ah.* Ezra's laughter in the car made sense. Paul had named his scooter Steed.

"Yeah, it was a real chick magnet," Simone said dryly.

"Get back to the part where you asked Mom out while she was on a date with another man," Ezra said.

Paul looked at Simone and his love for her beamed out of him like rays of the sun, reminding me of the way Ezra had looked at me on top of the hill. "She was the most beautiful woman I had ever laid eyes on. Poised, confident, intelligent—"

"You got all of that from looking at me?" Simone asked, leaning toward him.

"Absolutely. You strode into the diner like a queen who didn't doubt her place in the world. Intelligence, kindness, and humor shone from your eyes like beacons to this guy who'd lived in the dark for too long. It almost hurt to look at you."

"And you just had to ask me out?"

"I had to make you mine. I saw how awkward things were be-tween the two of you and knew your date wasn't the guy for you."

"And you knew you were the one for me?" Simone countered.

"No, but I wanted to be. I would've done anything to be deserv-ing of someone like you."

Simone reached over and brushed her hand over his jaw. "I'm so glad you rudely interrupted that horrible date. My parents were the worst at setting up blind dates."

"Doubt it," Ezra interjected, gaining their attention.

"Touché," Simone said. "You would've thought I'd learned from my parents' mistakes, but we always think we're so much smarter than our parents."

"I conveniently didn't include the straws when the waitress picked up their shakes from me at the soda counter. I'd caught Simone's eyes a few times, and I had a feeling she found me attractive. I had no way of knowing if she would approach me for the straws, send the putz over, or flag down her server, but it was my best shot at a few seconds alone with her."

Simone laughed. "I took advantage of the opportunity to speak to the most handsome, cockiest boy I'd laid my eyes on. He was the kind of boy my mom warned me about. One look and I was ready to—"

"Mom," Ezra said, cutting her off. "PG version."

Paul and Simone laughed while staring into each other's eyes. *So this is what a stable marriage and real love looked like.* My parents had never had this connection, and my mother had never remarried after my father died when I was ten. My heart cried out for this kind of relationship, and I must've released a little sigh because Paul and Simone turned and smiled at me, and Ezra squeezed my thigh beneath the table.

"Where were we?" Simone asked, sounding a little dazed from getting caught up in the emotions of the story."

"It was lust at first sight," Ezra said.

"Paul boldly asked me out on a date, and I turned him down."

"I wanted to argue, but she aimed her no-nonsense glare at me. I thought I'd lost my chance with my dream girl, but she returned to the diner the very next day with her girlfriends. They kept looking at me and giggling."

"What did you do?" I asked Paul.

"I held their straws captive, hoping she would approach me again," he replied.

"And I did," Simone said wistfully. "As I hoped, he asked me out again, and I said yes."

Ezra started laughing. "Now we're getting to the good part where Mom uses her stubborn glare on his behalf instead of directing it at him. Tell them about arriving at Grandma and Grandpa Clarkson's house."

"While I came from a very humble beginning, my sweet girl was born with a silver spoon in her mouth. I arrived on my scooter at what I would still describe as a mansion to pick up Simone. Joseph wasn't at all impressed with my denim jeans and leather jacket, but he nearly had a stroke when he saw Steed in the circular driveway. He forbade her to go out with a no-good loser like me."

"And I gave him 'the look.' He could threaten me all he wanted, but there was no way in hell I was missing out on a chance to go on a date with the only guy who had revved my engine."

"Gross," Ezra muttered, but I found it adorable.

"How long did it take for him to come around?" I asked.

Paul softly smiled at his wife. "He knew I wasn't all bad when I gave my only helmet to Simone to wear on our first date, his respect grew for me on the occasions I accepted his generosity even when it stung my pride, but he didn't fully forgive me until he saw Simone holding Ezra for the first time. He still blusters around and says she could've done better, but he's only teasing me."

"Mostly teasing," Simone added. "He tried to introduce me to the grandson of one of the residents living in his retirement community."

"That wily old bastard. Just wait until I see him again," Paul said, but there was no heat in his words. He was one hundred percent certain of his place in Simone's world.

The conversation flowed naturally while we finished dinner, and I was so relaxed that I didn't freeze up when Paul inquired about my degree.

"I'm studying for a Bachelor of Science degree in sociology and hope to become a counselor to help people within the LGBTQ+

community, especially the most vulnerable like homeless youth and those with HIV."

"That's wonderful," Simone said. "Ezra told us about a transition home called Ryan's Place. He said they do wonderful work there. Are you familiar with them? Paul is setting up a golf outing as a fundraiser for them in October."

Ezra squeezed my thigh again, signaling I could say as much or as little as I wanted to. It was my story to tell when, and if, I wanted to share it. It was nearly impossible to say anything with the lump of emotion lodged in my throat. Oddly, none of my feelings were shame. I wish I'd been smarter about safe-sex practices, but there's no reset button on life. My options were to wallow in self-pity or become a positive force in the world. I was proud of the work Archie did, grateful for my months there, and happy Ezra enlisted his parents to support Ryan's Place. There was no room for shame in my life.

"Ryan's Place saved my life," I said softly. "If not for them, I can't say for certain that I'd be sitting here right now. It's hard for me to imagine never knowing Ezra, or tasting these ribs, or anticipating your razzleberry jam, but it's the truth. It's not hard for a person to lose their will to fight when the world as they know it rejects them. I cannot survive everything I've gone through and not be a crusader for others who find themselves in the same position. I'm so grateful the two of you are joining the good fight too."

"Oh, Henry," Simone said, reaching across the table to cover my hand once more. I knew she must have a million questions, but she didn't ask a single one. She also looked at me with compassion and empathy, not pity or disgust. The back of my nose burned with impending tears. Ezra leaned over and kissed my temple.

"Well," Paul said with a thick voice, "I'm even happier about supporting Ryan's Place now." He lifted his glass of wine and tipped it in my direction. "Here's to the survivors and crusaders who make the world a better place."

We all lifted out glasses and said, "Cheers."

We were too full for dessert, so Simone insisted we take home the razzleberry pie she'd made even though Paul pouted.

"You're not getting my vanilla bean ice cream," he said fiercely.

Ezra laughed. "We'll stop by the grocery store on our way home and get some." Then he turned to me. "Unless you prefer whipped cream instead." I lifted my brow in surprise because he'd asked instead of assumed.

"I like either one."

"You'll also want some English muffins for the jam," Simone said. "There's no better way to start your morning than coffee and a muffin with this stuff on it."

Ezra's hand ghosted over my ass, but they couldn't see it from where they stood on the opposite side of the kitchen island. His gesture said he could think of at least one thing better than food to start his morning.

Simone refused our offer to help clean up, volunteering Paul instead. He groused, but it was all in good fun. They walked us out to Ezra's car when he announced we needed to get going. Simone pulled me into a lingering hug.

"It was so nice to meet you, Henry. I'm so glad we sucked at setting up our son on dates."

I laughed hard. "I'm happier about that than you are."

Simone released me so she and Paul could trade places. Ezra's dad squeezed me tight enough to crack a rib. "That's debatable," he said. "Nothing feels better than seeing your kid happy. You keep him in line, Henry. Know when to buckle beneath the glare and when to hold your ground."

Ezra laughed and said, "He already has that down to a science."

A full belly and happy heart made me sleepy on the ride home, but I fought it off. Ezra had given me the most precious gift—time with his parents and a glimpse at how a family should act. Ezra knew bits and pieces about my life, but he didn't know the full story. He had patiently waited for me to be ready. That time had arrived.

I waited until we were back at our favorite place inside his condo—the glorious tub. Maybe Ezra instinctively knew I was ready to come clean to him, and he ran a bath because he knew it would comfort me. Or maybe he knew speaking the words out loud would make me feel dirty. Either way, it was exactly where I needed to be. Once I was in my favorite position—sitting on his lap with my arm and legs wrapped around him—I began to speak.

"Our backgrounds couldn't possibly be more different, and I'm not just talking about the wealth. Your parents are so obviously in love with each other. It's just beautiful to witness." I released a sappy smile that Ezra couldn't resist kissing. "My father was an overbearing, loud-mouth drunk. A very mean one at that. They screamed and fought every single day." Ezra stiffened and held me tighter. "My father never laid a hand on me, Ezra, but he didn't have to. God, he was so scary." Just thinking about his thunderous roars made me shiver.

Ezra kissed my forehead. "I got you, baby."

"He died of sclerosis of the liver when I was ten. It was the first time I took an easy breath in the house, but the lessons he instilled in me didn't die with him. Disobeying my mother was out of the question. She turned deeper into her faith for solace, becoming a person I didn't recognize, which made me feel even more alone. I wanted to earn her affection and get her attention, so I worked harder at becoming the perfect child. Nothing was ever good enough, and I never got space from her because I was homeschooled. My only approved outings were to church and church events where she or other parents supervised us. I didn't start to rebel until I discovered how much I liked boys." I smiled at the memory then grinned when Ezra growled a little.

"I think you know the rest. I got a little wild at bible college of all places. Discovered a dating app and got reckless." My lips started to tremble, so I concentrated on centering myself and bringing my emotions under control. "I've learned a lot in therapy this past year, and I'm much stronger, but there are always going to be certain triggers or situations that send me to a dark space. Being my boyfriend won't always be easy, and I carry a lot of baggage. Sometimes I feel like it's too much. How could you want me when my own mother didn't?"

Ezra leaned forward and rubbed his nose against mine. "It's simple, Henry. She's a fool; I'm not. Give me all your baggage, I'm stronger than I look."

"Are you sure you want to hear the rest?"

"I do."

I took a few more breaths and pilfered a few more kisses before I found my courage to repeat the words I tried desperately to forget. I needed to purge them from my system. By the time I finished recounting the final day with my mom, Ezra was crying right along with me.

Then he picked up my favorite sponge and lovingly wiped away the shame, remorse, and ick the words made me feel. When he finished, Ezra cupped my face and stared into my eyes. "Henry, I need you to listen to me very carefully. Can you do that?" I nodded. "You are a miracle. You are beautiful. You have the purest heart. I'm grateful for the day you were born, because living in a world where you don't exist is unacceptable."

And because Ezra said it, I believed it.

Chapter Twenty

Ezra

I CHECKED MY PHONE FOR THE FIFTH TIME WHILE WAITING FOR MY DE-
partment meeting to start. Still no response from Henry. I knew
he'd picked up an extra shift at Mamma Maria's after his group
therapy session to cover for someone on vacation, but I couldn't imagine the pizza place was so slammed he couldn't check his phone. I'd
sent my message nearly two hours ago and was starting to get worried about him. It wasn't like Henry not to respond. I controlled my
breathing to combat the irrational fear rising inside me. He probably
forgot to charge his phone, and the battery died.

Knowing I would feel better if I could just hear his voice, I stood
up to step out into the hallway and call the landline for the pizzeria. I
turned and stopped dead in my tracks when I saw a man walking toward me with a purposeful stride. "Pres?" I asked in disbelief. "Is that
really you?"

"In the flesh," he said, smiling from ear to ear. I hadn't realized
how much I missed his charming British accent, his sparkling blue
eyes, and devilish grin until they were aimed at me. "If you would've
bothered listening to your messages, you would have known the university hired me as a guest lecturer for this year." Pres opened his
arms, and I stepped into them.

"Guilty," I said sheepishly, returning his tight hug. "I've been a little preoccupied lately." Images from the previous night flashed in my brain. Henry had been nervous about topping for the first time, but after some initial fumbling, he'd made love to me so sweetly it had left me speechless. I was desperate to see him and hold him again, which was why I kept checking my phone.

"I bet I can guess why," Pres returned, noting the way my mind had strayed away. "Are you free for drinks after the department meeting or are you otherwise preoccupied?"

"I, um…" I didn't know the answer because Henry hadn't responded to me. My phone buzzed in my hand, and I was relieved to see my boyfriend was texting me back. I sat back down in the seat I'd vacated, and Pres took the chair next to mine.

Again? Aren't you sick of me yet?

I nearly snorted when I read Henry's text. Fat chance, I thought to myself. To Henry, I said, *Hell no. Remind me to give you the spare key I revoked from my parents.* No remark came back immediately, and I second-guessed myself. *Too soon?* I asked. I was both relieved and nervous when those three dots popped up, letting me know he was responding.

Beside me, Pres chuckled. "Someone's got it bad."

Henry's message finally popped up. *Hell no.*

Which was he saying no to? I thought I knew, but I wouldn't pass up the chance to tease him. *You're not coming over, or you don't want a key to my place?*

Henry's response was immediate. *I meant it's definitely not too soon. I probably won't be there until a little after ten. Are you sure it's okay?*

See you then. I breathed a sigh of relief then tucked my phone away.

"Looks to me like you have plans," Pres said, flashing a disappointed grin.

"Looks that way." I couldn't say I was as disappointed as he was. My relationship with Prescott Stone was complicated. As much as I'd appreciated his friendship during one of the darkest and most humiliating times in my life, seeing Pres reminded me of the heartbreak and pointed out what a hypocrite I'd become. Dating a student is something I'd vowed never to do. If he found out, Pres would eagerly point it out to me.

"You don't have time for a quick drink with an old mate?" Pres countered, playfully batting long, dark eyelashes that made his eyes appear even bluer. "Just one tiny drink?"

I rolled my eyes at Pres's pouty expression. "I might have time for a quick drink if this meeting ends early enough."

"Alas, there is hope," Pres replied eagerly.

I hoped my smile didn't give away the mixed feelings I had about Prescott's presence. My tenure at the University of Cincinnati was supposed to be my clean slate, a chance to return to my parents' beloved hometown and start over. I never factored in a fragment of my troubled tenure in Connecticut following me. "We'll just see about that," I said. "Dr. Bronson hasn't even arrived yet, and the meeting was supposed to start five minutes ago."

"I'm betting on everyone keeping the questions and responses to a minimum so we get out of here faster," Pres countered smugly.

Looking around the room, I could see that Pres was right. The other professors in the department were checking their phones or watches and fidgeting in their chairs. Most of them hadn't taught over the summer, and they were clinging to their freedom for as long as they could. This department meeting was a reminder of the ticking clock counting down the number of days left. An image of Marisa Tomei's Mona Lisa Vito stomping her high-heeled boot on the wooden porch to signify her biological clock ticking came to mind, and a huge grin spread across my face. Henry would love the analogy.

Pres whistled softly, snapping me back to the present. "You've got the wandering-mind and private-smile thing happening. You've got it bad, my friend."

I might not be ready to broadcast my relationship with Henry, but denying the feelings existed felt wrong. "I do."

Pres's big smile didn't quite reach his eyes, and the uneasiness in the pit of my stomach grew. "You deserve it, Ezra."

I opened my mouth to force a friendly response, but Dr. Bronson entered the conference room. A collective sigh of relief echoed as the forty-something African American woman made her way to the seat at the head of the table reserved for the department chair. Instead of her usual bespoke suit, Regina wore a Little League baseball jersey with white capris and wedge sandals.

"I know. I know. I'm late and this is the last place you want to be with the summer break winding down, but my son's baseball game went into extra innings, and I couldn't walk away. If I had, I would've missed my baby boy driving in the winning run. I would have never forgiven myself."

A couple of the older, stodgy professors weren't at all moved while the rest of us congratulated her. Regina reminded me a lot of my mother—passionate about her career but fiercely devoted to her family. She turned around to pick up a stack of files on a small corner table, and the lettering on the back of her jersey made me smile. #1 Mom. She had been very open about her struggles to conceive a child, and there was no doubt in anyone's mind that motherhood would always come first.

"Let's get started," Regina said. "I'll see if I can't get you out of here earlier than planned to make up for my tardiness." That made the stick-up-the-ass professors look happier. "First off, I'd like to introduce our guest lecturer for the year. Dr. Prescott Stone, will you please stand up and introduce yourself to your fellow science professors?"

Prescott smoothly stood up, and every eye around the large table turned to him. At nearly six and a half feet tall, he was hard to miss. When you add in his dark hair, tanned skin, and piercing blue eyes, you got a strikingly handsome man who garnered attention everywhere he went. Even hetero men took notice and responded positively to him. I knew the minute he aimed his megawatt smile full of perfect white teeth at the people around the table because they all sat a little straighter. I grinned and waited for him to reveal his biggest weapon.

"Good evening, everyone. I'm not one to stand on formalities with my colleagues, so Prescott or Pres is fine, or Professor Stone is also perfectly acceptable if it makes you feel more comfortable," he said, his British accent sounding even smoother and more charming than usual. I saw a few mouths part and witnessed others fidget in their seats. I'd admit to having had a similar reaction the first time I saw him. Pres held his audience's rapt attention as he gave the highlights of his education and experience. Having an Oxford scholar join the department was an impressive achievement. "That's enough about me. I can see some of you are barely staying awake," Pres wryly said like he found it awkward to talk about himself. Self-deprecation was another tool in his arsenal; he whipped it out to ease people who were intimidated by him. It paired dashingly, as he'd say, with his urbane charisma to literally charm the pants off anyone he wanted.

"Thank you, Professor Stone. We're excited to have you join our team," Regina said, nodding at him. She wouldn't refer to him by his first name until she got to know him better. "I want to go over the schedule for the next few weeks. Labor Day is the second, and I'll give you the third off to recover, but I want everyone here on the fourth to meet their teaching assistants and go over your expectations with them. Normally, teaching assistants are grad students who can assist you with teaching responsibilities, but we shook things up this year and hired a few undergrads for those who don't plan to utilize their assistants in the classroom." She glanced in my direction because I always taught my own classes, and I was the one who approached her with the idea of hiring undergrads for professors like me who didn't need as much assistance.

The grumbling among the elitists in the group rankled my nerves because they were discounting these students without even meeting them. Any of them should consider themselves lucky to have Henry's sunny smile and eagerness to please brighten up their days. I suddenly remembered the way he'd started my morning off by sliding beneath the sheets to swallow my cock. His smile after he sucked me off wasn't sunny; it was downright wicked. *Don't go there, Ez. Not the place to get a boner. Not the kind of eagerness to help Henry will be offering.*

"These are quality students that I've personally interviewed. I'm asking for volunteers, but I won't hesitate to assign these assistants where I see fit." Regina opened the top file folder. "Beatrice Dexter is a third-year, undergrad student majoring in a Bachelor of Science degree in sociology. She was recommended by Professor Donovan." Regina then started reading off the notes she'd made about the attributes she liked best about Beatrice during her interview. Smart, funny, eager to learn, and arrives early were the keywords that stuck out to me. "Any volunteers?"

I raised my hand. "Beatrice sounds like the perfect assistant for me." As much as I wanted to work with Henry, I didn't trust either of us to behave.

"Thank you, Ezra. Next up is Josef Adnon," Regina said, quickly moving on to the next candidate to keep the meeting moving.

I glanced over at Pres, who quirked a brow because she referred to me by my first name while addressing him by his preferred title. Regina had a unique approach to running our department. She knew there were many grumbles about a younger, minority woman with less tenure being awarded the position, so she went out of her way to be respectful if they afforded her the same treatment. Some professors in the department would be highly insulted if she addressed them as anything less than doctor, where others preferred she use the title of professor. Then there were the ones like me who liked more casual interactions with their colleagues.

Doctor Mills raised her hand to choose Josef as her assistant and Regina moved on to the next candidate. Pres chose a student named Macy, and Professor Mansfield chose a student named Bixby. Regina had saved Henry for last, which was appropriate since I knew he was the best candidate. While I was confident they would all be exceptional assistants, none of them would dedicate themselves with the same alacrity as Henry would.

"Ezra recommended Henry Sullivan, and I can see why he thinks so highly of the young man." Regina read off Henry's education and career goals as she'd done with the others. I was eager for her to relay the notes she'd made during her interview. She smiled and stared down at her notes like she'd discovered something amusing she'd jotted down. "I wrote down, 'sunny disposition, warm heart, and an eagerness to please that rivals all others.' I hadn't meant to make the young man sound like a puppy." I nearly choked on my saliva, recalling the way Henry stared at the puppy play display at the Museum of Sex exhibit.

"Sounds like just the man for me," Pres whispered beside me, turning my stomach. "Too bad he's off-limits, right, Ez?"

"Right," I whispered back.

Meghan Millstone raised her hand to select Henry as her assistant, and I had to suppress a big sigh of relief. Meghan could be a strict, no-nonsense professor, but she genuinely cared for the well-being of her students and was a fantastic mentor for them. Meghan and Henry would make a great team. The tensions I'd been harboring melted away, knowing he would be in good hands.

Regina wrapped up the teaching assistant selection and moved on to the next item on her agenda, keeping a nice pace but still allowing for questions or concerns that cropped up. "We've reached the final item I want to discuss with you," she said, earning a smattering of applause. She bowed gracefully and said, "I know some of you have been looking forward to the back-to-school department party all year, and I finally have a location. We're gathering on September seventh from eight o'clock to midnight at the Kenwood Country Club, which is a gorgeous venue for all of us. The president had decided to extend invitations to your teaching assistants so they're made to feel part of the team and not just gophers who chase down your coffee.

Invitations will be going out to your assistants tomorrow via email, and I expect you to encourage them to attend when you meet them on the fourth. You'll be receiving the same email which will include the location details, entertainment, dinner menu options, dress code, et cetera. Don't embarrass me in front of the president with poor attendance because I have a very long memory, and there will come a time when you need a favor." She released a diabolical, cartoon villain laugh then clapped her hands. "Meeting adjourned, people."

I'd hoped the professors in the department would eagerly approach Pres and engage him in conversations which would allow me to beg out of my agreement to have a drink with him. They did politely introduce themselves, but instead of lingering with questions, they welcomed him to the team and said they were looking forward to getting to know him. *Well, damn.*

"Looks like we have time for that drink," Pres said, gesturing toward the exit.

"Looks like," I agreed with false cheer. "Have you found your preferred watering hole?"

"I only just arrived last Thursday," Pres said dryly, falling into step beside me.

"That's five days, so I know damn well you've found a favorite drinking place."

"Touché," Pres said. "The bartenders at Eleanor's make an excellent extra *dirty* martini." He'd put so much emphasis on dirty that it almost sounded like an invitation for something else.

"Boyfriend," I said, reminding him.

"Yeah, but you're all mine until ten o'clock," Pres said, his voice deep and wicked sounding. I stopped and turned to face him. Was he serious? "For *drinks.*"

"I thought I agreed to one drink," I countered.

"Why stop at one when we have so much catching up to do. I haven't been in the same room with you for over a year, and you hardly text, call, or email."

"Okay, *Mom*," I teased.

"I'm serious, Ez," Pres said, bumping his arm against mine. "I miss our friendship."

"I do too," I admitted. Pres had been the most amazing friend to me when my world turned upside down, and here I was acting stingy with my time. Why should I sit in my condo and twiddle my thumbs while waiting for Henry when I could share some laughs and a few drinks with an old friend? "At least my condo is in walking distance from Eleanor's."

"Good to know," Pres said, waggling his brows.

"Oh no," I said, shaking my head. "I'll put you in a cab."

Pres's frown was ridiculous. "You're no fun."

Henry thought I was plenty of fun. "Keep it up, and I'll stick to the one drink and leave you to find your own entertainment for the night."

Pres aimed a smug smile at me. "That hasn't been a problem for me so far. I really like the Queen City." Knowing he was screwing his way through the city eased the tension building inside me. What I thought was flirting had only been playful banter.

"I bet," I said, returning his smile. "How are you getting around?"

"Took a Lyft here. I'll call another one and meet you at Eleanor's so you can drop your car off and meet me there."

"Don't be silly," I said, waving him off. "Ride with me back to my place. We'll drop off the car and walk to Eleanor's together."

"It's a date then," Pres said happily.

"It's a plan," I countered. I only went on dates with Henry, except we hadn't been on an official one yet. But I had an idea to change that and couldn't wait to surprise him later.

Chapter Twenty-One

Henry

"HELLO, HENRY," GEORGE SAID FROM BEHIND HIS DESK. As friendly as the concierge was, his greeting lacked the same punch and response Ezra's stirred inside me. "You're looking a little tired tonight."

"Busted," I agreed. "It was a very long day." One that Ezra's tenderness would ease.

"Goodnight, Henry. I hope you rest well."

"Thanks, George. Don't work too hard." George's chuckle followed me to the elevator. He'd often told me his biggest struggle was staying awake all night long.

Once the elevator doors closed, I leaned back against the wall and closed my eyes. It felt like I hadn't stopped moving since I woke up at Ezra's that morning. I was tired, hungry, and borderline cranky, which meant I probably should've told Ezra I was going home after my shift instead of agreeing to come over. I could bitch to Jess without worrying about straining our relationship. But this was Ezra, and he was so good for me.

When I stepped off the elevator, I thought about the night Ezra stood outside his door waiting for me. The tenderness in his eyes and dark promise in his voice made me shiver hard. *Dark promise?* I had to stop reading Jessie's books when I got bored and find reading material better suited to me.

Being so close to seeing Ezra again was like a shot of adrenaline. By the time I knocked on his door, the exhaustion I'd felt during the elevator ride up had disappeared. The door opened fast, and Ezra tugged me into his arms, closing the door behind me.

"Hey, baby," he said.

"Um, that's new."

Ezra smiled. "Hello, Henry."

"Much better."

Something other than his greeting was different, but I couldn't put a finger on it until he kissed me and I tasted liquor in his kiss. Not the fruity stuff I preferred, but the stronger stuff I associated with serious drinks. I didn't like it at all and pulled back from the kiss. As far as I knew, Ezra didn't drink, or at least he never had in my presence during the time we dated. Then I noticed his eyes were a little red and glassy, his smile a little dopey.

"You've been drinking," I said.

"You caught me, Sherlock." Ezra's easy smile took out some of the sting from his words. "I enjoyed an extra dry and extra, extra dirty martini. It was so *dirty*."

I swallowed hard. "Just one?"

Ezra rolled his eyes up and tilted his head to the side like he was mentally counting his extra dry and extra, extra *dirty* martinis. I hadn't missed the emphasis on the word dirty and wasn't sure what to make of it.

"Four or five...maybe," he finally said then giggled.

"Wow," I said, stepping out of his arms. Suspicion and jealousy spread across my brain, forming ink blot images I wanted to deny but couldn't. I knew Ezra had attended a department meeting, but he'd told me they were stuffy and boring. "Did you drink these filthy martinis by yourself?"

"Ohhh, filthy sounds better than extra, extra dirty. Next time,

I'm going to order mine downright filthy," Ezra replied, ignoring my question. Was it deliberate or was his tipsy brain unable to string together multiple thoughts at once?

Maybe I should've let it go, but I couldn't. "And who will be drinking these downright filthy martinis with you?"

"Pres. You know, my friend who's guest lecturing at the school."

"Ezra, this is the first time you mentioned anything about your friend guest lecturing at the university." His secrecy only added to my suspicion. "You know, I think my being here isn't the best idea tonight."

"Whaaaat?" Ezra asked. "No. Don't go."

"I'm tired and cranky, and you're drunk. This isn't a good combo." I couldn't stand drunkenness. Ezra should've realized it was one of my triggers after I'd told him about my dad, but maybe that was on me for not being more specific.

"If I'd known you were going to be so immature about me having a drink with a friend, I wouldn't have invited you over tonight." *Immature.* He might as well have just kicked me in the balls; it would've hurt less. "I guess I can call Pres and see if he wants to meet me again. He didn't seem to mind getting filthy with me." *Filthy.* My heart fell to my feet. He'd already found someone else more suitable for him. Hadn't I known all along this would happen?

I flinched as if Ezra had hit me. "Maybe you should," I said, walking backward. Something in my expression must've penetrated his alcohol euphoria because remorse filled his eyes, and he reached for me.

"Baby, don't go," he begged. "I'm sorry. Nothing happened between Pres and me. We don't have that kind of relationship." I might've had less experience than Ezra, but I knew most relationships could be "that kind" under the right circumstances. Sensing he hadn't won me over, he started talking faster. "I didn't ask you to come over so we could argue; I wanted you to come over because I have a surprise for us."

Did he really think he could dangle a gift over my head and it would make up for his shitty behavior? "Ezra, I'm exhausted and hungry. You're drunk and a little mean. You should know how that makes me feel. I'm going home, and we can talk more tomorrow."

"Fine," Ezra said, releasing my arm. "Have a good night, Henry."

It was doubtful. "You too."

"I plan on it."

Ezra shut the door firmly behind me, and it felt like an omen. I wanted to cry but wouldn't allow it until I was someplace private and safe. My priority was getting a ride home. Jess had dropped me off on her way to a bar gig in Covington. I barely had enough money in my account to buy food after paying for my schoolbooks, so getting a Lyft was out. It was too far to walk, I didn't have change for a bus, and a taxi would cost me as much or more than a Lyft. I hated to bug Geoff, but he was my best bet. If he didn't answer, I'd call Des.

Stepping inside the elevator, I dialed Geoff's number. "Please answer. Please answer," I said when his phone started to ring.

"Hey, Henry, what's up?" he whispered into the phone.

"I need a favor, Geoff. I'm in a little jam."

"I'll be right there," he said soberly. "Um, where is there though?"

"I'm at Ezra's," I said just as the elevator door opened on the ground floor.

"Uh oh. I'll be right there."

I was glad to see George was busy talking to some tall dude so he wouldn't witness me leaving with my tail tucked between my legs.

"I just need to drop this off for Ezra Meyer," said the tall man with a familiar British accent. I ducked behind a large potted plant then peeked around the fronds to study him closer. Big and British turned his head to look at another couple coming off the elevator, allowing me to see his face in profile. He was the same guy I'd run into on Friday night. "He left his cell phone at the bar where we were having drinks," Ezra's friend, Pres, told George.

"Oh, how nice of you to return it. Let me call up and see if Dr.

Meyer wants you to bring it up," George said. Knock it off, George. The asshole said he was dropping it off.

"That's not necessary. Ezra told me he was expecting company," Pres told George, who'd already picked up the phone to dial the condo.

"Dr. Meyer. There's a gentleman at the desk who claims to have your cell phone." George listened for a second. "Yes, he's tall, dark, handsome, and British." George smiled at whatever Ezra said. "I'll tell him, sir." George laughed when he hung up the phone. "He said for you to bring it on up. He's in 1214."

"Well, I guess Ezra's plans changed, and I'm the lucky benefactor. Have a good night." The dickhead said it like he didn't plan to see George again until morning.

"You too, sir," George replied.

I waited until Pres was on the elevator and George turned to grab his coffee thermos off the back counter before I skirted out from behind the large plant and exited through the door. Feeling like fifteen kinds of foolish, I walked up the sidewalk to the same area Geoff had dropped me off on Friday night before I bumped into the guy who'd be sharing Ezra's bed. It took everything I had not to lose my shit and sob like the brokenhearted sucker I was. I told myself not to keep watching the door to Ezra's building because I was sure big and British wasn't coming back out anytime soon, but to my surprise, he came back out ten minutes later. I could tell by his body language he wasn't happy about his speedy exit, but I was deliriously so. I'd held back my tears of anguish in the elevator, but tears of relief spilled down my cheeks.

Ezra and I might've fought, but we weren't over until one of us said we were. He might've been drunk and disappointed with me, but Ezra hadn't betrayed me. There was still hope. Maybe in the light of morning, I'd look back and realize I had acted as immature as Ezra accused me of being. One argument didn't mean the end of us, but my heart was still racing, and my stomach was still queasy.

My phone vibrated in my hand, and I saw it was a call from Ezra. "Hey," I said softly.

"Come back, Henry." His voice was as soft as the sponge he loved running over my skin. "Where are you? I'll send a Lyft."

"I'm just down the street from your condo building waiting for Geoff to pick me up," I said.

"Geoff? Why'd you call him?"

My body stiffened with tension. "Because money is tight right now, and walking home isn't an option. It's okay for you to get drunk with a *friend*, but I can't call one of mine when I need a ride?"

"That isn't what I meant. I don't want to fight. I just want to hold you. Please?"

The idea of calling Geoff and telling him to never mind felt wrong. The tone for another incoming call sounded in my ear. I pulled the phone away from my ear and saw it was Geoff. "Geoff's calling me now, Ezra. Let me find out how close he is because I'm not going to drag him out of bed to get me then just tell him to turn around. Geoff might not answer next time I need help."

"There won't be a next time, baby," Ezra said firmly then hung up.

I tapped the accept button for Geoff's call and said, "Hey, Geoff."

"Please don't kill me, Henry, but I'm not going to be able to pick you up. My car is blocked in, and I can't find my mom's keys to move her car. Waking my parents up to ask for the keys isn't an option."

"It's okay. I'll just go back to Ezra's apartment. I'm sorry I bothered you."

"You're not bothering me. Are you sure you're okay with going back to Ezra's? I can order a Lyft for you on my app."

"No, buddy. I'm fine. I love you for it though."

"I love you too, Henry. Call or text me tomorrow to let me know you're okay."

I chuckled. "Ezra isn't dangerous."

"Tell that to your heart," Geoff said soberly.

I swallowed hard because he might not be wrong. "Everything will be okay," I said, unsure if I was trying to assure him or myself. "I'll text you tomorrow."

"Goodnight, Henry."

"Goodnight, Geoff."

I disconnected the call, slipped my phone in my pocket, then turned to walk back to Ezra's condo. I stopped in my tracks because the man I loved had decided not to wait and came looking for me. My heart raced as I walked toward him. Ezra opened his arms when I reached him, and I flung myself against his chest.

"I'm so sorry, baby," Ezra said, rocking me side to side. "Alcohol and I aren't a good mix, which is why I never drink. I'm too fucking old for peer pressure, so I have no excuse for my behavior. Please forgive me, Henry."

"I'm sorry too for overreacting," I said. "I don't want to be the guy who gets jealous when you do something with colleagues and friends."

"You mean like I do?" Ezra teased.

I pulled back and looked into his eyes. "You're not so bad."

Ezra leaned in to kiss me, but I flinched away, not wanting to taste the alcohol on his tongue. Smiling, Ezra said, "I brushed my teeth and gargled with mouthwash."

I pressed my lips to his without hesitation, loving the taste of fresh mint and Ezra. "Much better," I whispered after a long, lazy kiss.

"Let's go home," Ezra said, wrapping his arm around my waist and guiding me toward his condo. "You can take a nice shower while I make you an omelet. We'll get a good night's sleep, then I can tell you about the surprise I planned for us."

"Sounds perfect. Thank you."

"Thank you for coming back."

"There's no place I'd rather be."

Chapter Twenty-Two

Ezra

FEATHER-LIGHT KISSES ON THE BACK OF MY NECK TEASED ME TOWARD consciousness. At first, the butterfly-wing touches made me moan for more, but the moans turned to whimpers when I was alert enough to feel the street work going on inside my skull. Jackhammers dug into my brain, the vibrations sending misery through every part of my body. My limbs felt tight with tension like a rubber band about to snap, and my stomach pitched and rolled like I was at sea.

"Feeling rough?" Henry's voice was whispery-soft, but in my current state, he might as well have yelled in my ear.

"I'm dying," I whined. "This horrible morning-after feeling is the reason I don't drink."

"Are you sure it's not because you turn into a complete dickhead?"

"Yeah, there's that too. Henry, please tell me I got down on my knees and begged you for forgiveness last night."

"Groveling from your knees wasn't needed or wanted. You said you were sorry, and you meant it, which was all I needed."

"Ryder would say the situation called for a grand gesture," I said, carefully shifting closer into the big spoon Henry had formed behind me. The warmth of his bare skin was starting to make me feel so much better.

"Grand gesture?"

"It's the part in a romance novel where the dumbass hero has to step up his game and prove that he's both in love with his guy *and* worthy of his guy's love in return. According to Ryder, it follows an epic display of dumbass fuckery."

"You think last night qualifies as an epic display of dumbass fuckery?" Henry asked with a smile in his voice.

"Well, it's my biggest display so far, and you were nearly in tears when you left after I treated you horribly. It feels like an epic fuckery to me. I think there needs to be a grand gesture." I wiggled my ass against Henry's erection a little too enthusiastically then moaned when the jostling triggered another jackhammer session in my skull.

Henry chuckled softly then placed more kisses along the side of my neck while gliding his hand over my chest and abdomen, slowly inching to where I needed to feel him the most. "I don't think you're in any condition for *grand gestures* this morning."

"Maybe if enough blood floods south to fill my cock, it would relieve the pressure and misery in my brain. I think it's worth experimenting for the sake of science. Fuck me, Henry."

"You want me to slide my dick inside you for the sake of science?" Henry asked. "Or is relinquishing your control to me part of your *grand gesture*?" Henry slid his fingers down to tease the tightly trimmed curls at the base of my cock—his fingertips just grazing my thickening flesh.

"Both?" I replied breathlessly, pushing my ass against him more.

Henry licked a path up my neck then bit down on my earlobe. "Are you asking me or telling me?"

"Please, Henry," I whimpered. "Make it better."

And he did. His hands alternated between loving caresses and teasing touches as he worshipped my body. Henry only separated from me long enough to retrieve the lube and condoms from the bedside table drawer. I hated the chill that washed over my body during his brief absence, but he chased it away when he pressed his hot flesh up against mine once more.

"You're mine, Ezra. I need to hear you say it," Henry growled in my ear when he slid the first lubed finger inside me.

I gasped from both the intrusion and the possessiveness I heard in his voice. "Is that how I sound?"

"Like you could rip the limbs off anyone who dares touch me?" Henry asked. "Yes, that's how you sound."

God, it was true. Something about Henry triggered those primal urges deep inside me, and I acted on instinct instead of intellect. My need for Henry to belong to me sometimes frightened me. I'd been in love before, but my feelings for Henry were so much more intense, which increased the potential for devastating heartbreak. The stronger you loved, the deeper it hurt when everything exploded in your face.

Needing to steer myself away from morose thoughts that only made my head pound harder, I said, "At least I don't pee on your leg."

Henry's finger stilled inside me then retreated. "You think that's funny?" he whispered.

"A little b—Oh!" I gasped when Henry inserted two fingers inside my tight clench and pegged my prostate. "Baby, that's no way to discourage me."

"What if I finger your ass until you're nearly on the edge of orgasm then remember I have to be at work in twenty minutes?"

"I'm sorry," I said in a rush. "I take it back."

Henry's laughter rumbled through his chest, vibrating both of us. "That's more like it."

He took his time stretching me open before suiting up. "Need you now," I moaned when I didn't think I could take any more. Instead of rolling me to my back, Henry maintained our spoon position, bending my top leg up a little higher than the bottom for better access.

"Nice and easy," Henry whispered, pressing his cock against my entrance. It was only his second time topping, but Henry entered me with the smooth confidence of a practiced lover. Love did that to a person, and our bodies recognized our bond even if we never exchanged the words out loud.

"Yesss," I whimpered, fisting the pillow. The slow, slick glide in and out while Henry anchored me to him with a tight grip on my hip was pure perfection.

"Lazy morning sex for the win," Henry said before nipping at the sensitive flesh beneath my ear.

"Won't last long. Need your lips," I gritted. Turning my head, I gripped Henry's hair and pulled him to me for a hot, wet kiss.

Henry slid his hand from my hip up to tease my nipples while caressing my overly sensitized rim with a finger from his other hand, sending my pleasure sensors into overload. I released my grip on Henry's hair to fist my cock.

Henry broke our kiss. "Huh-uh," he said, knocking my hand away. "I'm in charge of your pleasure." Henry wrapped his fist tightly around the base of my cock, and I returned my hand to his hair, tugging the messy strands while whimpering against his lips. "You ready to come?"

"Please."

"Maybe," Henry said.

Dirty words, teasing touches, and the hottest kiss followed. I'd taught Henry many ways to please me, and he used all of them to rip the orgasm right from me, leaving me a shaking, spurting mess of a man. God, I loved what he did to me.

"That was the grandest of gestures," Henry said, lightly smacking my ass while easing his spent dick from inside me. "How about a science report. Do you feel better?"

"You have to ask?" I inquired, gesturing to my impersonation of a limp noodle draped across my bed.

Henry groaned. "I have to get up and get ready for work." He dropped a kiss on my shoulder then moved to get off the bed.

"Wait. Don't go yet. I have a grand gesture for you."

"Again? So much for Jess's joke about your recovery time," Henry teased. "I would much rather lounge around in bed with you all day, but it's not a fantasy I can fulfill today."

I rolled over and faced him. "My grand gesture isn't sex; it's a weekend getaway to Kelley's Island. I've rented a lake house for us. Four days of sun, water, food, and sex. We can spend as much time lounging in bed as we want."

Henry's smile was brighter than the sun streaming through the windows. "When?"

"This weekend. I wanted to surprise you with my plans for a Labor Day getaway last night but…well, you know what epic fuckery that was. Even better, we're taking my dad's Aston Martin." Henry's face fell, and he looked like he was on the verge of tears. "Baby, what's wrong?"

"I can't go this weekend, Ezra. I promised Maria I would pick up extra shifts because she has several people taking vacations. I don't want her working herself into an early grave because she's too kind-hearted to tell people no when she should. I'm so sorry."

"Surely, someone else can cover," I said. "How many pizza orders will there be this weekend? I wouldn't think she'd have a lot of dine-in guests either since everyone is at the river celebrating the last weekend of summer."

"It's one of her busiest weekends, and I can't—I won't—abandon her. Not the woman who sat beside me on the cold bathroom floor at Ryan's Place and lovingly washed my face with a cool, wet cloth when I was reeling from the side effects of my HIV meds. Maria means too much to me. I'm sorry, Ezra. I know I have a lot of baggage dragging me down, but—"

Moving quicker than was smart, I lunged across the bed and gathered him into my arms. "Don't you ever talk like that again, Henry. Never apologize for loving someone who selflessly cared for you when you were so sick. Never. Don't feel bad because I was pouting like a spoiled brat. We'll still spend the weekend together, and I promise you, it will be amazing."

I hated the doubt still lingering in the green eyes I loved so much. Words alone wouldn't be enough to chase it away. I needed actions and kisses. *Lots and lots of kisses starting right now.*

By the time Henry was dressed for work, all I saw when I looked in his eyes was adoration and reluctance to leave the happy bubble of my condo. Unwilling to listen to any of his protests, I drove Henry to work and cherished the long goodbye kiss he gave me before he exited the car. It was a temporary victory, and I began working on plans for a permanent one the second Henry stepped inside the doors of Hastings Law.

Chapter Twenty-Three

Henry

I STRESSED MYSELF SILLY OVER THE NEXT FEW DAYS, WORRYING EZRA would regret dating someone as unsophisticated as I was. Age difference aside, I couldn't just drop everything and leave for weekend trips every time he got the whim. I planned to scale back my hours at the pizzeria once school resumed, but until then, Maria needed me, and I desperately needed the extra income.

Ezra had been very understanding Tuesday morning when I'd told him I couldn't go on the trip with him, but I figured his empathy might fade the closer we got to the weekend. I'd never dreaded movie night before, but my hands shook when I unlocked his condo door with *my* key. I had convinced myself Ezra would resent me for ruining what sounded like a perfect vacation.

"You should go without me," I told him over the spaghetti and meatballs he'd made for dinner. Dread had filled me to the point where I couldn't even enjoy the thoughtful meal he'd made.

Ezra set down his fork and gave me an odd look. "By myself? What fun would that be?"

Ezra's happiness meant more to me than my own, which was the only reason I opened my mouth and said, "Maybe one of your friends is available. That Pres guy is new to town. It's doubtful he's made many friends." The idea made me want to vomit, but I wanted Ezra to be happy.

"He's made *plenty* of friends," Ezra quipped. "Besides, I don't want to go if you're not with me. I made the plans for *us*. I know better to plan ahead for next time."

Please let there be a next time. "Ezra, I don't want you to resent me."

"Never going to happen, baby." He sounded so sure, and I wanted to believe him. "I have some amazing things planned around your work schedule this weekend. Do you trust me, Henry?"

"I do."

"Then relax, eat your meatballs and sauce, and get ready for one of my favorite movies."

"*Pretty Woman?*" I asked forty-five minutes later when I was cuddled up beside him. "One of your favorite movies is about a prostitute?"

"She has a heart of gold," Ezra countered with a cheesy grin. "Come on; it's a classic."

"I love the movie, but I'm surprised you do."

"I'm full of surprises, Henry."

The stress of the week caught up to me, and I crashed hard not long after the movie started. Ezra woke me up with adorable kisses on my face.

"You're about to miss one of the best grand gestures in romantic comedies ever," Ezra whispered in my ear. I'd sprawled across his chest at some point, pinning him to the sofa. The firm hold he had on me indicated he wasn't the least bit put out that I'd used him as a human pillow.

"Climbing up the fire escape took balls," I said sleepily. "It doesn't look quite as rickety as mine."

Ezra's warm chuckle vibrated in his chest beneath my ear, lulling me back to sleep. I didn't know how much time passed before he woke me up again so we could get to bed. We didn't have sex on

Friday night, and he was sleeping too peacefully for me to disturb him when I woke up early the next morning to get a workout in before my shift at Maria's.

By the time I arrived at the pizzeria, I was feeling better than I had all week. Ezra hadn't been hiding his disappointment all week to make me feel better, and he was excited about the alternative plans he'd made for us. I loved being the first person to arrive because I enjoyed listening to music while prepping for the day. When "I Like Me Better" by Lauv came on the radio, I turned it up and started dancing around and singing while filling the ingredient tubs for our assembly line. I felt lighter than air as I swayed to my favorite song. When I executed a cute little spin move, I realized I wasn't alone.

Ezra leaned in the doorway watching me with a huge smile on his face. I was so happy to see him that it took me a second to realize he was wearing the same uniform as mine: green polo shirt with the Mamma Maria's logo stitched up by the left shoulder and a pair of black jeans.

"What are you doing here?" I asked, sounding a little breathless from dancing.

"You're here," was Ezra's reply. "You must really like this song. I've never seen you dance so freely. Not even at the club when we met."

"The words move me," I admitted. "They remind me of us."

"Really?" Ezra asked, straightening to his full height and stepping toward me.

"Really," I said, crossing the room to meet him halfway. "I like me better when I'm with you, Ezra." He sucked in a sharp breath, and I wondered if he thought the sentiment was too silly or too soon, but then a huge smile rivaling the Joker's spread across his face. "That looks almost painful," I said, reaching up to trace his lips with my index finger.

"Hurts so good," Ezra replied, nipping the tip of my finger.

I was quickly losing my ability to think about anything except getting Ezra naked, so I reined in my thoughts. "You told me what you're doing here but not the why you're here."

"The answer is the same. You're here, and I want to be with you."

"That required you to borrow a uniform?" I asked with a raised brow.

"This is *my* uniform," Ezra corrected. "Maria trained me this week while you were working for Des. I earned the uniform yesterday afternoon. I think she told me I was one of her best trainees."

"You trained to work here at Mamma Maria's?" I still couldn't believe what I was hearing. I had to be dreaming. "Why? And please don't say it's because I'm here."

"Maria is important to you, so she's important to me too. You said she needed help, and I wanted to help her while spending time with you. I'm donating my weekend earnings to a charity of her choosing."

"This is the big surprise you had planned?" I asked incredulously.

"This is only one surprise," Ezra countered. "You're not upset, are you?"

"Upset that you used your last few days off before school resumes to learn the ins and outs of working at a pizzeria just so you could help out a person I love like a mother?" I asked.

"Well, when you put it like that, my actions do sound pretty cool."

"Pretty cool?" I asked. "Try fucking awesome. Hell no, I'm not mad."

"Good," Ezra said with relief. "It felt like I was intruding into your world a little bit, and now Mamma Maria's is one less place I haven't touched."

I waggled my eyebrows. "I want you to touch me everywhere," I said. Ezra responded with a deep, long kiss that made my blood hum.

"Okay, you two," Maria said when she walked through the rear door a few minutes later. "I can see I'll need to keep you separated today. Ezra, if you can behave, I'll allow you to help Henry set out the food prep stations. If you can't be trusted, there's plenty of other things to do in the dining room. The napkin holders on each table need refilling, as well as the Parmesan cheese and red pepper flake shakers."

Ezra winked at me then smiled over my head at Maria. "I can't be trusted to behave."

Maria laughed. "That's what I thought. You get extra points for honesty. Do you remember where I store the napkins, Parmesan, and red pepper flakes?"

"Yes, ma'am," Ezra told Maria.

"Get to it then. After that, I'll need you to check the straws, lids, and cups."

"On it." Ezra saluted her then dropped a kiss on my forehead before heading to the supply closet.

Maria walked over to me and pulled me into a hug. "He's a keeper, Henry," she said.

"He is," I agreed.

"What do you mean, you've never slept in a tent," Ezra said eight hours later when we were in his car headed to his parents' house. "What about church camp?"

"We had rustic cabins with rickety bunk beds. Damn things squeaked something fierce if you tried sneaking in someone else's bed or even took care of your own business privately."

"You like to rile me up deliberately and make me jealous, don't you?" Ezra asked.

"You're jealous of my fist?" I asked in disbelief.

Ezra snorted. "Have you forgotten your confession about losing your virginity to Geoff at church camp?"

"No, but it didn't happen in a cabin we shared with ten other boys."

"Then how do you know about the squeaky sounds the beds made when boys climbed into bed with other boys? And where did Geoffrey debauch you?"

"Debauch?" I asked. "Have you helped yourself to Jess's historical romance novels?"

"Are you avoiding my questions by asking your own?" Ezra challenged.

"I don't want you to think poorly of me," I said.

"Never going to happen, baby," Ezra said with a confidence I didn't feel.

"We used the guest pastor's office, which happened to be Geoff's dad during our week at camp."

"Whoa," Ezra said. "That's an interesting form of lashing out against tyrannical parents."

"Pastor Daily would kill us both if he ever found out," I said, sheepishly.

"He won't touch a hair on either of your heads," Ezra replied fiercely. "Jesus, I can't imagine growing up in the kinds of homes you did."

"We didn't know there was another world out there," I said with a shrug. "We were homeschooled and were only allowed to socialize with other kids from our church. No cable television, video games, cell phones, or internet were permitted in our homes. When I finally found some freedom after I went to bible college, I went a little wild. My act of rebellion is something I'll have to manage for the rest of my life." It amazed me how far I'd come in a year. I could think and even speak about having HIV without self-loathing following, and none of it would be possible without the remarkable people around me, including the guy gripping my hand as if I might float away. "That's enough heavy talk," I said. "I'm looking forward to camping up on the ridge with you tonight. I noticed you only packed one sleeping bag."

"Busted," Ezra said sheepishly. "I can borrow an extra sleeping bag from my parents if sharing one with me is too much cuddling for you."

I chuckled. "I practically sleep on top of you as it is."

"I like it that way," Ezra purred.

The Meyers' farm was every bit as beautiful during my second visit, maybe more so because I'd seen the true beauty of the people residing inside it. It was dinnertime when we arrived, so we shared a meal of delicious smoked beef brisket with all the trimmings with Ezra's parents before he led me to the barn and taught me how to saddle Bourbon Baby.

Ezra kissed my cheek when we finished and said, "Grip the saddle horn with your left hand, put your left foot in the stirrup, then pull yourself up and swing your right leg over the saddle."

"Where's your horse?" I asked.

"I thought we'd ride Bourbon Baby together since you're new to horseback riding."

"Oh, how Kip and Clarissa of you," I said, batting my eyelashes playfully.

"I bet I can make you scream up on that ridge in ways good ole Kipster can only dream about," Ezra said smugly.

"He's mostly talk," I agreed. "You're a man of action."

"You got that right. Ready?" Ezra asked.

"I hope I don't make a fool of myself," I said nervously.

"No one will laugh at you here, Henry. I promise."

I replayed his instructions in my head then awkwardly seated myself on the saddle. Bourbon Baby took a couple of steps, and I tensed up. "What's she doing?"

"She's responding to your nervousness, baby. Relax and breathe. I still have the reins. Bourbon Baby isn't going to bolt with you on her back."

"She's a retired racehorse," I pointed out. "Bolting is what she does best."

"She wasn't a very good racehorse if that helps." Bourbon Baby nickered like she understood what Ezra said.

"Way to piss off our horse, Ezra."

"She's not mad," he said, rubbing her velvety nose and cooing to her. "She knows she's the most beautiful girl in the world. She would've been the best racehorse in the country had it not been for lackluster training, isn't that right, Baby?" Bourbon Baby's ears twitched, and she tossed her head a little from side to side. "She said yes."

"Climb up on here, and let's get to it before I lose my nerve."

Ezra grinned wickedly. "I love it when you talk dirty to me." He quickly climbed up behind me with the natural grace he exuded in everything he did. Unsure where to put my hands, I held on to Ezra's thighs. "I like this a whole lot," he murmured in my ear. Then he clicked his tongue and gave the reins a light tug. I gasped and tensed when Bourbon Baby started an easy trot but relaxed into Ezra's body and enjoyed the ride.

Ezra guided the horse down several trails through the rolling, dense woodland. He showed me a creek on one trail which turned into a small waterfall farther down on another one. Birds and tree frogs serenaded us during our adventure, making me feel like we were two princes in our own private kingdom. When dusk approached, Ezra guided us back toward the homestead.

"Would you like to take over the reins?" he asked. "Bourbon Baby is gentle, kind, and very patient."

"Sounds like someone else I know."

"Brat." Ezra's breath ghosted over my ear, making me shiver.

"I'd love for you to teach me."

Ezra showed me the best way to grip the reins and demonstrated how to steer her in the direction we wanted her to go. "Some horses need a firm hand, but Baby doesn't. Try it," he said encouragingly.

I held the reins firmly but gently in my hands then clicked my tongue like Ezra had done when he wanted her to get going. Bourbon Baby started on an easy trot, and I couldn't stifle the joy I felt. She followed my commands to go right, left, and stop.

"You got it," Ezra said proudly, tightening his hold around my waist. "Let's head back to the barn, so we can untack Baby and give her some TLC then pack the Wolverine for our trip up to the ridge."

"I can't wait."

We gave Baby plenty of water then removed her tack before giving her a thorough brushing, first with a sweat scraper then two other types of combs and brushes before Ezra was satisfied she was properly cared for. Ezra looked like he was packing the Wolverine for a weeklong camping trip instead of an overnight sleepover on the ridge.

"This looks so *Red Dawn*," I said.

Ezra looked up from arranging all the stuff in the cargo hold in the rear. "Original or remake?"

"Um, original. Swayze, duh."

"Good call," Ezra said then shrugged. "I like to be prepared for contingencies."

"Such as?" I asked, picturing marauding bears or a swarm of bloodsucking mosquitos.

"S'mores." Ezra packed a hell of a lot more than ingredients for s'mores. He tossed me the keys to the Wolverine then headed to the passenger seat. "By now, you know I love it when you drive."

Driving up to the ridge felt a lot more dangerous than coming back down, especially when I realized how dark it got in the woods even before the sun fully set. Ezra told me where to find the switch for the headlights, which eased my nerves a lot. I parked about the same place Ezra had the last time, and we backpacked the goods the rest of the way.

"Okay, maybe I packed more than we needed," Ezra said after the third trip.

"I'll forgive you once I'm holding a s'more in my hand."

We worked together pitching the tent, then Ezra rolled out memory foam to lay in the bottom, which would provide a nice cushion for sleeping. "I bought Coleman LED citronella lanterns. They illuminate the dark with pretty colors and keep the mosquitos away. You know how they like to bite my ass."

"You have plans to expose your bare ass to the night air?" I teased.

Ezra winked in the fading light. "The tent is for sleeping only, Henry. I'm going to lay you out beneath the stars and… Oomph." I tackled him to the hard ground and straddled his hips. "I thought you wanted s'mores."

"Later. I have something important I need to tell you." Suddenly, my nerve left me while Ezra lay smiling up at me with anticipation.

Ezra cupped my cheek tenderly. "Ditto."

I narrowed my eyes suspiciously. "You don't even know what I was going to say."

"I do too."

"What?" I challenged.

Ezra smiled smugly. "You were going to admit you're in love with me."

"And your response was ditto?" I asked in disbelief. It sounded familiar like a scene from a movie I'd watched with Esther and Archie. "Oh my God, Ezra. Were you quoting *Ghost*?"

"'Swayze, duh.' I was trying to ease your nerves. Wanna try it again?"

"I'm not really in the mood for a confession now," I said with a sniff.

"I bet I can get you in the mood again," Ezra said, rolling me over on my back so fast it left me breathless. "Feeling shy? I'll go first. You are everything I've searched for in a partner but never found. You make me see things in a different light, and I want to spend every day making the world a better place for you. I love you, Henry."

"Wow," I whispered as tears pooled in my eyes.

"Pretty epic, huh?"

His smugness made me laugh, and it loosened my tongue. "You make me feel like I can be and do anything my heart desires. I'm proud of who I am when I'm with you. You had me at 'Hello, Henry.' I love you so much, Ezra."

Salty kisses turned into moans of pleasure as Ezra made sweet love to me under the setting sun in our private paradise. Afterward, we toasted marshmallows on the mini propane stove for s'mores and took turns telling the silliest ghost stories that still managed to keep me awake long after Ezra fell asleep in our shared sleeping bag. With a mild night and no sign of bad weather, we decided that sleeping under the stars sounded romantic. And it did until every rustling tree in the wind made me think one of Ezra's killer ghosts was going to get me.

"I can't sleep with your heart pounding so hard against my back," Ezra whispered before he rolled over and faced me. "Do you want to go back down the ridge? We could crash in one of my parents' guest rooms."

"And ruin your plans? No way," I said passionately. "I just need you to exhaust me so I can fall into a deep sleep."

"Would you like to discuss quantum physics?"

"I said exhaust me, not bore me," I countered.

Ezra chuckled against my neck then rolled until I was pinned beneath him once more. Instead of parting my thighs and fucking me, Ezra unzipped the sleeping bag to give him enough room to ride my cock until we were lying together in a quivering heap.

"That's the trick," I whispered sleepily. Ezra chuckled as he removed the condom from my spent dick and cleaned us both up before nestling against me once more. If the ghosts were going to get me in my sleep, at least I would die knowing I was truly loved for the first time in my life.

Chapter Twenty-Four

Ezra

"**D**O YOU NEED ANYTHING ELSE BEFORE I GO TO LUNCH, DR. Meyer?" Beatrice asked.

I looked up from my desk and found her standing in the open doorway. Beatrice was everything Regina had described her as and more. I was confident we were going to work great together.

"I'm good here," I replied with a smile.

"Would you like me to bring you anything?" she asked.

"I'm meeting a colleague for lunch soon but thank you for your offer."

Beatrice smiled like she wanted to say something but wasn't sure she should.

"Is something wrong?" I asked.

"Wrong? No. I just wanted to say I'm happy to assist you this year. There are already issues between teaching assistants and their professors. I'm relieved we're not among them."

I glanced at my watch and said, "Already? It's not even noon yet." I hoped my joke hid the worry brewing in my mind. Was Henry among the teaching assistants having issues with their professors? Surely not. I was confident he and Meghan would make a great team.

"Already," Beatrice confirmed. "I think everything has settled down now that a few professors have swapped assistants."

"I'm glad things are working out well for us too," I said with a friendly smile. "Enjoy your lunch."

I discreetly looked for Henry as I made my way to Pres's office. I wouldn't pull him aside to have a private conversation, but I'd be able to tell how his day was going with one quick look. The man I loved would be a horrible poker player. I was disappointed when I didn't spot him anywhere. Pres's door was closed, but I knew I hadn't missed him because I could hear him talking inside his office.

"Come in," Pres called out after I knocked on his door.

I inhaled a deep breath then released it before plastering the happiest smile I could muster on my face. Prescott hadn't been pleased with me when I hadn't asked him into my condo the previous week, and even more unhappy I'd turned down his weekend invites. I'd told him once I had plans with my boyfriend, but that didn't seem to bother him. I had the impression Pres wanted me and whatever anyone else wanted was inconsequential to him. Asking him to have lunch with me felt like the right thing to do if I wanted to maintain our friendship. While the jury was still out on that one, I didn't want to risk burning my bridges too soon.

My smile faded when I opened the door and stepped inside Pres's office. He and his teaching assistant looked at me with very different expressions on their faces. Pres looked delighted to see me and spent an unusually long time raking his eyes over my business casual attire. He acted as if he'd never seen me in anything besides a suit. Pres's teaching assistant, on the other hand, glared at me.

"Ezra, I believe you already know Henry Sullivan?" Pres said jovially. Too jovially for my liking, and I grew suspicious. Did he know my true relationship with Henry, or was he saying that because I was the one who recommended Henry for the job? "As you know, Henry was supposed to be working with Professor Millstone, but my assistant took one look at me and freaked out."

"Because?" I asked.

"My size made her uncomfortable, but she was too worried about insulting me to request a change. The last thing I need is an assistant who is afraid to be alone with me, so I talked to Regina this morning. And now I have Henry," Pres said with an unreadable expression on his face.

"It's good to see you again, Mr. Sullivan," I said, walking toward Henry with an outstretched hand.

Henry's stricken expression made me sick to my stomach, but luckily, he masked his anguish before Pres could see it. He accepted my hand, gave me a weak smile, and said, "Likewise, Dr. Meyer."

I fucking hated the formality and the awkwardness thickening the air around us. "Pres, are you ready? I have a lot to do, and I have an appointment later this afternoon I can't miss." My *appointment* was a trip to Kings Island with Henry. I wanted to be with him as much as I could before school started and occupied most of his time.

"We wouldn't want that," Pres said dryly, looking between Henry and me. He *did* know, but I wasn't sure how.

Picking up on Pres's mood, Henry stiffened and looked at me with wide eyes, begging me to believe he hadn't betrayed us. I fucking hated the situation we were in but felt powerless to do anything about it. Gathering his binder slash planner up from Pres's desk, Henry looked at Pres. "Is there anything else you need from me, Professor Stone?"

"That's right," Pres said, nodding. "You also have an appointment this afternoon you can't miss. Um." Pres paused like he was thinking. "I can't think of anything, but I'll email you if I do." Pres smiled at Henry, but it was brittle instead of friendly. Then he turned toward me with barely concealed disappointment, which made me want to back out of our plans. I knew it was better to get the conversation over with. "Not again," he muttered when he passed by me on his way out the door. A darted glance in Henry's direction let me know he heard it too and was jumping to all kinds of conclusions.

I wanted to stay and clear things up with Henry, but Pres felt like a ticking time bomb that needed diffusing first. "I'll explain later," I said, begging for Henry's understanding. Tears filled his eyes, but he nodded. I turned quickly and caught up to Pres down the hallway.

Pres maintained a brisk pace when he set off for Dante's Bistro, and because of the difference in our heights, I practically had to jog to keep up with him.

"Are we going to talk about what's bothering you?" I asked, trying to make small talk.

Pres looked around and made sure no one was within hearing distance. "I cannot believe you, Ezra. Of all people, you know better than to get involved with a student. Wasn't the fallout in Connecticut bad enough for you, or are you a fucking masochist?"

"The situations aren't at all the same, Pres," I said.

Prescott stopped suddenly and stared down at me, anger radiating from him. "A professor fucking a student spells disaster, Ezra. Always. You know this."

"It's different with Henry."

Pres rolled his eyes and kept walking. "Like I've never heard that one before. You're the worst fucking kind of hypocrite, Ezra. Rationalizing your actions to justify plowing a sweet, tight hole."

"Watch how you fucking talk about Henry, Pres. I love him."

Pres released a harsh breath. "I think I'm going to be sick. How stupid can you be?"

"You're sick with jealousy," I hissed. "You thought this was the chance for us you've been waiting for, Pres. Don't bother denying it. You've been coming on to me since the night of the faculty meeting, not wanting to take no for an answer."

"Fuck you, Ezra," Pres growled then stormed off toward the bistro.

"Don't you hurt him, Pres," I called after him.

Pres stuttered to a stop then pivoted to face me. "The fact you think me capable of such pettiness shows me just how wrong I was about you." Pres shook his head when I didn't comment further, then turned and walked away again.

I didn't call after him even though his parting shot struck a bull's-eye, nailing me right in the heart. Rather than walk to a different restaurant, I headed to the cafeteria to pick up a sandwich, chips, and a soda to take back to my office. I wanted to be alone until it was time for me to meet Henry at my condo to change clothes and head out for an afternoon and evening of fun. *Like Henry wants to go anywhere with you now after that shit show.*

Up ahead in the hallway, I saw Henry duck into a bathroom. Knowing it was probably a mistake, I casually altered my course and entered behind him a minute later. Henry's eyes widened when our gazes met in the mirror. It felt like déjà vu.

"Are you okay, Henry?" I asked after confirming we were alone.

He briefly closed his eyes and shook his head. "No, Ezra, I'm not okay."

"I know you heard what Pres said, and you're jumping to conclusions—wrong ones, I might add."

"He didn't mean to imply that this isn't the first time you had an affair with a student?" Henry boldly asked.

"Please keep your voice down," I begged. "I've never had an affair with a student, Henry. That isn't at all what Pres meant."

"Then what did he mean?" he asked angrily.

"We can't do this here, Henry," I whispered.

"We shouldn't be doing *this* anywhere." Henry's voice registered his disgust, but I wasn't letting him give up so easily.

"I'm going to send an email to Beatrice to let her know I'm leaving early to take care of important matters. I expect to see you at my condo within an hour so we can work this out, Henry," I said firmly.

His brow shot up. "And if I don't show?"

"There's no place you can hide where I won't find you." My voice was low but firm, letting him know I wouldn't budge. I closed the distance between us, relishing the way Henry's body trembled from my proximity.

"You fight so dirty," Henry whispered, lips trembling. "You know I can't resist that voice."

"I love you, Henry. I'll fight any way it takes to keep you." I took every ounce of restraint I had to prevent me from pulling him into my arms and kissing him. "One hour."

Henry nodded, and I left before my control snapped.

I shot an email to Beatrice then packed my briefcase with my laptop and the files I'd been reviewing before my failed attempt at lunch. I didn't realize how hungry I was until I reached my condo. It was doubtful Henry had eaten either, so I ordered our favorite soups and paninis from Dante's with a specified delivery time. Then I paced the floors of my condo, waiting for Henry to arrive. I should've told him the truth about what happened in Connecticut when we first started dating but reliving that time in my life wasn't something I liked to do. For Henry, I'd bare my soul because he deserved to have the best, and I couldn't give it to him without coming clean first.

It wasn't long before I heard his key turning the deadbolt. I was relieved I didn't have to track him down, but that died when I saw his expression. Dread? Resignation? Fear? He stood across the expanse of the living room, his body squared and coiled with tension. His fingertips twitched, reminding me of gunslingers facing off against each other at high noon. Was that what we would become? Instead of bullets, we'd shoot angry words at each other. *Fuck no.*

"I'm about to tell you something very personal and hurtful, and I'd prefer to do it while sitting next to you on the sofa instead of squaring off against you across a room." Henry's resolve wavered, and he met me halfway. We sat facing each other on the couch instead of sitting side by side. "I would also like to touch you while I talk. Is that okay?"

"Of course," Henry said thickly.

I laced my fingers through his then leaned forward, touching my forehead to his. "Pres and I taught at the same small university in Connecticut alongside my former fiancé." I paused to let that sink in. Henry tensed, but he didn't say anything. After a few seconds of silence, he squeezed my fingers, encouraging me to continue.

"The three of us were best friends, and Pres was the one I turned to when I discovered Ben was having an affair with a teaching assistant. It wasn't just any teaching assistant; it was *my* teaching assistant, Garrett."

"Ezra, I'm so sorry."

I nodded then blew out a shaky breath, wanting to get the truth all out in the open while I still had the nerve. "Ben knew how I felt about professors having sex with their students, and I thought he shared my same views. I learned how wrong I was when Garrett purposefully left his computer open at his desk, hoping I would see the email exchange between him and Ben who was using a personal email account I didn't know about."

"Oh no," Henry said, scooting closer until his folded legs overlapped mine. "What did you do, Ezra?"

"I was too stunned to say anything to Garrett when he returned from lunch, but I went looking for Ben's secret email account and evidence on his phone later that night while he slept. It wasn't hard hacking the account since he used the same password for everything. What I found was…" I shook my head. More than a year later, the humiliation still stung me.

"You don't have to tell me more if you don't want to, Ezra," Henry rushed to say. "I understand why you were so reluctant to get involved with me. I'm so sorry they hurt you." Henry tugged one of his hands free so he could caress my jaw. "I'd never betray you like he did."

I nodded because I knew he wouldn't. "There's more you need to know so you can understand why Pres is so pissed at me right now."

"He's pissed because he wants what's mine," Henry said fiercely. I suspected he was right, but Pres hadn't admitted it when I'd given him the chance.

"It doesn't matter if he does," I said, rubbing the back of my hand over his cheek. Henry practically purred when he leaned into my touch. "The things I found in Ben's email account shocked me, Henry. Not only did I learn he was having an affair with Garrett, but I also found pictures of them together in the bed I shared with Ben. Garrett was trussed up on our bed with neck ties Ben bought me as gifts. Imagine the horror I felt knowing the tie I'd worn to work that day had been used to tie one of Garrett's ankles to a bedpost."

Henry gasped and tears spilled down his cheeks. "I don't think I want to hear anymore."

Brushing the tears away, I said, "I'm sorry, Henry, but I need you to hear the full story."

"I can't imagine it gets worse," he countered.

"Much worse. Garrett wasn't the only student Ben had cheated with or took pictures of, and I found email exchanges where Ben had suggested these men use sexual favors or send nude pictures of themselves for extra credit when their grades were failing."

Henry gasped, and I knew he was recalling the teasing exchange we shared in my office before we started dating. "I didn't really mean it."

"I know you didn't, Henry." I leaned forward and kissed his trembling lips. "Even if Ben had been joking with the students, it wasn't something I felt comfortable keeping from the university."

"What happened?"

"I printed the emails without the nude photos and turned them into the chancellor. I did it without letting on to Ben or Garrett that I knew anything." I released a huge sigh. "Maybe if I handled it better, the fallout wouldn't have been as disastrous."

"What happened?' Henry asked.

"Garrett threw a cup of hot coffee in my face after getting expelled from school. Ben took his golf clubs to my car while I was having dinner with my parents at the country club later that night. The chancellor had checked the students' grades and test scores against the dates on the emails, and Ben had solicited sexual favors in exchange for better grades. He was fired on the spot and very angry at me. Rumors spread faster than a wildfire, and I couldn't go anywhere without people whispering and looking at me with either pity or contempt. Ben and Garrett took every opportunity to pour gasoline on my broken heart by sending me photos or videos of the two of them together. It was the worse time of my life."

"And Pres fits in where?" Henry asked.

"His friendship helped me through it. Well, his friendship got me drunker than what you witnessed the other night, but the rest of the time he was my rock. He's disappointed in me right now, Henry. He thinks I'm a hypocrite who cast aside my convictions the first time a student caught my eye."

"He's wrong about us," Henry whispered.

"I'm completely in love with you, Henry. Ben abused his position of power for sex. There's nothing similar between the situations there, but Pres isn't completely wrong. I might not have doctored your grades due to our relationship, but I convinced the department chair to hire undergrads as teaching assistants and recommended you for one of the positions."

"Oh no," Henry said. "Why would you take that kind of risk?"

"Because I believe in you and wanted to find ways to help you pay for college. I set this in motion and recommended you for the position before we started dating. Unfortunately, the school won't see it that way. I don't know how to fix this, Henry, but I will."

Henry looked at me with so much sadness in his eyes. "Ezra, maybe we—"

I cut him off by pressing my lips firmly against his. "There has to be a way, and I will find it."

The landline rang in the kitchen. "That's going to be the concierge desk calling to let me know our delivery is here. I haven't eaten, and I was certain you hadn't either."

"No," Henry agreed. "I'm still not feeling that hungry."

"I ordered your favorites from Dante's," I said over my shoulder on the way to the kitchen.

"Maybe I could eat a little," Henry said. "I don't think I'm much interested in going to Kings Island this afternoon though. I think I've had enough roller-coaster rides for a day, even if they were only the emotional kind."

"Those are the worst kind," I said wryly. I picked up the phone and approved sending up the delivery guy. I returned to the couch and squatted beside Henry. "Please give me time to figure something out. Don't give up on us, Henry."

"I won't." Henry smiled, but it didn't quite reach his eyes. Was he afraid to hope? It felt like he was slipping away, and I was powerless to stop it. If there is one thing a control freak hates the most, it's feeling powerless. The only way to take back the power was to come clean to the school about my involvement with Henry. It wasn't going to be easy, but he was worth it.

We are worth it.

Chapter Twenty-Five

Henry

I EXPECTED PROFESSOR STONE TO LECTURE ME, OR EVEN TREAT ME harshly, when I reported to work the following morning, but he didn't. He remained professional, cool, and aloof, even though I felt his eyes on me, watching and judging my every move, hoping I would fuck up so he could point it out to Ezra and say, "See! He's no good for you, and here's the proof." But that wasn't what happened. When I screwed up, he didn't take advantage and rub my nose in it; he calmly told me what I did wrong and showed me how to do it correctly. When I did something right, he praised me.

By Friday afternoon, I relaxed a little. He could be biding his time to say something about my relationship with Ezra, or he could've just decided to mind his own business. I didn't want to think poorly of the man, but I'd seen his body language both before and after he went up to Ezra's condo. He had strode toward the elevator with confidence, clutching Ezra's phone in his hand, thinking it was the key to get him into Ezra's bed. Fast-forward ten minutes later, a dejected and very disappointed man had exited the building with the option of finding a different man to work off his frustrations with or take care of business himself. I hadn't cared which he picked because Ezra had chosen me.

I reminded myself of that whenever I made the mistake of comparing myself to the big Brit. Prescott Stone was sexy, smelled like sin, had a boxer-melting accent, was highly educated, and appeared to have a similar background as Ezra's, which made him the better bet for the long run. The depressing thoughts weighed heavily on me until I reminded myself Ezra loved *me*; he chose *me*.

Even though Professor Stone hadn't acted aggressively, my body was tense from anticipating the anvil that had to be hovering over my head. The only thing standing between me and a crushing blow was a frayed rope that was a few threads away from losing the battle. The thought triggered the memory of Ezra and me watching a marathon of *Bugs Bunny* instead of going to Kings Island. He'd been horrified to learn my parents had deprived me of watching the cartoon because they thought it was too violent.

The memory of what happened afterward made my face heat. I'd heard the term toe-curling sex, but I witnessed it firsthand when my calves were propped up on Ezra's shoulders, giving me a perfect view of my feet when my body tensed just before I came.

I had to bite my lip to keep from giggling in Pres's office when I recalled Ezra quoting the show's closing tagline after he came hard. "'That's all, folks!'"

Knowing I had to get away from Pres's watchful eye, I said, "I'm going to get something to drink. Do you want anything?"

"No, thank you."

The room swayed a bit when I stood up too fast, and I gripped the edge of my desk to steady myself.

"Are you okay, Mr. Sullivan?" Professor Stone asked.

"I think my blood sugar is just a little low. I ate lunch, but it didn't have the right balance between carbs and proteins."

"You sound so much like *him* already," Professor Stone murmured. "Are you diabetic? Is that the emergency ID bracelet you're wearing?"

I looked down at the platinum ID bracelet with my name etched in red on one side and my HIV status on the other. Ezra had given it to me, and I recalled the adoration in his eyes when he secured the clasp before running his finger over my name. Heart thundering in my chest, I dreaded the reaction when I answered Professor Stone's question. I wasn't ashamed; I just didn't want him making trouble for Ezra and me.

"I'm hot trauma is what I am."

"You're beautiful trauma, baby."

I let Ezra's convictions wash over me and chase away the fear. "No, sir, it's to let first responders know I'm HIV positive in case of an emergency." Another thread snapped and the anvil swayed.

I had to give credit where it was due. He could've said many things, any number of them derogatory, but he didn't. He nodded and said, "That's very wise."

"Thank you," I replied, unsure what else the situation called for.

"I'm just about ready to wrap up my workday, so you can too," Professor Stone said. "Will I see you at the dinner tomorrow night? You did get your invitation, right?"

"Yes, sir. Thank you. I'll be there." I had wanted to decline the invitation, but Ezra wouldn't hear it.

Pres rose from his chair and nodded curtly. "I'll see you then."

I don't know what made me do it, but before Professor Stone could reach the door, I blurted out, "How did you know?"

Professor Stone stiffened and turned slowly. I didn't need to be more specific; he knew what I meant. "When I ran into you on the sidewalk down the street from Ezra's, I knew I was looking at a guy who was experiencing the blush of early love. Not paying attention to where he was going and smiling down at his phone like it held the world's best treasures. I didn't know it was Ezra's condo building you were heading to that night. Running into you was just a coincidence, if you believe in them." I wasn't sure I did. "Anyway, I saw you step off the elevator the following Monday evening, but you were too miserable to see me. I didn't know you belonged to Ezra then either until you overheard the conversation between the old guy and me and hid behind the plant to eavesdrop." And I thought I'd been so savvy. My face heated with humiliation. "I could see your reflection in the glass panels of the framed artwork behind the concierge desk."

"His name is George; he's not just some old guy," I said.

"I won't lie to you, Henry. I had every intention of capitalizing on whatever mistake you'd made. I whistled happily riding up in the elevator, knowing I was finally getting my chance. Then Ezra opened his door looking as miserable as you did. He refused to let me in, declined coming out for another drink, and said something about making a grand gesture to make up for epic fuckery. I had no idea what the hell he was talking about, but I knew I had no chance with him that night."

"Then you met me on Tuesday and realized how Ezra and I met."

"I—" Professor Stone released a frustrated sigh and ran his hand through his immaculately styled hair. "It doesn't matter what I *think*, but I *know* this: if you fuck him over in any way, I promise you'll regret it."

Professor Stone looked like he was carved out of stone right then. I'd call him Mount Determination if we were on friendly terms, but we weren't and most likely would never be. "I hear you."

"See you tomorrow night. I assume you have a suit to wear?" he asked, raking his eyes over my body.

"Several," I replied calmly.

He gave me a curt nod and left. I collapsed back down in my chair and laid my head against the cool surface of my small desk in the corner of his office. It was the first easy breath I'd taken all day. It was Friday; movie night. I refused to allow work stress to come between Ezra and me. I pulled out a protein bar and a bottle of water from my backpack to tide me over until dinner then finished up my tasks. I had places to be and people to love.

Ezra was in the kitchen smashing potatoes in a larger serving bowl when I arrived at his condo. "Hello, Henry." *Damn.* How could two words make me want to rip my clothes off?

"Hello, Ezra. Something smells delicious," I said, sniffing the air appreciatively. "What is that?"

"Meatloaf," Ezra said excitedly. "It's my favorite comfort food."

"I think it could become mine too."

"This is my mom's recipe. She's played around and updated many of her recipes over the years, but this one has always stayed the same." Ezra set the potato masher aside and opened the oven. "Perfect." He slid on two oven mitts then pulled the glass baking dish out of the oven and set it on the marble counter.

"Wow. That looks as good as it smells. I've never eaten meatloaf with melted cheese on top."

"Then you haven't really lived," Ezra said, dropping the oven mitts. He pulled me to him for a kiss. "Welcome home, baby."

It wasn't the first time Ezra had referred to his condo as my home, and it never failed to send thrilling shivers down my spine. It made me crave things with him—a shared home and life where hiding our love was no longer necessary and no one could pull us apart. *Maybe someday*, my heart whispered.

"Did you have a good day?" I asked.

"I had a great day," Ezra replied happily. "What about you? Did *you* have a good day?"

I could tell him about the conversation I had with Pres, but it would only make him mad. Well, he might laugh about my ridiculous attempt to hide behind the big plotted plant, but he would find no humor in Pres's warning. I noticed Ezra nibbling on his bottom lip, which was a rare sign of nervousness from him.

"What's wrong?" I asked.

"I have a surprise for you after dinner, but I'm worried you won't like it."

"Ezra, you don't need to keep giving me surprises. I feel bad because I can't afford to do the same thing for you."

He caressed my face. "You can't put a price on the gifts you give me every day."

"Some would argue with that," I replied wryly.

"I meant your beautiful heart. I hope you will love my gift and accept it, but I understand if you don't. I'll return it without an argument."

I kissed his smiling lips then picked up the electric handheld mixer. "Let me finish the mashed potatoes. I did this a lot at home, and I think I'm pretty good at it."

"I'll heat up the green beans then."

I loved cooking with Ezra. It had amazed me how quickly we caught on to one another's quirks and habits. Like everywhere else, we just clicked.

"Oh my God. This *is* the best meatloaf. I'll never eat it without cheese again."

"Thank you. I'll be sure to pass your compliments along to my mother."

We chatted about our day and the plans we'd made for the weekend. I was dreading going to the country club in one of my secondhand suits while everyone else would be decked out in elegant clothes. On the other hand, I was excited to catch glimpses of Ezra in his element. I was eager to see how he mixed and mingled with people. Was he as friendly and relaxed as he was with me, or was he coolly cordial?

After dinner, Ezra took me into his bedroom where a black garment bag lay on his bed. I recognized the name of the men's department store and knew whatever was inside would be gorgeous and expensive.

"Ezra," I said softly.

He silenced further protest with a lingering kiss. "Will you just try it on and see how it feels before you tell me no. Maybe let me snap a picture so I can stare at it on the nights you're not here?"

"Suit porn?" I asked.

"Henry porn," he countered.

I knew I should refuse the gift, but I was dying to see what he picked out for me. "I'll try it on, but I'm not committing to keeping it."

"Fair enough." Ezra walked to the bed and unzipped the garment bag. He removed a charcoal gray suit, lavender shirt, and a lilac-and-gray-plaid tie. There was even a pocket square made from the same fabric as the tie. "What do you think? I picked these colors because they'll look amazing with your green eyes."

"It's a beautiful suit, Ezra."

Truthfully, I'd never owned anything as nice and my fingers twitched to touch the fabric. Was the tie made of silk? Did the shirt feel as soft as it looked? I wanted to wear the suit more than I would've imagined. I wanted to walk into the country club and look like a man who deserved to be on Ezra's arm, even though it wasn't possible yet. If I ever hoped for it to happen, I needed to start setting the stage. The faculty dinner was the perfect place to prove I belonged in his world. Months of joking aside, I really felt like Eliza Doolittle.

"Can I try it on now?" I asked.

"Of course. Would you like any help?"

I shook my head. "Um, would you think it was silly if I wanted you to wait and see me in the suit tomorrow?"

Sensing a victory, Ezra's mouth spread into a wide grin. "If that's what you want. The tailor will make any necessary adjustments in the morning if you feel it doesn't fit comfortably."

"Get out and let me try it on," I said, making a shooing motion.

"Fine. I'll get the movie ready."

Once Ezra left, I undressed and tried on my suit, carefully handling the pieces like they were constructed of the rarest materials. They couldn't be more precious to me if they were. When I finished, I didn't recognize the guy in the mirror. He looked taller, stronger, wiser, and certain of his place in the world. I admired the graceful lines of the suit, marveling at how perfectly it fit my body. After staring at myself for a few minutes, I carefully removed the suit and returned it to the garment bag before hanging it in Ezra's closet.

"Well?" he asked eagerly.

"It's perfect. Thank you."

"You're welcome, Henry. Ready for the movie? I chose *Buffy the Vampire Slayer*."

I straddled his lap and set the remote control aside. "Not yet."

"What did you have in mind?"

"I have so many emotions building inside me, Ezra. I feel like I'll burst if I don't let them out."

"Baby, you've come to the right place. I know just the thing."

"I just bet you do."

"Wow, this is swanky as hell," Beatrice said from beside me. She'd asked me to attend the dinner as her friend, and I jumped all over the chance. I liked her personality and quick wit, but I adored the way she respected Ezra. He'd chosen his assistant well.

We looked around at the elegantly dressed people socializing and drinking before dinner. I hoped like hell Ezra wasn't drinking. I had a sudden image of me diving across the room and knocking a downright filthy martini from his hand. I stifled the laugh until Ezra could laugh about it with me.

"I feel like a fish out of water," I confessed. I'd strode into the place with confidence until I saw all the people in attendance. I expected a few dozen, but it looked like there were at least a hundred people or more. I didn't spot the one I wanted to see most though.

"You look so handsome, Henry," Beatrice said.

"Thank you, Bea. You look really pretty tonight." She'd been a nervous wreck when she picked me up at my apartment but had relaxed during the drive to the country club.

"I'm ready for yoga pants and an oversized tee," she said. "Add in a glass of wine and a smutty romance book, and I'd call that the perfect night."

"It does sounds great," I admitted. "Well, I wear shorts to yoga instead of tight pants, but the rest is great."

"You're so funny, Henry."

"I try." I bent my arm and offered it to her. "Shall we mingle, milady?"

"Yes, milord," Beatrice said, slipping her arm through mine. "There are a few other teaching assistants hiding over there in the corner. I can hear their knees knocking from over here."

"Sounds like the best place for us to be."

We joined the other assistants standing off to the side and struck up a conversation about our week. I could feel Ezra's eyes on me, but I didn't dare turn around and search the room. My emotions were running too high, and I'd give us both away. Instead, I chatted with my new friends, and after a few minutes, I no longer felt nervous.

When they announced dinner was ready, our little group followed the larger one toward the dining room. I spotted Ezra walking with Regina, or Dr. Bronson, as I knew her. He was completely at ease with her, laughing at whatever story she was telling him. If Ezra wasn't the one keeping a watchful eye, then who was? I turned my head slightly to the right and locked gazes with Prescott Stone. He raised his glass in a silent toast, but I couldn't tell if he was admiring my suit or being a dickhead. Both were a big probability.

Ezra was seated at the far opposite end of the dining room as me. Our eyes connected briefly for a second before someone approached him to say hello. I couldn't stand there staring at him with puppy eyes, so I took my seat and really threw myself into enjoying the night. By the time dinner ended, most people were hitting up the lovely bar for more drinks and either mingling on the grounds or gathering in groups to talk some more.

I'd had two glasses of wine at dinner, which was more than I was used to drinking. I wasn't drunk, but I was warm and feeling a bit buzzed. I just needed a few minutes in cooler air, so I stepped out the French doors and onto the large patio off the back of the country club. There was a set of stairs in the center and off both sides leading to different areas of the sprawling property. I heard hushed, angry voices coming from the steps leading toward the impressive flower gardens. I recognized Ezra's voice and knew I should go back inside and mind my own business, but he was my business.

I treaded lightly down the steps until I could get close enough to make out who he was talking to and what they were arguing about, although I had a pretty good idea.

"You're making a fool of yourself, Ezra," Pres hissed. "You can't keep your eyes off him while he doesn't seem to even notice you're here."

"Keep your voice down, Pres."

"Did you buy your boy his fancy suit?" Pres asked. "Didn't he own anything nice enough to wear? Or do you just like playing dress-up?"

"Shut the fuck up and stop calling him my boy. What's the matter with you?"

"What kind of future can you possibly have with this kid? You jeopardize your job if anyone finds out. How long do you think he's going to settle for being kept a secret? He's an unsophisticated *child*, Ezra. You need a *man* you can be proud of."

"That's you? You're the *man* for me?" Ezra asked snidely.

"I love you, Ezra. I have for a very long time," Pres said, making bile churn in my gut. "Why can't you see we'd be so good together?"

"Listen to me very carefully, Pres, because we're not having this conversation again. I love Henry. I want to be with Henry. I don't care if you approve or not. I would be honored to enter any room with Henry on my arm. My family adores him, and I want a life with him. I'm sorry if that hurts you, Pres, but I've never led you on. I've never pretended to have romantic feelings for you."

"You haven't even tried," Pres countered.

"The feelings are either there or they aren't. Henry is who I want to build my life with. I've already requested a meeting with Regina on Monday morning. I'm going to come clean to her and let the chips fall where they may. This will be the last time I deny what Henry means to me." Tears of joy and relief cascaded down my face.

"You're throwing your life away for a piece of ass—one you can't even fuck raw. What's the point of a monogamous relationship if you can't fill his tight hole with your cum. You really want to settle for wearing condoms for the rest of your life?"

The other comments were ones I'd expected him to say, but I took the last one like a sucker punch to the gut. Pres had used my honesty as a weapon against me. I actually staggered back a few steps until I regained my steps. *Disgusting. Filthy.* I felt like I was going to puke.

"You son of a bitch," Ezra growled. A second later I heard a hard thud followed by a sickening crunch.

"Fuck! I think you broke my nose," Pres yelled.

"You stay the fuck away from him," Ezra yelled.

Snapping out of my self-pity party for one, I dashed around the end of the tall shrubs and found Ezra squared up with his fists at the ready to hit Pres again. The Brit stood a few feet away covering his nose to no avail because blood gushed out from beneath it, spreading down his crisp, white shirt.

"Ezra," I said starkly, running to block him when he advanced on Pres. "What are you doing?" I gripped his biceps hard, hoping to penetrate his rage.

"Fucking up his life," Pres said, his voice sounding nasally beneath his hand.

"Shut up," Ezra and I both yelled at the same time.

"You need to beat his ass a little quieter. I heard you arguing as soon as I stepped outside," I said.

"You two deserve each other," Pres said, stomping toward us. "Don't bother reporting for work on Monday, Henry. You're fired."

"You can't fire me, jackass," I retorted.

"We'll just see about that," he said over his shoulder as he left Ezra and me by ourselves.

"Son of a bitch!" Ezra said, pulling free from my grasp and shaking out his fist. "That hurt. Bastard's square jaw felt like punching concrete."

The reality of the situation hit me. Ezra not only risked his career by getting involved with me, he risked getting arrested for assault because he defended my honor. I loved him more than my next breath, and that meant I needed to let him go.

Reading my expression, Ezra firmly said, "No, Henry." He reached for me, but I stepped away from him. The wounded look from my rejection made me temporarily waver in my decision but hearing rapidly approaching footsteps prodded me to do what was necessary.

"He's not wrong, Ezra. You deserve a man you can be proud of, grow old with, and not have to worry about latex barriers preventing you from getting sick. I can't let you ruin your life for me. I'm not worth it."

"You're worth everything. I love you, Henry. Please don't do this to us," he cried.

"Love isn't always enough. You'll only resent me later." I looked around for another exit when the footsteps got closer. I wouldn't allow him to get caught with me in a compromising position. Spotting a break in the shrubs, I began jogged toward it. "You have to let me go, Ezra," I said over my shoulder.

"Never," he said passionately.

I ducked between the bushes just as I heard Dr. Bronson's voice. "Ezra, what the hell is going on? Did you punch Dr. Stone in the face?"

"He had too much to drink and tripped," Ezra said calmly. "Regina, I don't think our conversation can wait until Monday."

Dr. Bronson let out a long sigh. "Let's go find a drink and quiet corner."

I waited long enough for them to reach the country club before I returned inside. The place was buzzing with excitement, and I figured their imaginations were running wild.

"Henry," Beatrice said. "Did you hear what happened? Dr. Meyer punched Dr. Stone in the face."

"Really? I heard Dr. Stone had too much to drink and tripped."

"Oh," Beatrice said, sounding disappointed. "I guess that makes more sense than mild-mannered Dr. Meyer laying him out." She studied me closely for a second. "Have you been crying?"

"Allergies. I had too much wine and went outside for some fresh air. There are flowers everywhere out there. Beatrice, I hate to ask, but do you think you'll be ready to leave soon?"

"Oh, my friend, I was just about to ask the same. Yoga pants. Wine. Book. I'm dying in this place."

By some miracle, I kept my shit together until I let myself in my apartment. Jess was home on a rare Saturday night. She whistled when she saw my suit, but it turned into an anguished gasp when she saw my face.

"Looks like I'll be kicking his ass after all," Jess said.

I burst into tears and dropped onto the couch beside her, crying my heartache against her shoulder. "Hurts so bad, Jess." She wrapped her arms around me tighter, letting me cry until there was nothing left but dry, wracking sobs.

"It gets better," she whispered against my hair.

I wished I could believe her, but I didn't think this pain would ever go away.

Chapter Twenty-Six

Ezra

REGINA HAD BEEN DISAPPOINTED IN ME WHEN I TOLD HER WHAT happened, but she had also been kind. "This would be so much easier if you were already a tenured professor."

"I know," I'd said with a resigned sigh. "I realize that tenure at UC might be off the table in the future, but there are other universities." Regina had narrowed her eyes. "My mom has a lot of connections at Xavier, and I'm sure she wouldn't mind making some introductions."

"You're willing to leave the university for Henry?"

"I am."

Regina asked me to take the rest of the weekend to think about what I really wanted before I took irreparable actions. I didn't need to think; I knew what I wanted. *Henry.* I agreed to her request because she deserved my respect, and not because I thought my relationship with Henry was over. There was no way in hell we were finished.

"It's not just about what you want," Regina had said, accurately reading my expression. "Did you read the essay Henry wrote when he applied for the teacher's assistant position?"

"No. I wasn't aware an essay was required."

"I had reservations when you suggested we hire undergrads as teaching assistants and decided to implement additional processes to make sure the best candidates were chosen. Each student was required to submit a written essay about their chosen career field, and I used their essays as the deciding factor on who I hired." Regina had leveled a reproachful gaze at me. "One allegation I cannot make against you is that Henry was hired because of your recommendation. I hired Henry because the words he wrote kept me up all night long, alternating between tears of sorrow and tears of pride for a young man I'd never met. He titled the essay *Beautiful Trauma*, and I now know who one of his heroes is." Through my tears, I saw Regina rapidly blinking to fight hers off. "What you want matters to me, Ezra, but not more than what Henry wants. I'm going to email the essay to you when I get home, even though I shouldn't. I want you to read it and think about what he's risking. The best outcome we can hope for Henry is academic probation, but he could lose any credit hours he earned based on your influence. Right now, I don't think that's many."

"It's none," I'd countered. "His grades in my class weren't that good because I was especially hard on him."

"That's not a confession I wish to hear. It's a potential lawsuit against the university should Henry decide your involvement harmed his grades too." Regina had taken a deep breath. "You could lose your job, Ezra. I will go to bat for you, but there are no guarantees in this climate. Even if you keep your job, you will lose respect among some of your colleagues and students. I need you to really think this over before you meet me on Monday morning."

"I will."

After I left the party, I'd wanted to drive to Henry's apartment and begin patching things up between us, but I went home instead. I didn't need to reconsider my decision, because I knew it was the best one. True to her word, Regina emailed a copy of the essay to me along with the welcome news that she'd received a resignation letter from Pres that went into effect immediately. That was one less thing Henry and I would have to worry about when we returned to school.

I took my tablet out on the balcony Henry loved so much and read the words Henry had bled onto the page.

He started off his essay by briefly describing his strict upbringing and controlling parents and how it impacted his decision-making skills as a young person finding freedom for the first time without any knowledge of the risks he faced. My heart shattered as he described sitting in a clinic with his friend Geoff, who held his hand when a doctor told him the bad cold he couldn't shake was actually the early onset symptoms of HIV. I already knew about the fight he'd had with his mother, but it didn't soften the blow when I read the words.

"Who would love me if my own mother couldn't? I thought I'd lost my will to live and my worthiness of love. Somehow, I kept putting one foot in front of the other, and it led me to Ryan's Place where Esther waited for me with a hug and Archie inspired me to use my heartache to help others. Then I met Maria, who became the mother we all wished we had. I kept putting one foot in front of the other, grateful for the people who loved me along the way. Then I met him—the man who changed how I viewed myself because of the way he saw me.

"Where I saw weakness, he saw strength. Where I saw trauma, he saw beauty. Where I saw negative equity, he saw worth. Millions of people are walking around not realizing that their personal trauma may be a part of them, but it doesn't have to define them. I want to work with kids who find themselves in situations like mine. With guidance and love, I can help turn their trauma into something beautiful too."

If Regina thought reading Henry's words would change my mind, she was wrong. It made me want to double down on my efforts to prove I was worthy of his love and help him achieve his dreams. I tossed and turned all night, forming a plan. I not only had to come up with the world's best grand gesture, I needed to find a way to protect Henry's academic career. I could do both with one phone call, and I did it before the sun fully rose.

"Ezra, it's not even seven o'clock yet," Mom sleepily said when she answered the phone.

"I need to hire your legal skills," I told her.

"Are you in trouble?" Mom said, going from annoyed mother to mama bear on high alert in a heartbeat.

"What's going on?" I heard Dad ask sleepily. "Is everything okay?"

"I'm fine," I said.

"He said he's fine, Paul," Mom told Dad.

"I'm more worried about Henry, Mom. I have a meeting on Monday morning with the department chair to formally admit to my involvement with Henry."

"I'll represent you both," Mom said. "What time shall I be there?"

"Eight thirty," I replied.

"I'd like to meet with you both today to discuss our strategy," Mom said.

"That's another problem, but I'm hoping Dad can help me out. Will you hand him the phone?"

"He wants to talk to you, Paul," Mom said.

"Ezra, is everything okay?" Dad asked, sounding worried.

"Not quite, but I have a plan." Then I told him about my grand gesture and explained how he could help me.

Dad laughed heartily and said, "Attaboy, Ezra."

Chapter Twenty-Seven

Henry

SLEEP WAS NIL. APPETITE WAS ZILCH. DESIRE TO LEAVE MY BED WAS nonexistent. I couldn't force myself to sleep, but I dragged myself out of bed once the sun came up, got dressed, and started a pot of coffee before making scrambled eggs. I was doing the one-step-in-front-of-the-other thing that saw me through my last heartbreak. I was proud of my effort until I pulled a jar of Simone's razzleberry jam out of the refrigerator to smear on my English muffin and promptly burst into tears.

I texted Maria to let her know I had a really late night and wouldn't be riding to church with her and Esther. She assumed I was exhausted for good reasons and shot back a winking emoji.

"I wish," I said out loud in the tiny apartment kitchen.

Nervous energy pulsed through me, and I had to find a way to work some of it out of my system. I tried meditation, but none of the techniques I tried muted the buzzing in my brain. I didn't feel up to facing people and wanted to avoid the gym. Cleaning the apartment from top to bottom seemed like the best way to wear myself out enough so I could get some sleep. I popped in my earbuds but the first song that came on when I was stripping my bed was "I Like Me Better." After another round of tears, I decided music wasn't a good idea either, so I flipped on the small television in my room. It seemed like every movie Ezra and I had watched over the past two months was playing on various cable channels. I wanted to view the song and the movie selection as signs Ezra and I were supposed to be together, but hoping had only led me to heartbreak. I shut the television off and laid the remote on the coffee table.

"No music or movies," I said. "Guess I'll have to rely on my inner dialogue to entertain myself while I clean."

"Your external dialogue with yourself is entertaining the hell out of me," Jess said, catching me off guard.

I whipped around and found her leaning in my bedroom doorway with a smirk on her face. "What's so funny?"

"You're adorable, Henry."

I snorted. "If you say so."

"Why don't you just call Ezra?" Jess asked. "I'm sure you can work this out."

"I don't want him throwing away his life for me, Jess. He'll resent it."

"I call bullshit. That man is crazy about you."

I narrowed my eyes suspiciously. "You were ready to skin him alive a few hours ago. What's changed?"

Jess shrugged casually. "I've seen the light."

"What?"

"New day; new perspective. Haven't you learned any of that in your new age practices?"

"Meditation and yoga have been around a long time," I countered. "What's really—" *Beep. Beep.* I whipped my head toward my bedroom window. "What's that? It sounds like a horn." *Beep. Beep. Beep.* It got louder, then I noticed the hum of a small engine. "What the hell?" I asked.

Jessie started giggling. "I guess you better go see."

Beep. Beep. Beep. "What's this jackass doing?" I groused when I looked out the window. "Some idiot is steering an ancient scooter down the alleyway with one hand and holding a bouquet of flowers in the other."

"Who is it?" Jess asked.

"I can't tell. He's wearing a helmet." The white scooter stopped just beneath my fire escape, and my heart recognized the identity of the rider before my brain could comprehend. Ezra killed the engine and climbed off the scooter then removed his helmet. He looked as tired as I felt, but Ezra's smile was the most beautiful thing I'd ever seen.

I opened the window and climbed out onto the rickety-looking fire escape.

"Hello, Henry," he said in the voice I loved.

"Hello, Ezra," I said, an answering smile creeping across my face. How had I ever thought we were through? "Are we having a *Pretty Woman* moment?"

"More like a Pretty Henry moment."

"Play hard to get," Jessie whispered behind me.

"I heard that, harpy," Ezra teased.

"Must be the new hearing aid you bought, geezer," Jess countered.

Rather than be offended, Ezra tipped his head back and laughed. "I'm coming up, Henry." Then he began the slow climb up to my window.

"I'm not so sure about this," I said to him as the metal structure creaked.

"I am," Ezra confidently said, gaining another foot closer to me. "Nothing and no one keeps me away from you. Not rusty fire escapes, not so-called friends, and certainly not a college administration." A few more feet and he was standing in front of me. "I choose you, Henry. I'm always going to choose you."

I fisted his shirt and pulled him through the window and into my arms.

"That's my cue to leave," Jess said. I heard the door shut a second later.

"You're deciding for me, huh?" I asked.

"You know how I like to take charge." Ezra leaned forward, rubbing his nose against mine.

"It's one of your most endearing qualities," I said, savoring the warmth of his embrace.

Ezra chuckled then kissed my forehead. "I bet you won't be saying that in another forty years."

Forty years. Happy tears filled my eyes. "What about school and the asshole?"

"The asshole resigned immediately. We'll never have to look at him again," Ezra said.

"And the school?"

"I'd already scheduled an appointment to meet with Regina on Monday. After the altercation in the garden, I escalated my confession. We're meeting with her at eight thirty on Monday with our lawyer."

"Our lawyer?" I asked. "That sounds like we're going in with our guns blazing."

Ezra kissed my lips to soothe me. "My mother is formidable, and she has a vested interest in the outcome."

"Simone is representing us?"

"She adores you, Henry, and there's no way she's letting either of us get railroaded. We're not exactly the first two people to find ourselves in this predicament. I'm sure her presence won't be necessary, but it won't hurt us either. She invited us over for a family dinner slash strategy session."

I groaned. "I can't face your parents."

"You have to because I need to return Steed to Dad. I thought he was nervous about letting me borrow his Aston Martin. It turns out his sixty-year-old Vespa scooter is more valuable to him than the car that cost him six figures."

"Oh my gosh! He still has Steed after all these years?" I asked.

"My parents know how to hold on to the things that mean the most. *You're* what matters the most to me. I can teach at another university, but I could never find another Henry. Take me back."

As if there were any doubt. "You had me at 'Hello, Henry.'"

Epilogue

Henry

Three months later...

"THIS BIRTHDAY CELEBRATION IS MUCH NICER THAN THE ONE I set up last year," Geoff said beside me.

Ezra had rented out half of Rinella's to celebrate my twenty-second birthday. His family was there along with my friends from school and Ryan's Place plus Ezra's friends on the faculty that had stuck by us, including Regina Bronson. It was rough at first, but Simone had been fierce and amazing when she brokered an agreement that everyone could live with. Ezra kept his job but was placed on probation, and I was stripped of my Biology of Human Sexuality credits and also placed on probation. The two of us frequently played naughty professor and slutty student in the privacy of our own home.

"Geoff, without your celebration, none of this," I said, gesturing to the gathering of people, "would be possible. I love you, man. Thank you for always sticking by me."

"There's no place I'd rather be," he said. "You deserve this life, Henry."

"Hey, new roomie," Jess said, flopping down in the empty chair beside Geoff. "All set to move in tomorrow?"

I'd officially moved in with Ezra the previous week, leaving my old room vacant. Jessie couldn't afford to pay the rent on her own, and she was afraid to place an ad online or in the paper for a room-mate. Geoff had been an obvious choice. He was tired of living a lie and ready to step out of the closet.

"I'm nervous, but ready," Geoff said, his eyes searching the room for a handsome, black man who seemed to reach Geoff in ways no one else could.

"Good," Jess said, patting him on the shoulder.

I looked for Des, too, but couldn't find him. Ezra and Archie were also missing. What were they up to?

"Hello, birthday boy," Simone said, moving to sit on my other side. She kissed my cheek.

"Hi there," I replied, leaning into her one-armed hug.

Paul joined us, sitting on Simone's other side. "Having a good time?"

"The best," I told him.

"Um, Henry," Geoff said beside me. "Don't look now, but there's a sexy, silver fox checking you out."

I laughed. "It feels like I've heard this somewhere before."

"Nine o'clock," Geoff mock whispered.

I turned my head, and Ezra stood on the far side of the room with several drag queens, including Archie and Des, standing behind him. "What's going on?"

"Looks like a flash mob," Jess said.

"I Like Me Better" started playing, and Ezra and the queens start-ed dancing my way. I laughed when the queens shouted "the Queen City" over New York City in the lyrics. They took their time dancing between the tables, but Ezra kept his eyes locked on mine with every step he took. When he finally reached me, he held his hand out to me while swaying to the beat. I placed my hand in his, and he pulled me up to my feet.

"Hello, Henry."

"Hello, Ezra."

We kissed and danced together while the crowd cheered. When the music ended, Ezra dropped to his knee in front of me. He pulled a ring from his pocket and said, "This ring has been in my family for three generations, gracing the ring finger of some of the strongest, most incredible men I know. My great-grandfather and my grandfather have both worn this ring as a symbol of faith and fidelity, and now I'm offering it to you. Will you be my forever?"

"You're *asking* me?"

Ezra laughed. "I'm trying here; work with me."

"Yes, Ezra, I will be your forever."

Ezra slid the ring on my finger then kissed my hand before standing up and tugging me back into his arms. "You know what this means?"

"We're getting married?" I asked.

"Henry: fifty; Ezra: one million."

The End!

Other Books by
AIMEE NICOLE WALKER

Only You

The Fated Hearts Series

Chasing Mr. Wright, Book 1
Rhythm of Us, Book 2
Surrender Your Heart, Book 3
Perfect Fit, Book 4
Return to Me, Book 5
Always You, Book 6
Any Means Necessary, Book 7

Curl Up and Dye Mysteries

Dyeing to be Loved
Something to Dye For
Dyed and Gone to Heaven
I Do, or Dye Trying
A Dye Hard Holiday
Ride or Dye

Road to Blissville Series

Unscripted Love
Someone to Call My Own
Nobody's Prince Charming
This Time Around
Smoke in the Mirror
Inside Out

The Lady is Mine Series

The Lady is a Thief
The Lady Stole My Heart

Queen City Rogue Series

Broken Halos
Wicked Games

Standalone Novels
Second Wind

Coauthored with Nicholas Bella

Undisputed
Circle of Darkness (Genesis Circle, Book 1)
Circle of Trust (Genesis Circle, Book 2)

Acknowledgments

First, I need to thank my husband and children for their constant support and encouragement. It's not easy living with a writer who often disappears into a fictional world for long periods of time. They do so many things to help me out so that I can realize my dream. I love you guys more than words can ever express.

To my creative dream team, thanks seem hardly enough for all that you do. Miranda Turner of V8 Editing and Proofreading, thank you for your tireless work, feedback, and many laughs while editing. Jay Aheer of Simply Defined art is an incredible artist, and I love how she brings my words to life. Stacey Blake of Champagne Formats is also an amazing artist who does incredible interior formatting, illustrating, and designing for e-books and paperbacks. Judy Zweifel of Judy's Proofreading and Jill Wexler do a great job of proofreading and polishing so my manuscripts shine.

To my lovely PA, Michelle Slagan. I'm not sure how I ever did this without you. I love you to the moon and back!

I want to thank the Brittany for being a wonderful critique partner and Rachel and Melinda for being amazing alpha readers. And to my betas, Kim, Dana, Jodie, Michael, and Laurel, I appreciate your honest feedback. I love working with you all.

About
AIMEE NICOLE WALKER

Ever since she was a little girl, Aimee Nicole Walker entertained herself with stories that popped into her head. Now she gets paid to tell those stories to other people. She wears many titles—wife, mom, and animal lover are just a few of them. Her absolute favorite title is champion of the happily ever after. Love inspires everything she does, music keeps her sane, and coffee is the magic elixir that fuels her day.

I'd love to hear from you.

You can reach me at:

Twitter—twitter.com/AimeeNWalker

Facebook—www.facebook.com/aimeenicole.walker

Instagram—instagram.com/aimeenicolewalker

Blog—AimeeNicoleWalker.blogspot.com

www.ingramcontent.com/pod-product-compliance
Lightning Source LLC
Chambersburg PA
CBHW020756250626
47155CB00003B/1092